GOD WENT LIKE THAT

GOD WENT LIKE THAT

A NOVEL

YXTA MAYA MURRAY

CURBSTONE BOOKS/NORTHWESTERN UNIVERSITY PRESS

EVANSTON, ILLINOIS

Curbstone Books
Northwestern University Press
www.nupress.northwestern.edu

This is a work of fiction. Characters, some places, and some events are the product
of the author's imagination. However, the novel is based on a 1959 nuclear reactor
disaster and two later fuel incidents that occurred at the Santa Susana Field
Laboratory in Simi Valley, California. The author was inspired to write this book
after reading the report *Santa Susana Field Laboratory Former Worker Interviews*
(November 2011), issued by the Department of Energy, https://www.etec.energy.gov
/Environmental_and_Health/Documents/WorkerHealthFiles/Former_Worker
_Interview_Final_Report.pdf. Further, the massacre at Pohang, South Korea,
described by "Carlos Mejia," was made public knowledge after the declassification
of the *USS DeHaven*'s official diary. See Associated Press, "Report: Korean War-Era
Massacre Was Policy," *CBS*, April 14, 2007, https://www.cbsnews.com/news/report
-korean-war-era-massacre-was-policy/. Mejia's description of the ocular experiments
on rabbits that occurred on the *DeHaven* is also corroborated by the historical
record. See Department of Defense, *Operation Hardtack* (1958) at p. 133,
https://apps.dtic.mil/sti/pdfs/ADA136819.pdf.

Printed in the United States of America

10 9 8 7 6 5 4 3 2 1

Library of Congress Cataloging-in-Publication Data
Names: Murray, Yxta Maya, author.
Title: God went like that : a novel / Yxta Maya Murray.
Description: Evanston : Curbstone Books/Northwestern University Press, 2023.
Identifiers: LCCN 2022045192 | ISBN 9780810146020 (paperback) | ISBN
    9780810146037 (ebook)
Classification: LCC PS3563.U832 G64 2023 | DDC 813.54—dc23/eng/20220919.
LC record available at https://lccn.loc.gov/2022045192

To Dr. Eila Skinner and
Dr. Tina Koopersmith

So many difficulties were encountered that, at least in retrospect, it is quite clear that the reactor should have been shut down and the problems solved properly. Continuing to run in the face of a known Tetralin leak, repeated scrams, equipment failures, rising radioactivity releases, and unexplained transient effects is difficult to justify.

—Report of the Santa Susana Field Laboratory Advisory Panel, October 2006

CONTENTS

ENVIRONMENTAL PROTECTION AGENCY, COMMUNITY INVOLVEMENT INTERVIEWS IN RE SANTA SUSANA FIELD LABORATORY, SIMI VALLEY, CALIFORNIA

TO: JENNA BAYLOR,
Regional Supervisor,
Environmental Protection Agency,
Region IX (Pacific Southwest)

FROM: REYNA RODRIGUEZ,
EPA Community Involvement Coordinator,
Region IX, San Francisco, California

DATE: JUNE 20, 2020

I. INTRODUCTION

On July 13, 1959, scientists and technicians struggled to secure an experimental nuclear reactor located in the Santa Susana Field Laboratory, a facility that stood on a scrubby, shining hillside in Simi Valley, California. The men labored on the Sodium Reactor Experiment (SRE), a nuclear reactor that employed liquid sodium to cool heat generated by radioactive fission. Dressed in white jumpsuits, they bustled around the massive and tubular SRE with jumpy gaits, as if wire springs had been stapled to their shoe soles. Their anxiety was understandable, considering they strove to encourage the reactor's combustible neutron population by withdrawing slim, steel boron control rods from the SRE's core. The proliferating neutrons' energy expanded at a steady pace until all at once it burst into a frantic miasma. Nuclear watchdogs later called this effect a *power excursion*, meaning that the heat and power generated by the reactor spiked to a deadly level. The technicians immediately inserted more control rods, which bristled atop the reactor like porcupine quills, so as to decrease the neutrons and dampen the reactor's power.

Months earlier in the reactor's run, physicists detected a temperature elevation, which impelled them to inspect a mesh used to filter impurities from the furnace's catalysts and coolants. Their pale faces flinched when they found a sticky black substance on the mesh's webbing. After a brief calculation, they identified this muck as corroded tetralin, an ordinarily colorless hydrocarbon that chilled the infernal sodium. Tetralin, they discovered, changed into a thick ebony gum when churned within the heat of the reactor. The workers scrubbed all visible waste from the reactor's workings, but in the weeks after their discovery of the leak the coagulated chemical continued to block the reactor's tubes and channels, through which the sodium traveled. This caused the sodium to heat to an extraordinary degree. On July 13, the percolating effect damaged the reactor's core, which held rods containing nuclear fuel. Radioactive gas wafted from the reactor and into the laboratory. Santa Susana's entire staff scrambled about in an effort to contain this partial meltdown.

Neither the physicists nor their technician helpmeets wore much in the way of protective gear; film footage taken at the time reveals them grappling with reactor machinery while sporting little more than the aforementioned jumpsuits. They washed the lab and sunk cameras into the reactor in an attempt to discern their error. Meanwhile, the gases spun and charmed the air within the building. The scientists evacuated these radioactive fumes by venting them into the outer atmosphere, usually at night. This expulsion occurred for weeks.

The gases spread a film around the lab and inserted their mysteries into the men's blood and bones. They floated down onto the bedroom community of Simi Valley and sank into the region's groundwater.

Residents wouldn't learn of the disaster for two decades. They ascertained these facts only in 1979, the same year Three Mile Island's Unit 2 reactor melted down and Ronald Reagan announced his run for president.

Simi Valley is the color of gold bullion. Its luster is caused by the region's weeds and shrubs that have died back under the always-sun, but if viewed in a mood of either the extreme optimism that arrives reportedly in one's greenest youth, or the morbid skepticism that can descend in early middle age, the valley's hills and defiles look almost worryingly radiant. I myself didn't grow up with a bedroom view of these glittering steppes. I lived on Ridgegate Lane, which cuts through the central part of town, the should-we-say more affordable part of town. My mother, Sonia Rodriguez, worked as a cleaning lady in Simi Valley from 1978 to 1993, decades after the '59 catastrophe. She scrubbed the floors, did the laundry, and washed the walls and windows of the large, boxy homes that presided over the verdant plains of Simi's Wood Ranch Parkway and Santa Susana Knolls. We lived six minutes from the now-decommissioned laboratory, residing in the Shadow Ridge Apartment development, a name that struck me as poetic during the years I resided there.

I was a quiet child. My test scores spiked and cratered to bizarre levels; I had a tendency toward depression that found relief only in reading novels or fusty tomes on natural science, which became a personal passion. My mother strove to assist my rich inner life even as she cultivated her own operatic tendencies, such as making lavish hand gestures and elegantly smoking the thinnest of cigarettes. She also coddled me because by my thirteenth year I fell ill with an undiagnosed condition that left me confined to bed. Mom, herself afflicted eventually with a chronic cough that made her work as a cleaning lady difficult until it proved impossible, lifted my spirits by bringing home little gifts suited to our hothouse tastes, mostly paperbacks for me and wine and perfume for her. I spent my "good" days going to school or scrubbing floors alongside her, but on my increasing number of "bad" days I rested at home while paging blearily through a book and breathing in my mother's signature scent, L'Heure Bleue.

When I could, though, I'd sail outdoors, driven by my reveries. I turned on the rubber hose in the apartment's astroturfed backyard and pretended I lived in a forest, like the lush Shropshire glades that first inspired Charles Darwin to study the enigmas of nature or the groves of fresh pines and brilliant maples that provoked Henry David Thoreau to live in solitude on the edge of Walden Pond. I simulated these Edens by spraying the hose into the air. A mist descended from the cloudless sky. I closed my eyes and lifted my face as the moisture floated onto my cheeks and lips. I fantasized away Simi Valley's withered grass and charcoal skies, replacing them with a vision of soft, clean rain and unburnt flora.

This game seems to have saved my life when I turned fourteen years old. I'd just read John Muir's *My First Summer in the Sierra* for the fourth time. I wanted to scale the heights of Cathedral Peak and bravely swim the length of blue Mono Lake when not building a cabin by hand or reading Emerson by the light of the moon. My problem began during one hot school day in October. I'd spent the morning sweating in my bedroom, but by the afternoon, fever throbbed painfully throughout my body. I heaved myself from my covers and went out our front door. I wandered toward the lawn and its rubber hose to refresh myself with my pagan rituals. But I soon found myself staggering around the apartment complex in a confused search for my mother, who at the time buffed floors several miles away.

After a blurry interval I stumbled into the eastern quadrant of the development. I passed the open door of a "cottage luxury" unit. A very old, white-haired woman wearing a housecoat and felt slippers sat in a plastic chair positioned on her concrete porch steps. She and I had crossed paths before, though I usually avoided her, as I'd once seen her slash at a smoky cloud of trashcan crows with a shovel. When she saw me now, she shook her head. I lurched in the breezeway. The sun pounded down and I blinked dazedly into the heat.

"How's it going there, little sister?" the woman asked.

"OK, I guess," I rasped.

"Shouldn't you be in school?" she said.

"My mom's going to write me a note," I replied.

The old woman nodded. "Ah, you're Sonia's girl. The poorly one."

"Where is she?" I croaked. "I have to tell her something."

"Are you all right?" the old lady asked.

I stared at the ground, mesmerized. The concrete passage between our apartments had become an unexpected host of swirling black blobs.

"Child, come inside," the old lady said.

The woman rose, shoved aside the chair, and pulled me into her dark apartment. She guided me into a parlor filled with fine mahogany furniture and sat me down on a small green velvet sofa packed with lacy pillows. I tried to blink away the black blobs and focus on the silver-framed photographs placed on the coffee table and hung in clusters on the walls. Some revealed a young man who wore a bow tie and had a brush-cut. These pictures were in black-and-white and had been taken long before. The other, color, photographs showed a young fellow with blond hair and a gentle smile who posed in a prom tuxedo. Then I didn't see anything at all because I lost consciousness.

"Drink this," was the next thing I heard.

I opened my eyes to find myself collapsed on the sofa. The old woman held a glass and coaxed me to take a few sips of water. She laid a wet washcloth on my brow. I saw that her white hair floated out from her head, as if loneliness so filled her thoughts that her bangs didn't want to be close to them.

"I don't like these guys looking at me," I blithered, about the men smiling out from the photographs.

"That's just my husband, Jason, and that's my son Rob," the woman said. She peered at me with her huge, blue, filmy eyes. Brown spots dappled her fragile face, so that she looked like a deer.

"Are they here?" I asked.

"Oh, no, honey, they're gone now," she said. "My Jason, he was at the lab and so, you know, he got sick on account of the poison. And then my Rob, he didn't work at Santa Susana, but I guess he got the poison, too, because it's just everywhere, it's all over the place, and they're never going to get rid of it."

"I don't want to be here," I said, not understanding her. "I want my mom."

I sobbed as the old woman put a thermometer in my mouth. She held me down for several minutes and then extracted the glass tube and squinted at it. She retrieved her spectacles from a nearby table and put them on. Looking at the thermometer again, she stood up quickly and began jostling me.

"All right, sugar," she said, heaving me off the sofa. "Let's get you to the doc."

"I want to go to sleep," I whispered, before passing out again.

I woke six days later in a white room. The old woman was gone. Beeping metal machines flanked me like robot sentries. I could hear my mother weeping in the hallway. Time passed as my mind attempted to clear itself from a gloom of drugs. Somewhere, separately—that is, with a knowledge I didn't feel intimately but rather remotely, as if learning my status from the murmurs of a stranger who possessed greater access to and interest in all the relevant facts—I understood something very bad had happened. I peered down at my torso, which was swathed in bandages. I saw that my left, bruised arm was attached to one of the machines with the aid of a plastic tube. I realized slowly that I was fastened also to a battery of other cheeping and grinding engines of indeterminate function. Nurses hurried in and out of the room. My mother appeared suddenly next to me, crying and coughing with violent shudders that drew the attention of a nearby doctor.

Within my trance, I glanced up and discerned that my room's east wall bore a window, which looked onto a vision of Simi Valley's gold hills. At that moment, an outdoor sprinkler turned on, as if a person subject to curious ideas about the world held a hose beneath the window and sprayed it into the air. A diamond mist filled the bullion-bright square. The water drops tapped on the glass and doused the sunny sky. My mother cried and coughed again while answering the doctor's questions. I closed my eyes. I sailed out of the hospital room, away from my mother, the doctors, my body, and the entire brassy radiance of Simi Valley. I floated through my mental fog until I spied a green isle, which resembled the emerald quiet of Muir Woods. I sailed on crystal breezes until I reached that better world, where pain was replaced by singing birds and perfumed flowers, and my parched lips were drenched by the blue water of pure lagoons and soft white showers.

Today, as a thirty-two-year-old Community Involvement Coordinator for the EPA, I understand that I'm not the only person in the world who might escape into daydreaming when confronted with unmanageable facts. This tendency appears so universal that it shouldn't strike us as surprising when a mortally wounded fourteen-year-old girl hallucinates heaven when stunned on Roxycontin and strapped to a phalanx of monitors in a Simi Valley ICU. Nor, for that matter, does it seem odd to me that a conflicted bureaucrat might write in panicked tangents while introducing a dossier of interviews that she conducted regarding a sixty-years-long radionuclide contamination in her hometown. Still, I think we can all agree that it's deeply alarming when wealthy businesses and powerful governments retreat into legend when faced with difficult truths:

Forty-seven days after the Sodium Reactor Experiment's 1959 partial core meltdown, one of the Santa Susana Field Laboratory's owners, being the commercial nuclear technology developer Atomics International, issued a joint press statement with the U.S. Atomic Energy Commission. These organizations described the July 13 incident in confusing jargon and the passive voice—*a parted fuel element was observed*—and misled the public about the danger they now faced. *The fuel element damage is not an indication of unsafe reactor conditions. No release of radioactive materials to the plant or its environs occurred and operating personnel were not exposed to harmful conditions.*

The lab continued to operate and serve as the site of further disasters despite this nightmare and its cover-up. The Santa Susana Field Laboratory amounted to two different divisions, each dedicated to Herculean technological inventions. One section, operated by Atomics

International, conducted nuclear reactor trials, and the other, owned by an American rocket production company called Rocketdyne, Inc., busied itself with rocket testing. Within the space committed to the nuclear reactors stood the now-infamous Area IV, which held the Sodium Reactor Experiment as well as nine other reactors, including the SNAP8ER and SNAP8DR, which were designed to power space missions. In 1964, and then again in 1969, the SNAP8 reactors suffered catastrophic fuel damage that released an undocumented amount of radioactive pollution into the region. In addition, Area IV accommodated a "hot cell" that hosted a radioactive fire in 1971, and an open-air "burn pit," wherein lab managers dumped radioactive waste for decades.

But no one informed the public of these calamities, either.

Meanwhile, the surrounding populations of Simi Valley grew and multiplied, developing from a sparse farming community into a city housing more than 61,000 people in 1970. By 1974, many of the scientists who'd presided over the 1959 meltdown were dead and forgotten, but the unburied revenants of radioactive and rocket fuel detritus continued to float up from Simi Valley's terrain like ghostly reminders of their lives. The toxins percolated from the groundwater and possessed the groundcover and tingling soils now spreading far afield of the lab site. As of yet, no reports of cancer clusters troubled the local news, and residents bathed, drank, and swam in the local waters with calm confidence. The laboratory persisted in testing nuclear reactors, though it appears to have put its rocket program on hold after the undisclosed SNAP8 accidents. It now employed 750 Simi Valley residents.

Southern California citizenry's faith in the goings-on at Santa Susana remained so high that Hollywood production companies filmed their shows on the site through the 1970s—*Barnaby Jones*, *The Six Million Dollar Man*, and a series I loved on reruns, *The Bionic Woman*. Neither did the press question the site's safety: On December 28, 1978, the *Los Angeles Times* exulted that, *After more than a decade of silence, Rocketdyne has reactivated its 1,800-acre rocket test facility in the mountains between Thousand Oaks and Canoga Park . . . While the earth trembles and canyons echo the engine's roar, the only evidence that a test is being carried out is the billowing cloud of steam produced by the liquid hydrogen, liquid oxygen fuel.*

One year after that account was published, the same year as the mishap at Pennsylvania's Three Mile Island, a meddling UCLA engineering lecturer named Daniel Hirsch obtained a cache of papers that had been leaked from the Santa Susana lab by a former Atomics International employee. These files disclosed details of the 1959 meltdown and the risks the people of Simi Valley and the nearby San Fernando Valley had lived with in ignorance for all of this time. Mr. Hirsch and his researchers gave the papers to the press, and in 1979, the first news reports of the SRE meltdown surfaced. KNBC investigative reporter Warren Olney, who would later become the bespectacled and avuncular star of public radio's *Which Way, L.A.?*, broke the story:

We've obtained films and documents that showed what happened when a nuclear reactor suffered an accident twenty years ago, young, auburn-haired Olney told a startled audience. *The reactor was located about five miles from what's now the Topanga Plaza Shopping Center, twenty miles from Van Nuys, and thirty-five miles from downtown L.A.*

The period that passed after I woke in an ICU situated twenty miles from Van Nuys, and thirty-five miles from downtown L.A., is difficult to recount. There exist no films or documents that could ever come close to showing what happened to my mother and me during this era. The only way to summon the catastrophes that punctuated my personal entry into the 2010s, in order that you, Regional Supervisor, might fathom the experience of being killed or nearly so by environmental toxins, and how my intimacy with such shocks makes me either the best-suited or least-equipped governmental investigator to submit this file on the EPA's Community Involvement Plan at Santa Susana, is to write about it here, on my computer, in a way that makes sense.

But how exactly should I do that?

Having thought long and deeply on this important question, I've concluded that there are two ways of describing what happened to me next.

The first method that I might use to describe my illness and my mother's death is by far the most favored. This style uses the language of logic and linear time, which is to say, the language of power, the impoverished language of law and bureaucracy:

On December 10, 2010, when I was twenty-two years old and had been in remission from a urinary-tract carcinoma for three years, my mother perished of lung cancer. The causes of our health crises remain obscure and unsubstantiated, though one theory posits that we suffered dangerous exposures from contact with groundwater that had been contaminated by runoff from the Santa Susana lab. Another hypothesis holds that my mother's habit of smoking matchstick-thin Capri cigarettes doomed us both. A third postulate suggests that the deadly flaws in our bodies came about through a combination of both of these causes, though whether they may be weighted equally or not remains undetermined.

Which is to say, my mother died. I lived. Two weeks after her funeral, I received a scholarship from and later attended Cal State Los Angeles as an Environmental Geoscience major, with a minor in English literature. Upon graduating, I drifted through Los Angeles in a haze of grief and hypochondria. Two years plodded by. After making a brief stab at law school, where I learned that there exist no real federal rights to clean air, clean food, and clean water, I grew afraid for my mental health and applied rather hysterically to the EPA. Here, I hoped to work toward that paradise described by Muir and Thoreau, whose visions had so soothed me in the Simi Valley ICU. I soon found myself attached to the Superfund Taskforce. My superiors assigned me to the post of Community Involvement Coordinator at the EPA's San Francisco Region 9 office, where I solicited input on the question of how the agency should best restore its Superfund sites. Subsequent to an initial period of what might be described as either culture shock or retriggered trauma, I manufactured concise and bloodless summations of interviews I conducted with the enraged casualties of trichloroethylene poisoning in Sunnyvale, volatile organic compound exposure in Torrance, and radioactive thorium in Oxnard (just to name a few). This idyll of obedience lasted until the 2018 Woolsey Fire blew through the Santa Susana Field Laboratory on its destructive path toward Pacific Palisades and Malibu, quite probably re-releasing radionuclides into the atmosphere by burning contaminated vegetation, and leading to the crisis that resulted in the document that you, Regional Supervisor, hold in your hands right now.

The second method of describing what happened to my mother and me is this:

When I was ten years old, my mother took a day off work, and I didn't go to school. At this point in our history, each of us enjoyed good health.

My mother was petite, 4 feet and 11 inches. She was also perfectly made, with curved dark legs and small breasts. As a girl back in Guadalajara, she'd worked for a time as a singer and ballerina in a cabaret of ill repute. She modeled her act on the performance styles of two goddesses, Marlene Dietrich in *Blue Angel* (1930) and Dolores del Rio in *The Red Dance* (1928). Kicking, leaping, and belting out the lyrics to *You Make Me That Way* while wearing a silver dress, my mother bewitched temporarily an American named Gerry, who brought her to a motel in Simi Valley. He impregnated her with me before returning to his wife and disappearing into the wilds of Fresno, or Long Beach, or the City of Industry.

At home that day, my mother poured herself a glass of sauvignon blanc and stepped into one of her most fashionable dresses, a slightly tattered blue chiffon gown decorated with feather trim. We lay in bed together, she drinking and tugging out one of her Capris from its pack, and fiddling it in her fingers.

"Do you know how the angels talk?" she asked me, in Spanish.

"No," I said.

My mother stretched out her legs, languorously, and lit her cigarette. "They don't talk at all. They sing."

"Why?"

"Because God didn't like to listen to them complain. When he gave birth to the angels from his womb, a long time ago, before the earth existed, before the sky, before the desert, before the moon, they were perfect. They flew through the stars, chatting to each other in numbers and poems, 'cause that's how angels think, about the higher things, the beautiful things. But sometimes they were still sad. The angels worried like the rest of us, about this and that. What would happen when they died. Getting old and sick, or losing their jobs. Or not having anybody to love. Most of all, they missed their brother, Satan, because he'd made them laugh, laugh, laugh! Satan was the funniest angel of them all. He'd make them drink martinis and dance in a motel room to radio music, and clap his hands and say *olé!* But God didn't like that bastard. Not because old terrible Satan was a woman-izer, though. And not because he stole people's money or drank all their whiskey, or broke their stupid hearts. God cast Satan into hell because he was the most pain-in-the ass complainer of them all. The angels were so scared they'd have to follow their brother into the fire, but that didn't stop them from groaning about how that pinche God never cared if they cried, or about how scared and lonely they felt. And so God went like *that*"—my mother flicked her wrist, causing the smoke floating from her Capri to confuse the air—"and then, every time the angels opened their mouths, they found they couldn't bitch any more. Instead, all they could do was sing. Joyous songs! Ah, the most pretty songs. Songs without meanings. *Coo coo coo cooooo*, like that. After the angels lost the power to speak, they stopped worrying. Since they couldn't say *why do bad things happen* or *why is there so much pain*, they forgot the questions and became free."

"But what happens when we pray to them?" I'd asked.

"Oh, baby, it's been so long since they forgot how to talk that they can't understand us now," my mother said, closing her eyes. "That's why those fools never answer." The muscles of her legs flexed, and she moved her shoulders to a silent music, so that the ghost of the girl who'd danced in silver in Guadalajara made herself briefly felt. Mom took a long drag of the Capri and exhaled. The cigarette smoke threw a thin white veil over our small, dividing bodies.

Despite Warren Olney's blockbuster report, public fears over Santa Susana didn't surface until 1989, nine years before my mother told me her story about the singing angels. The previous winter, the Department of Energy ordered an investigation of the area's soils and groundwater. The resulting published study revealed contamination at several locations. Simi Valley citizens, who as usual watered their lawns and drank from their taps, soon found themselves fending off anxieties that hatched in their minds like tiny spiders. They hurried to the store to purchase Poland Spring and Perrier bottled water (the latter of which was later found to contain elevated levels of benzene). They froze on their porch steps at the sight of their children running through the sprinklers. They crouched in their beds, gritting their teeth while praying to a heaven that could no longer comprehend human language. The Lord is my shepherd, I shall not want. Yea, though I walk through the valley of the shadow of death, I will fear no evil. For thou art with me. Thy rod and thy staff they comfort me.

Federal and state regulators said Thursday that toxic contamination of groundwater is moving from Rockwell International's Santa Susana Field Laboratory toward Simi Valley, Beth Barrett of the *Los Angeles Daily News* wrote, despite these divine entreaties, in the waning days of '89. *The report said there was no immediate health risk.*

The residents of Simi Valley tried to believe the government's reassurances. As humans tend to do in the early stages of catastrophes, they continued to live, work, give birth, frolic, and die in the community as if immune to its dangers, while quelling their terrors with alcohol and television. This quiescence shattered in the 1990s, when the California Department of Health Services and UCLA issued studies reporting that Santa Susana's lab workers had higher rates of lung and lymph cancer, and that an increased risk for certain carcinomas had been detected in nearby communities. Several lawsuits followed, particularly after Boeing, Inc., purchased the land in the mid-1990s. Nevertheless, the EPA didn't designate the area a federal Superfund priority, which would have allowed the agency to clean away the radioactivity or force responsible parties to take action. Top officials explained that under a now-lapsed 2007 consent decree, Boeing, NASA, and the Department of Energy shared responsibility for the area, and so presumably the federal government didn't consider EPA intervention warranted. We may note with interest that, due to cuts in EPA funds, the agency failed to monitor Santa Susana for five decades, and allowed the reckless owners of Atomics International and Rocketdyne to regulate themselves.

The Woolsey superfire ignited in Simi Valley on November 8, 2018, at 2:24 P.M. According to news reports, the fire began at the now-dismantled Santa Susana lab site, possibly because of a malfunction at Southern California Edison's in situ Chatsworth substation. The location of the fire's origins appears to rest in a drought-parched plot of land within a thousand yards of the SRE's partial meltdown. The flames spread to the surrounding weeds and brush and detonated. Before pushing toward Bell Canyon, the Santa Monica Mountains, and Malibu, the conflagration burned freely through the former lab's position, whose terrain remains infected with the nuclear waste and assorted other deadly toxins spilled there so many decades before.

Woolsey proved doubly dangerous to the people of Simi Valley because of the exceptional hazards created by radionuclide intoxication. As revealed in a 2015 Chernobyl study, radionuclides sink into groundwater, which is then tapped by groundcover. Wildfires that appear in the area will likely burn the turf, which releases the plants' toxins into the air.

People in Simi Valley circulated these studies and many of them felt afraid. In January of 2019, residents petitioned the EPA to conduct its own investigation of the reasons behind the longstanding Santa Susana contamination and whether the Woolsey Fire spread toxins to their neighborhoods. You, Regional Supervisor, reacted to these requests by instructing me to solicit, via web postings, interviewees from Simi Valley in order to gauge the community impacts of the combined effects of Santa Susana and Woolsey. My efforts, as you explained in an email, would prepare the way for the remediation that will follow the lab site's long-delayed but upcoming inclusion on the Superfund National Priorities List. Behind closed doors, you also suggested to me that we might use these interviews as opportunities to measure local interest in pursuing Federal Tort Claims Act lawsuits against the United States for our failure to make the site safe despite our awareness of its dangers.

I started to work on this project immediately, though, as you'll see, I deviated from the strict formulas dictated by the EPA's community engagement script. This playbook instructs Coordinators like myself to ask victims narrow questions such as "What is your opinion of the government's commitment to cleaning up hazardous waste at the XX site?" and "What contacts have you had with government officials about the site? Do you feel that these officials have been responsive to your concerns? Why or why not?" Having discovered that there exists an approximately zero percent chance that any of my interviewees would succeed in a lawsuit pursued against the government due to overwhelming immunity shields the state erects around itself, I also realized that after living in this administrative fug, I had to relearn how to do something as basic as listening to the people I encountered, an attention they deserved even if their grief and fury compelled them to narrate horrors that veered far beyond my administrative or emotional capacities. I believe I've finally attended to these individuals with the devotion that is their due, though it's taken me over a year to deliver this finished product, an exercise that ordinarily would have taken me three weeks using traditional methodology.

During my first year at the EPA I learned that most of the passionate and meandering statements made by victims of hazardous waste exposure are irrelevant to the task of developing an effective remediation plan. While engaging interviewees in various places of environmental pandemonium, I taught myself to deflect my subjects' most incandescent accusations, which included the indictments that their losses could never be made whole, that I needed to listen to the *whole story*, and that justice must be done. Rather than reply that I could offer the complainants no retribution or salvation, I found myself forced into a panicked sympathy that, after a difficult period, began to blossom into an anxiety that these people threatened the balance of my mind. Within the interviewees' red-faced rages and blustering denunciations, during which they might excitedly bash at the table between us or break down into a misery so deep it turned them savage, I detected intimations of the bright confusions that had once caused me, in the ICU, to levitate from my broken body and fly to the island of John Muir's most luminous descriptions. This desperation coalesced within me as if it were a vapor and formed a shimmering screen between me and my subjects. In those moments, I understood that if I crossed over that mist I'd reenter a place where one can encounter a pain so exquisite it deprives us of language, even our own names. I thus learned to treasure my job, as it helped me contain this nemesis within the cage of prefabricated questions and curt administrative conclusions.

That pleasant era seems to be over for me now, though. Since the Woolsey Fire, I've been made to remember everything that happened to my mother and me, and today face a reckoning for my participation in this farce. My mother was correct, as it turns out. Those who find themselves undefended by the powerful will pray to unhearing angels, such as I became upon assuming the mantle of a government official. The question the following dossier of interviews seeks to answer is whether this fate can be altered, or whether it forms an inescapable part of the paradox and mirage that we call our laws and our democracy.

II. RESULTS

INTERVIEW WITH CARLOS MEJIA

NOVEMBER 20–23, 2019
CANOGA PARK, CALIFORNIA

[NOVEMBER 20]

You've come to see me. Did you bring the children, sweetheart? No? Let me look at you, my sweet, Schatzi, my darling—

Oh. You're not my daughter.

I see, yes.

No, no, no, no, of course I understand. You are from the government. Give me a moment, please.

There's no need to apologize. I was only drifting and when I woke, I wasn't really myself.

You want to know about—that. Yes, right. I sent an email about this, didn't I? After Heidi asked me to, she's the night nurse. And I wrote that note to you, explaining the problem with the reactor.

It's because the nurses saw the EPA's message to the lab's former staff. They said, didn't you once? And I admitted that a long time ago, I worked there. They said, Mr. Mejia, you should tell the government. The agency is doing an investigation. They're interviewing people who have information. The nurses are afraid after that fire, you see. I tell them that I'm sure it's fine, that it's all cleaned up. It's not true, as you know. But I don't want the girls to worry about things they can't change.

Well, how nice to have a visitor. Sira, Sira. May I have a tea? Would you like one?

Two teas, please, Sira.

It's been sixty years. But I know that it's all still there, where we left it. The radiation is what I mean. And here you finally are. To ask me about it. You should have asked me years ago. Thank God my daughter lives far away.

I was there for thirty-three years, not counting '60. That's the year that I left to take care of Walther.

Walther Becker, dear. Dr. Becker. I assume you are here to ask about him.

My name is Carlos Mejia. I was an electronics technician in Area IV. At the Santa Susana laboratory that was stationed not fifteen minutes away, in Simi Hills.

I was born here? No. In Guanajuato. I came to the U.S. in the late '40s, and just missed World War II. I was too young to fight, yet. I had to wait for Korea. Long before I ever heard the words "Santa Susana" or the name "Dr. Walther Becker," I enlisted in the navy, which is, I suppose, where my story starts. Back then, I was blessed with complete ignorance about nuclear reactors and the effects of radionuclide exposure upon the fragile association of tissue and thoughts that we call a human being. Though I did learn other, quite terrible things during my service.

I began as a lowly mess crank on the USS DeHaven. Oh, in the early days, it was heaven on that boat. The DeHaven was filled with young men so thrilled to be fighting for their country that their skin fairly sparkled with the joy of it. It felt like the beginning of my real life. My father had been disappointed in me, I'm afraid to say. And my brothers wouldn't have anything to do with me, except in the most horrible way. So, yes, I very much enjoyed being a sailor, which meant finally enjoying the esteem of other men.

I became eventually a radio technician, second class, under the command of one Steve Dickinson. Even though I was a Mexican laboring in the most miserable nadir of the chain of command, Steve gave me the chance to work with him because I brought him coffee every day, and he noticed my talent for absorbing the patois used to record comms in the log. Our station was the Primary Tactical radio circuit, what we called the PriTac, which was down by the DeHaven's scullery, far away from the guns. Steve taught me the old prowords, with their funny euphemisms, such as how *be advised that* meant that one should probably panic, or how *casevac* required the immediate evacuation of casualties. How *contact* meant killing people and *send it* meant to open fire upon the enemy or whomever one wanted destroyed. But, as I said, I did remain there, by the scullery, with Steve, at the PriTac, below deck, away from the shooting. And so, just in case you're wondering, you can rest assured that I did not personally make contact at Pohang, where we engaged with those refugees.

Pohang. In South Korea. You must have heard about this, Miss Rodriguez. It's what the *DeHaven* is famous for now since the declassification. Yes, I know the reason why you have come to talk to me, but how can you understand what happened at Santa Susana if you do not first learn about the war?

As I was saying before your interruption, the travesty occurred on, what, September 1, 1950, two weeks before the invasion at Incheon. The *DeHaven* was patrolling the shore for insurgents. We were given orders to open on any moving body of Koreans, even the Southerners. The army warned us that the enemy could be hiding in disguise amongst the most peaceable-looking people. Steve was the one who received and was to relay the command. The admiral said that a group of two thousand civilians or purported civilians was stranded on Pohang beach. The refugees had torn off their shirts and waved them in the air at us. The people thought that we would save them.

Steve said, *say again, say again.* I remember his face when he understood what the Shore Fire Control Party was telling him, that we should fire on the camp. He began yelling, and crying, and I felt embarrassed for him. I stood next to the dish washers, who'd all gone mute with fear. But the hairs on my arms stood up. I saw this as an opportunity to distinguish myself. I told Steve that we had to obey orders! He called me awful names, and then stared at the console as if he had suddenly lost his senses. I ran to the TF commander. That stooge screamed at me when he had trouble understanding my accent but in the end I conveyed the information. I felt very important. Back in Guanajuato I had expected to become the farmer of a ruined hayfield presided over by a madwoman. But now I was an American. Now I was a man. I took the headset from Steve and continued transmitting instructions. Within the hour, hundreds of people were dead.

[*In Spanish*] When the shooting stopped, I could not breathe. It took all of, twenty seconds? I don't know. I couldn't think. It was if I had no mind. I finally went on deck and saw what we had done. Above, the sky was a pretty blue. The clouds sifted through the air, layered over with stinking smoke. A breeze ran across my face. I breathed in powder fumes and asbestos. It was too quiet, as if I'd gone deaf. I looked around at my mates. The brave men with the glittering skin now had blank faces, as if they'd died along with the others. I heard later that some of them refused to shoot. I always wondered if those gunners regarded themselves as innocent.

The water, in the ocean, was red. Ruby red. I saw what the waves held. And it was impossible. The crime we had committed. Many women. Many small children.

I did not feel it. Not until much later. Instead, as I stood there looking down at the jewel-bright, pink-red water, I had the strangest thought. It was, *I've seen that color before.*

Isn't that odd?

Still, there was no time to lose your head over it. I ran back down to the PriTac and Steve and I began logging in comms. He didn't speak of the massacre again. Neither did I. And after a day or two, we'd all moved on to other things. We were getting ready to support the amphibious landing on Wolmido. The offensive at Incheon.

We killed and captured thirty-five thousand people there.

[*Pause.*]

[*In English*] I'm sorry, what was that? Oh. Again with this. The problems at the laboratory. The role that poor Walther played in it. You do seem in quite a rush for me to confess to you about that specific tragedy, Miss Rodriguez. It appears young people these days do not have the patience to let a story unfold at its natural pace, which requires some decorum on the part of the listener.

Yes, at Santa Susana it was a disaster and a great many people died. However, I don't feel like talking any more right now. I'm not feeling all that well, suddenly.

I am tired.

Sira? Sira?

That's fine. Yes, that will be better.

Tomorrow would be best.

[NOVEMBER 21]

[*In English*] I will tell you all about it. But I have to finish the one story, when I was explaining about the awful—and what I saw in the water—and then I will say what happened at the lab. First, though, I must speak about my mother. Whom I did mention yesterday.

My mother was an alfalfa farmer. Her name was Serafina. She inherited our land from her own mother. When she married my father he moved in and they had four strong sons. And then they had me. Alfalfa is a forage crop, bright green with purple-blue flowers. Cows eat it, and horses. Ranchers will pay a great deal for quality alfalfa to keep their herds healthy, and my family had been farming it for seventy years already. Alfalfa sprouts make a good tea, which stimulates the appetite. Its blossoms are beautiful and sweet. Another name for the alfalfa is *lucerne*, which comes from the Persian word for lapis lazuli. *Lājward*. When I was a child, my mother realized that I was different from my brothers and so she sent away for books on history, poetry, mathematics, botany. Lucerne was introduced to the ancient Greeks during the Persian invasion, an assault by sea, commanded first by Darius and then by his son Xerxes, who grew so enraged over the intransigent Hellespont that he ordered his men to whip the waves with chains. *Bitter water, Xerxes the king will pass over you whether you want it or not, you are a turbid and briny river.* Already, as a boy, I was connected to the bitter ocean, and to men who believed that they could control the powers of nature.

The alfalfa flowers were a perfect, pure azure color, denoting its name. We grew the crop in all seasons, and could've had eight to ten cuttings per year, if we'd wanted. Later, when my mother ran off my father and all of my brothers, she had a weakness for letting it grow, so that the air was perfumed with this indescribable scent, fresh and with the tang of wet soil, like a truffle. Like a tree. And then the blue flowers winking everywhere.

She was a madwoman because she chose me over them. I won't bore you with the details. Let it suffice to say that my father and my brothers saw in me a Greek bearing and found themselves unable to appreciate that classical influence. Not that I had any idea why my papa beat me while my brothers offered clever suggestions for how best to inflict his punishments. Once, he whipped my head, back, and shoulders with his belt until I nearly died.

When I woke in my bed, many days later, I discovered that Mother had persuaded them all to leave with the aid of the family rifle. Shortly afterward, while I still healed from my injuries, she stopped cutting the hay. Slowly, our farm became a kind of paradise. She was Eve, and I was Abel. Or maybe I was Cain, the farmer and wanderer who was marked by his sin and confusion.

[*In Spanish*] I don't know the first time that I saw my mother wandering naked through the grass, but I know I thought it was wonderful. She was a pagan. Cottontails had begun to appear in the field, attracted by the alfalfa. My mother was like the blue-skinned fertility goddess Mayahuel, patron of the name-day Tochtli, the day of four hundred rabbits. She would move through the grass as the sun sparkled down and laugh as the creatures sprang away from her. *Stop all that reading*, she'd call out. *Come be with me.*

And so, once I was well again, we would walk naked through the field together, quietly, feeling the plants brush against our skin. In July, after the heaviest rains, the fragrance would rise from the ground and soak my mind with pleasure. I felt the warm, wet earth between my toes. My mother rubbed the mud against her skin, and I did, too. The grass glinted with water drops, twinkling like stars, and the bunnies leaped and trembled at our feet. Desire entered me like a color. Not that cool blue of the flowers.

Eventually it occurred to me that what we were doing was sinful. I didn't know that I would never again experience another person in so innocent a way as my mother. It was that color, drenching me, the desire I didn't understand. It baffled me. It led me astray. I felt ashamed.

When I was sixteen, my mother caught one of the rabbits in her arms. The animal was not like the others, which were brown and brindle-colored. This rabbit was all white, with striking pink-red eyes.

She hugged the rabbit against her chest and looked at me, smiling. I knew already that I would be leaving home soon but hadn't told her so. I needed to escape from her perversity, I thought. I looked at her from across the long grass. The blue flowers shone with the darkness of the Persian lapis. The bunny lay against her skin like a stripe of snow. Its one visible eye was like a ruby jewel.

I love you, she said to me.

[NOVEMBER 22]

[*In English*] Have you ever seen the films of the atom bombs? The ones exploded at the Pacific Proving Grounds? The whole world faded into a terrible brightness. A great rushing explosion of vapor detonated, forming a white Taj Mahal in the sky. Then a copper-bronze tree shot up from the ocean. This tree of knowledge was black and twisty and full of evil. Demons and serpents hid within it. Birds careened across its boughs and fell dead from the clouds.

In my last mission for the navy, my job was to help determine whether Heisenberg and Oppenheimer had actually invented God. The Yahweh of Moses. You recall what would happen if the prophet gazed upon the face of the Lord. We hoped for a similar effect.

What I am talking about is this: On July 31, 1958, the U.S. Joint Task Force Seven performed an experiment with a 3.8 megaton hydrogen bomb called Shot Teak. The protocol occurred above Johnston Island, in the Pacific Ocean, as part of Operation Hardtack. The rocket we used for the test was a Redstone, an advancement from the German V-2, the invention of Wernher von Braun. Its engine was built by the Rocketdyne Company, with whom I would soon work so closely at Santa Susana. I remained attached to the *DeHaven*. We were stationed about 209 klicks away from the island, working on the part of the experiment that had to do with the effect of the blast on the retina. The objective was to study the aurora, the size of it, the amount of light it shed, how far it could be seen, and for how long. And whether we would be able to blind the enemy by detonating a weapon at high altitude.

It was considered bad form to use people and so we used rabbits. They came in cages that the seamen placed on the decks. Shot Teak evacuated its energy within fifty milliseconds, while the fastest that a human can blink is, I believe, one hundred milliseconds. A person exposed to the aurora unexpectedly would not be able to avoid blindness by closing their eyes. Of course, the rabbits were incapable of doing so anyway, on account of the conditions of the experiment. All of the rabbits were brown or brindle-colored, but one, I recall, had white fur.

I was laughing at first, watching the boys set it up. I was twenty-six years old. I want you to imagine a boat full of young men about to watch a rocket blast into space and toss a blazing sun down from the stars. I had been initiated into my true nature by then, years back, during Korea. It wasn't a problem in the navy if you knew how to be discreet and were very, very lucky. Unlike my father and brothers, no one in the service cared about whom I happened to share my free time with, or if they did, they didn't say, at least not to me. They knew that they might need me to save their life. I am gilding the truth here, I'll admit. But even if homosexuals were not the most respected sailors in the navy, on the *DeHaven* I was an acknowledged part of the crew. We all stomped about with our shirts off, flexing and joshing. During shore leave, we'd storm into the bars, our white teeth gleaming like fangs as we called for beer and wrestled with women and boys.

And we all guffawed together when we watched the seamen put the rabbits out on the decks. We made jokes about the Easter Bunny, I recall, and also sex. Even as I was wisecracking, however, I felt drawn to the creatures hunkered on the deck, with their eyes pulled open. They mesmerized me with a dreadful feeling. A memory. I bent down and peered at the white rabbit through the bars in its cage. I watched it shiver. I must tell you that it is ridiculous for a man to suffer for vermin when he has helped human beings die. But I froze. I didn't hear the call that we were to hustle below decks for the detonation and would have been blinded myself if the Master at Arms hadn't yanked me by the collar and thrown me beneath the hold.

What I can't remember is this: Was the rabbit's eye rosy before, or just after? That clear, dark, pink-red color, like a ruby.

I now know that albinism doesn't create pink eyes per se, but rather dilutes the pigment in the eye, so that one can see a reflection of the capillary blood beneath the salt waters of the cornea. Perhaps this is why, when I crouched to look at the creature in its hutch, my chest began to burn. My literal heart clenched with a brief, intense pain that spread throughout my limbs.

After the test, I went back on deck to look at the white rabbit again. I watched as the seamen lugged the animal, and her sister specimens, off in their crates. I began to feel ill once more, as if an old, dormant disease had flared suddenly inside all my organs. I tried to walk it off. I went back to work. Having been promoted the year earlier, I now supervised my own team of junior radiomen. I spent the rest of the afternoon attempting to read their logs and otherwise communicate coherently with them.

That evening, in the mess, as I stood in line for dinner, I began to perspire and shake. It felt as if my body filled slowly with molten lead. My mind fragmented into violent abbreviations. I collapsed. For three days I lay in sick bay, vomiting and weeping.

I could not recover. After a navy doctor examined me back in Honolulu, he did mention Section 8 but kindly enough recommended me for "early release on compassionate assignment" so that I might still find work in civilian life.

I separated from the navy soon after.

[NOVEMBER 23]

[*In English*] After I wandered adrift in California for a while, an old navy buddy who had worked with von Braun at Fort Bliss recommended me for an opening at Santa Susana. Von Braun, dear. Wernher von Braun, the Nazi and rocket scientist. The man who developed the V-2 with Jewish slave labor at Peenemünde. It was common after the war for us to work side-by-side with German scientists and indeed the most abysmal sort of Fascist on account of the postwar mania for collecting Rhineland experts on the two core Cold War obsessions, missiles and fission. Operation Paperclip, Operation Alsos, Project 63, all of them desperate efforts to capture the Führer's best minds for our own labs. Some of these immigrants did well, translating easily from their supervision of the Mittelwerk death-pits to their new book-lined offices at Redstone Arsenal. Others had a more difficult time, stalked as they were by the traces of the dead and their own terror that they were condemned to hell for the deeds and misprisions they had committed in Germany.

I was an electronics tech. When I arrived at Susana I was given a mop but then some alert fellow thought to give me a mathematics test, which led to my swift installation in the newly built Area IV, home of the Sodium Reactor Experiment. The site was divided into regions for rockets and nuclear testing. The rockets, in Areas I–III, were ruled by the jaunty von Braun and his fellow Paperclipper, Dieter Huzel, both of whom I would sometimes see sunning their snowy shoulders amongst the chaparral blooming on the area's buffer zones. The reactor, in Area IV, was the province of Dr. Walther Becker, Hahn's acolyte and the visionary who theorized that a nuclear reactor could operate at a higher rate of utility when cooled by liquid sodium rather than water, which possesses a higher vapor pressure. After a modicum of training I found myself assigned to Walther's duchy, which was amply funded by the Department of Defense.

The SRE was a twenty-foot reactor located beneath the floor of Building 4059's high bay, shielded by concrete vaults. The concrete created a barrier against the reactor's radiation, but it prevented us from seeing what was happening inside. These hidden workings could be dangerous if a problem arose. My job was to regularly test the stability of the metals out of which the SRE had been constructed by plunging samples into the reactor and irradiating them. I worked with titanium and also beryllium, the latter an earth metal that scatters neutrons. It is sweet to the taste, is found in emeralds, and, if inhaled, has the same effect on the lungs as the strangling phosgene gasses that appalled Hitler during the Great War. I found the work absorbing, which I hoped would cure my increasing fixation on the idea that I was due for some sort of blood atonement.

It cannot be said that I was well. At the very end of 1958, I took a small apartment in Simi Valley, on Cottage Drive. It had a bed, a stove, a toilet, a sink, a closet, a floor full of splinters, and walls that I painted a blinding white. I spent my nights with my face turned toward that blank expanse. Upon waking, I ate a breakfast of plain toast and coffee, and then drove a rented Ford to the lab. Once there, I slipped into my overalls and readied my samples. I worked quietly, staying apart from my chummy fellow techs, and listened to the mingled sounds of German and English float around me. Not a word of Spanish was spoken there, unless one counted the cleaning staff, who were mostly silent, like me. I measured the samples' radioactivity with a photo multiplier tube and a scaler, which reminded me of checking the doneness of a cake. I input the data, and then placed the specimens on a workbench, where they would be collected by the physicist in charge of the experiment. As often as not, this scientist would be Walther.

"And your name is?" he asked me after some weeks. We both stood in the lab. Dr. Walther Becker was tall, thin, pale, blond, and forty-five years old. He had dark blue eyes and translucent pale lashes. A long neck. He bore the abstracted expression of an amateur classicist, which he had been in Berlin, in addition to dogsbodying for the great Otto Hahn at the Kaiser Wilhelm Institute for Chemistry.

"Carlos Mejia," I said.

"Mejia," he repeated, trying to pronounce it.

We looked at each other. He was taller than me, much taller. I gazed up at him, my dead eyes flickering. The moment lasted.

"You will have a beer with me, if you like," he said.

"All right," I said.

Days later, we arranged to go to a pub about twenty miles away from the lab, without either of us mentioning why we chose a location so far afield. We sat across from each other at a small table, sipping our lagers in the beery gloom. At first we spoke very little. Around us, heterosexual couples nuzzled and laughed. We sat with straight backs, smiling hopelessly at one another. The foam of our lagers looked like small clouds, exploding.

"It's no use," I finally said.

Walther nodded, holding my eyes with his. "The war."

"Korea, for me," I said. "And other things."

"I understand," he said.

We looked out the pub's window. It was November, and mournfully sunny.

"Why?" I asked.

"Why, what?" he said.

"Why do you understand?"

Walther didn't answer at first. He continued gazing at me with his lapis eyes. For a moment, he looked as if he would run away or cry. But then he forced that expression from his face. He shrugged and said, "I am a scientist, but I am also a sinner. My errors began when I was very young, and fell into an admiration for a man whose science promised too much. I am speaking of Doktor Otto Hahn, the discoverer of nuclear fission, along with Professor Lise Meitner, na sicher. Do you know that in the last days of the war, while Hitler kissed and cradled the PPK he would soon use to kill himself, Herr Doktor hid with me, his wife, and his several children in Tailfingen, the land of half-timbered houses and the most vile cowards the world has ever seen? Hahn and I had been selected for acquisition by the American Colonel Boris Pash, lately the guardian of the Manhattan Project, who had made it his mission to kidnap German physicists before Stalin could get to us himself. In late April of 1945, Colonel Pash and his team of commandos crossed into enemy lines, which was no small feat, considering that Germany was still patrolled by Nazi youth, the Wehrwolves who marched not only beneath the swastika but also the death's head set aflame against a black flag.

"Colonel Pash pushed across the countryside to Heidelberg, then to Haigerloch, beating back those small bands of savages. In a cave set within a white field of edelweiss, he and his men found an unusable reactor cobbled together by Heisenberg's men, which they destroyed with grenades. Pash's team then divided into two parts without discerning the irony of the gesture, and from Haigerloch a group of fourteen soldiers cut their way to Tailfingen. Doktor Hahn and his family and I had been hiding there for one month already, starving within the dusty rooms of a bunker. As I am so obviously strong of brawn and a born hunter, Hahn had assigned me the task of hunting for our food and gathering water and edible grasses. This job I fulfilled with maximum ineptitude, wandering the fields like a lost soul as I searched out rabbits and attempted to strangle them with my bare hands. Doktor Hahn and his wife and children would watch me from out of the windows of the Institute, waving to me whenever I looked back, panting and empty-handed. I had more luck with the grasses, and the flowers, and a few fruits and nuts that I managed to stuff into my pockets and roast back at the Institute over the flame of a Bunsen burner. While I cooked them their dinner, my charges attempted to give me advice on how best to catch a coney with string, or how to knock a fat bird out of the sky with a rock. 'You are too slow, Walther,' they said. And, 'You run very stumblingly, like an ox.'

"So, I was quite delighted when Colonel Pash finally stormed the Institute with his terrifying soldiers, who found me roaming about the daisies one morning, clutching a piece of granite and peering confusedly into the sky. They tackled me, screaming, and pressed their guns to my head while I fainted in their arms. Later that afternoon I woke in a Jeep surrounded by Doktor Hahn, his wife and ghastly children, and learned that the army had discovered our cache of uranium and had also acquired Doktors Bagge, Korsching, von Laue, von Weizsäcker, and Wirtz, as they would soon collect Heisenberg himself. After a short stint in England, we were all transferred to a crumbling chateau in Versailles, the Chateau de Chesney, where the beds were hard, the food was lukewarm, and the manly American guards glared at us, sick with boredom.

"Never in my life have I heard the grumbling of so many great men. Doktor Hahn was the worst offender of all. Though I'd expected to be given a reprieve while among the company of the Americans, he soon expedited me to the boundaries of the property to find fresh berries and herbs for his meals. The physicists complained constantly—about the food, the lack of beer, the beds, the paucity of books—but when they were not harping on in this way they became collectively fixated on their own physical culture. The air of Versailles is much more golden than any weather that might be discovered in poor Germany, and the physicists commenced to race about the gardens in all manner of undress, with their skinny legs pumping and their loose pale bellies flouncing under the sunbeams. While Truman readied to translate Hahn and Meitner's discovery into a storm of death over the peoples of the East, Hahn now indulged in a second childhood, demanding treats of me when not prancing about the Versailles tulip trees. 'Ha ha ha ha,' he cackled, as he ran past me of a morning, wearing nothing but flimsy white underpants, as I clutched apples or pears in a sack made of my tattered shirt. 'Ha ha ha ha ha.'"

Walther ceased speaking and took a sip of his beer, his bangs falling into his beautiful eyes.

"Why are you telling me this story?" I asked, laughing for the first time since Shot Teak.

"So that you know that I am ruined," he said, smiling softly at me.

"But you are heading up this important lab," I protested. "You are in charge of the reactor."

"I am hoping to make some little amends through my work," he said.

"Well, I am ruined, too, if you care to know," I said. I hesitated, and then reached for his hand beneath the table.

"I very much doubt that," Walther said, squeezing my hand back.

And so it began. At first we were very chaste. We would walk together in the evenings and the weekends, in the back trails amongst the local hills. We clambered over rocks and little streams, sweat pouring down our bodies. We studied together the redbush monkey flower and the desert dandelion, the flight of the red-winged blackbird and the tracks of the mountain coyote. After the small seasonal fires the black patches of burnt ground would flame with the orange poppy. Within the florid fields we discussed art, music, physics, the Greeks.

Walther had read even more than I—the Bible, all of the ancients. He taught me many things. How Sophocles had been the first person modern enough to ask what a man was and admit that he did not know the answer. Had Oedipus the King been broken by his combat with the Sphinx, and became not one man but two: a man of fate and a man of mistakes? In some way, Walther said, the problem of fission has plagued the arts and the sciences since they were invented, and the secrets of life and death will be divined within the myriad divisions that created the earth and its woes. The splitting of the mind from the body, for example. The rupture of the cell during meiosis. The separation of Adam's rib. The bursting of the uranium nucleus into two daughters. The severance of peoples into good and evil. And Plato's allegory of soulmates, that old story that humans were cleaved by the gods and are cursed to search the earth for their other half.

I left my squalid bedsit and moved into Walther's bungalow on Tapo Canyon Road. We would caress each other deep into the blue hour of the night. I recall one evening that February [*in Spanish*]—we had been out walking and shuddered within the dry cold that scours the winter air here. Once home, we took a hot bath. The atmosphere grew silky with mist. Walther put on a Bach LP, Suite No. 3 en ré majeur. I would like to be able to explain to you what passed between us. Was it that he bent over me with such tenderness that I remembered the alfalfa on my skin and could bear finally the memory of my mother, laughing? Was it that when he loved me, I understood suddenly that what had happened between my dear mother and myself had been the most guiltless expression of affection? He gripped onto me; he fucked me. I saw his gleaming face, which hid something from me. I reached up and pulled on his arm, his shoulder. My hands slipped on his wet skin. He said my name, in his curious, garbled way. He welcomed the unsung places in my body with a melancholy force. And I missed my mother so, so much. I told him that, in media res. I said, Walther, you have made me realize something.

During nuclear fission the uranium nucleus is bombarded with neutrons and a miracle occurs: the nucleus splits into two daughters who bring forth energy as well as three new neutrons. A chain reaction begins. You will forgive me for describing my love for Walther Becker in such unlikely terms, since I lack any other manner of speaking that might do it justice. All forms of language are abbreviation. What I am telling you is that the love I felt for him was a miracle, which gave birth to a new energy. I wanted to have a child with him. I wanted to marry him.

"You are my husband," I said.

He wrapped his hands around my face and said, *yes, yes, yes*. He kissed my eyes.

[*In English*] As for your question.

On July 13 of that year, 1959, I was stooped over a beryllium sample in the lab when an alarm erupted. I looked up. I could hear the sound of men running. I rushed out to the control room, which was separated from the high bay by thick glass windows. Engineers surrounded Walther, who stared at the gauges. The meters all revealed arrows tipping into the red.

"Scram, scram, scram, scram!" he yelled.

A young engineer named Maurice, who had black hair and black glasses, slammed his hand on a button and pressed a host of other controls. This shut down the SRE.

For an hour and a half afterward, the men inspected the reactor with their robot-like machines. Then they turned it on again. The SRE now worked normally.

Later that night, or rather, early the next morning, Walther would barely speak. In our house, he stared at the floor, his eyes darting and his mouth a thin quiver.

"None of the tests that I've done revealed any problem," I told him.

"Some quirk in the system," he muttered, as he drank the third of four scotches.

A week later we realized that the high bay was filling with radioactive gases. That is, that the SRE was somehow leaking from its fuel elements.

You couldn't see it, of course. But the radiation alarm would sound and our film badges had begun to turn black.

"Bleed the gas," Walther ordered the engineers and the techs. They expelled the fumes to the outdoors, at night. They did this for weeks and, even so, we wouldn't enter the control room except when absolutely necessary.

"Is it safe?" I asked him, one night, in bed.

"It is not safe," he said, his face withered against the sheet.

"I mean, is it safe to release the gases outside?"

He rolled over and did not answer for a long time.

"If I don't, everyone could die," he said.

For the next few days, Walther stopped sleeping almost altogether. I would wake up to see him staring at the ceiling.

"Remember that story I told you, about Doktor Hahn?" he asked, once. "About when we were interned at the Chateau de Chesney?"

"When he ran around like a fool," I said, curling around him. I began laughing. "When you tried to kill birds with stones and those awful children barked orders at you."

"I made it into a comedy, but I should not have," he said.

"It doesn't matter now," I said, touching him.

He shook his head. "I haven't told you anything at all."

I thought of my own story, but it was not one that I wanted him to hear. "You don't have to tell me anything."

He closed his eyes. "I wish I had been killed during the war."

I clutched at him, unsure how to respond. Finally, I said, "You will fix the reactor, Walther."

"I want you to stop coming to work." He began arguing with me.

But I would not leave him there, alone.

"We will shut it down," Walther said a week later. "We must look inside." This was July 26. He had called a meeting of all the techs, janitors, guards, researchers, reactor operators, scientists, and engineers in the lab. "But we have to sanitize the high bay first. No one can be there for more than two hours at a time."

We cleaned the high bay in shifts. We brought in buckets, Bactine, soap, buffing sponges. Eventually we realized that the buffers only moved the contamination around the floor and did not absorb it. We began to use Kotex sanitary sponges. It sounds absurd, but we didn't joke about it.

I scrubbed radiation off the high bay's floor on my hands and knees, trying not to breathe. Most of us did not wear special clothing except for booties and rubber gloves. We had some hazard suits stored in a hutch outside, but there were too few to go around, I can't say why. After two hours I would take my soaked sponges and place them into a lead-lined container. A janitor later disposed of them somewhere. The burn pit. The ocean.

Eventually the counter revealed a deep decline in the radiation levels. Walther ordered Maurice to accompany him to the control room, where together they would use an instrument called a *coffin* to inspect the fuel elements in the reactor. The coffin had a grappler that would open the reactor through a pneumatic process that prevented the release of core radiation. It would then extract the elements, place them within its lead container, and seal them beneath its safety shield. Everyone but Walther and the young engineer was to leave the vicinity.

"Get out," Walther told me, looking straight into my eyes.

We all filed out of the building. We stood on the hot hillside, sweating. The men from Areas I–III evacuated. I saw von Braun and Dieter Huzel scurrying off, carrying their satchels. Hours passed. Many of the men from Area IV went home. Others were too terrified to leave— they had families in Simi Valley and the San Fernando Valley, and wanted to know the threats. I stood apart, looking down at the hills, drinking purified water from a canteen.

At around eleven o'clock that night the lab's door burst open and Maurice came racing out, his glasses askew.

"It broke, it broke," he shouted.

"What broke?" we all asked.

"Everything," he said. "The coffin's safety panel is open."

"Where's Dr. Becker?" I yelled.

"I don't know," Maurice said.

I ran to the hutch, right outside the lab, where we kept six hazard suits. I put one on. I ran into the building and down the hallway, screaming. Later, I learned that when Walther discovered the coffin's safety shield had broken he bolted into the high bay, without a mask, and without protective clothing, not that it would have saved him. He struggled manually with the opened coffin, which contained several melted fuel elements spilling radiation into the room. Something had gone wrong with the machine and its safety shield had raised. He'd forced it shut and then tried to escape.

I found Walther in a passage close by the exit. He'd fallen as he'd tried to make his way out. He lay on the ground, breathing with his mouth open. His eyes were closed. I reached down and grasped him with my gloved hands. I put both arms around his waist and dragged him out.

The radiation spread to a mile's radius. All of us on site that day were contaminated.

And then others were, too, weren't they? For decades the site has remained polluted. And it remained a secret for twenty years.

I took care of Walther. The accident destroyed his blood and his skin. He was not very concerned about it. But he did bother over other things.

A day before he died, he struggled in his hospital bed and tried to grab at my hands. He was crying.

"I wasn't one of them, but I didn't try to stop them," he managed to say.

I knew what he meant. "Walther," I said. "Please calm down."

"It's the same thing."

"It's not," I said, wretched.

"It is, it is."

At the end, I lay next to him. He was too delicate to touch. He breathed so lightly, like a small animal.

"I was made for you, and you were made for me," I whispered into his ear. "I for you, and you for me."

"Yes," he gasped.

He died soon after.

I kept waiting for it to happen to me. Maurice died. Seven of the techs. Three of the engineers. Five janitors. Four guards. Three more physicists. Later, it spread to the people living at the base of the hill.

Walther had left me his house. I haunted it like a spirit. I would find myself drifting through the suburbs wondering why I was not dead. The radiation, the beryllium. Later, in the 1960s and then in the 1980s, I was diagnosed with an aggressive skin cancer, then lung cancer. But, as you can see, I prevailed. The doctors don't know why some people can resist exposure to that level of radiation. The only thing that I can tell you is that the people who survived were not necessarily the ones who deserved to.

I went back to the lab. I did not know where else to go. I was promoted to head tech. I worked and slept. I endured my medical treatments. I subsisted in this way for years. Then, in 1965, Area IV had a Christmas party at Lupe's Mexican Restaurant in Thousand Oaks, and my colleagues obliged me to go. One of the engineers, Alfrid Fischer, had a spinster sister, who attended. Anna. It was a beautiful night. The walls were hung with stars and spangles of red, green, and gold. Merry rock music played. Men and women danced in a cleared area toward the back. Anna sat at a table while the men caroused around her, ignoring her. She was tall, taller than me. She had a long, pale face and an abstracted expression. She had clear blue eyes. A large nose. Light, nearly white, hair, which hung in loops at the sides of her face.

I observed Anna for a long while. I decided that the resemblance was as good a reason as any to make some sort of last lunge at life. I approached her, shyly. "Would you like to dance?"

"Not really," she said, in her German accent, laughing.

I sat there with her, throughout the party. We talked and drank.

"You are a hero, I hear," she said, after an hour or so. "The man who saved poor Walther Becker's life."

"That is not true, on either count," I said.

"I also hear that you are a homosexual," she said, smiling.

"Yes," I said.

She smiled. "I like you, Carlos." She pronounced my name perfectly. "You are a gallant."

I began laughing, as I had laughed with Walther when he told me the story of Doctor Hahn.

"You will have a beer with me, if you like," I said. "On another night."

She looked at me with her shimmering eyes. "All right," she said.

We courted in our own way, after that. We went to the zoo, to the aquarium, to the mountains, skiing. I liked Anna very much. I would pick her up in my Ford and take her to French restaurants, where we would talk about everything. I told her about Guanajuato, the alfalfa fields, and what I had felt there. I told her about what I had done in Korea. She listened quietly, and kissed my hands.

"It's all right," she lied, kindly. "You only followed orders."

On another night, she drank a great deal and recited to me the details of her job as a child-minder. "I am in charge of two gremlins, a boy and a girl, who are themselves the products of the most monstrous parents. Behind my back, they call me *the Nazi*. The girl has a distressing tendency to lose her toys. I will be washing dishes, or ironing shirts, and all at once the air will be rent by screams. The first time I heard this alarm I dashed around the house, screaming myself, certain that the child was being murdered. But she had only misplaced her favorite doll, a poppet called 'Mimi,' which has grisly muslin limbs and a deathly china face with ice-blue eyes. 'Tell the Nazi to find it,' I heard the father say, from the bedroom. My brother, Alfrid, is so terrified by the prospect of having to support me that I could not afford to quit. And so I stalked through the house, searching for Mimi. The entire time the child continued shrieking. The family followed me, into the kitchen, into the living room, uselessly, though giving me multiple tips on where I should explore. 'Look in the toilet,' the brother said. 'Look in the closet,' the mother said. 'Look in the attic,' the father said. I investigated all of these places as they continued trailing me, the father dragging his demented daughter along until I grabbed the girl into my arms and escaped into the backyard. There, I found Mimi half-buried in a makeshift grave that the brother had made and forgotten the day before. The child immediately ceased her howling and raced around the lawn, holding up the doll and laughing madly. The family was so overjoyed at the cessation of the noise that they all piled on top of me, shouting that I was the best governess in the world and the most precious Nazi. Rolling there, on the grass, beneath them, receiving their accolades and insults and embraces, I began to laugh, albeit a bit hysterically. That was the happiest I had been all year," she said. She looked at me. "Until I met you."

The next day, I went to a local jeweler's and bought Anna a small diamond ring, an oval-cut surrounded by two tiny baguettes. A week later, I took her to one of our French restaurants. As the waiter filled the water glasses, I brought out the box and placed it on the table.

She opened my offering and gave me a sly smile.

"Do you understand what I can give you?" I asked.

"Yes," she said.

"Do you want to?"

"Yes," she said.

We got married. Alfrid was relieved to be liberated from the menace of a dowager sister, and did not give us any trouble about his suspicions of my true inclinations, which I will say I did pursue occasionally through the years, though with the utmost delicacy. The necessary mechanics between Anna and myself were, for their own part, duly managed. And, soon enough, the much hoped-for cell divided into a daughter: Anna became pregnant with our child, Schatzi. As soon as my wife told me the news, I moved us to Long Beach, to get us as far away as possible from the radionuclides and the trichloroethylene that had migrated to the Valleys. On account of the SRE's partial core meltdown, the area was embedded with tritium, strontium-90, cesium-137, and uranium-235. It gets into the groundwater. It infests the shrubs and grasses and soils. When fires come, or floods, the contaminants spread toward the suburbs and the city. It has remained like this ever since 1959. I don't know why they never cleaned it up.

We had forty good years together until my wife died of cancer in 2006. I was unable to protect her from that. My daughter moved to San Francisco, where she is now a mathematician and married to a lovely woman. They have three sons. A year after my wife passed, I came back here to live in Walther's house, which I had never sold. And then, a few months ago, I came to this hospice.

[*In Spanish*] My daughter, Schatzi Mejia, was born on July 19, 1968. The birthstone for July is the ruby.

That night, when the nurses finally allowed me into the birthing room, I marveled to see Anna hold our tiny, wrinkled child to her breast. Without speaking, I bent down to embrace them both. I closed my eyes and inhaled the scents of saltwater and blood and my own worthlessness. As I listened to our daughter's cries, I remembered that one perfect night with Walther. I pressed my lips to my daughter's face and recalled how, when he had adored me with his strange strength, I had traveled back in time, far before Korea, to the alfalfa field. Standing there, with Anna, with Schatzi, with the memory of my beloved, I was also in the presence of my shining mother, who held the white rabbit with the bright red eyes.

"I love you," I said.

INTERVIEW WITH ELISA OUMAROU

JANUARY 10–12, 2020
CHICAGO, ILLINOIS

[JANUARY 10]
The first time I saw Benjamin at the Santa Susana Field Laboratory, I wore a white skirt, a white polyester blouse, low-heeled sandals, and nude stockings that didn't match my skin color but were all I could get my hands on. This was 1966. Summer. Hot, it was then. I was unhappy. I didn't have much in the way of friends. Wasn't good being with other folks, except my father. But Ben, he reminded me of somebody, though I couldn't say who. And he had this expression like he'd seen me before. My people are fallen from the "upper crust" of El Salvador and Cameroon. That gave me a face that made Anglos comfortable, which explains why I could get a job there in the first place. Anyway, Ben looked at me in a certain way, with a different intelligence than other people at that lab. And it made me feel good.

Do you have a light? Do you mind?

There, that's better.

No, Ms. Rodriguez, I'm not here to talk about myself. Whatever I went through, that's private. My business. It's not for your report. But you *do* need to know about Ben. Dr. Benjamin Augustine. When I saw the government's email, it brought all that back. That's why I replied. Because—I want—I want you to know—what happened.

[*Closes eyes for several seconds, then opens them and nearly smiles.*]

I wore this white skirt that went below the knees, that's how much of a mouse I was. I was twenty-three. Tucked my hair into a bun. I had thick, long eyelashes. Large on top. Large bottom, which I hated. Long legs. I see now that I was a pretty girl. The only problem being, I'd already given up on myself. I felt all pent up, not knowing who I was. I did know I didn't want to be a secretary. I was bad at figures, bad at typing. I was a useless person—always drawing in my notebooks, making ink washes, doodling. It took Ben to bring me out of the prison I'd put myself into.

Santa Susana's engineering department hired me on as a secretary. Building 38. I worked as a repro-typist. I used an IBM Selectric typewriter. I typed up studies and letters and made the engineers' travel plans, their reservations. The day I met Ben, my boss, Kathleen Monroe, started hassling me about mistakes I'd made in a report on the Sodium Reactor Experiment, something about the coolant. I'd run from her office to the typing pool to make the corrections with Mistake Out, but I got so angry I started crying. Must have looked a fright. Back then, when I was a kid, I'd get puffy and red when I became upset, red up to my eyeballs. I don't know what Ben saw in me that day.

He stood in the hall. Turned out the report I messed up was late and he had walked the distance from Building 4143 to fetch it. Put him in a bad mood. He'd come to yell at Kathleen. But when he saw me clutching at myself and sobbing so dramatically, he smiled.

I stopped fussing when I saw him, too. He was tall, big. Had a couple decades on me. Wore a gray suit, white shirt. A blue tie, I think. Black shoes. Dark hair, very short. Freckles across his nose. Large brown eyes. Soft mouth.

He tilted his head at me, and I had this sense of déjà vu.

"I'm so sorry, Doctor Augustine," Kathleen said. "I'll get the girl to do it right away."

"All right, then," Ben answered, while still keeping his eyes on me. He laughed a little and then left.

Kathleen sucked in her cheeks when she saw me staring at the empty place where he'd just stood, like I'd been struck in the head. "Is there a problem, Elisa?"

"Not at all, ma'am," I said, running off to my desk, and not bothering about her and her bad manners any longer—my head was filling with notions of that man already.

"He's married," she called out after me.

[*Winks, then gets up and goes to her kitchen. Comes back with a bottle of white wine and two glasses. Pours only one when I decline.*]
Salud.

My father's family comes from Douala, like I was saying. I look more like my papi, in my features. He was a dandy. Liked a drink, a new suit, a fine hat. He supported us by laying pipe. When I was a child, he'd whisk me up in his arms and say, "Who's my little kumquat?" until I screamed from laughing. My mother shook her head at us from the bedroom doorway and then went inside and we wouldn't hear from her for the rest of the night. Papi and I danced to "Lipstick on Your Collar" and "Lavender Blue." We'd play pinochle and he'd let me cheat. Early in my life, I learned from them that there were happy people and there were sad people. Now I know that women have it harder, and that's why she got depressed. But, back then, I worried that I would be one of the sad ones. The disappointed ones. Like her.

So, when I saw Ben looking at me like that, I jumped. Chance at happiness. But I didn't barely know how to get it started. I started reading ladies' magazines for tips on how to get fixed up. I taught myself how to do a beehive from Nancy Wilson on the cover of *Ebony*. Saved my quarters and got a pair of blue pumps, with three-inch heels. I bought some Moon Drops and Nadinola's so I could be cute like Twiggy. And some White Shoulders. That bunk took up almost all my paycheck.

I'd wobble around Building 38, trying to lure Ben back to the typing pool with my mental vibrations. I didn't know the location of his office and felt too scared to ask. But it was wonderful to feel that hope. That I would run into him. I looked for him around every corner. It gave my life a new sensation. At night, I'd lie in bed, naked, and shimmy around the sheets, pretending that he had his hands on me. I'd heard his voice when he'd spoken to Kathleen, and it was deep. I wanted to hear him call my name. Actually, I barely knew what I wanted, as my mother brought me up very strict and my father left that all to her. And before that, the boys who might have shown me a trick or two found me shy and awkward. So, me hankering after Ben, it was just instinct.

I'd occasionally see Ben after work, when he walked through the back lot to his car. He stood straight, dignified. His clothes looked crisp and neat, unlike the other scientists, who appeared rumpled and unmarried. I did a carpool with Kathleen, Shauna, Patricia, and Wiletta—we rode to work in Kathleen's VW Bus, even though she drove like a lunatic. She lived all the way down in Long Beach and could pick us up and drop us off, as long as we helped with the gas. We'd set out together at five o'clock, heading to the secretaries' parking spaces. When I'd spy Ben, I'd whip up ahead, trying to get his eye. Sometimes I'd see him nod just slightly, as if he could feel me, but he would never turn around, never smile, not after that first day. Sometimes an engineer or a custodian jogged up to me and I'd have to bat them away. I'd stand there alone and watch Ben get into his car, a shiny green Lincoln, and drive off.

"Making a fool of yourself," Wiletta said, once, as we all drove home.

"Hussy," Kathleen said, pumping on the gas like that VW was a souped-up Mustang.

"He's got a family," Patricia said.

"He looks good, though," Shauna said, nudging me.

"I'm not doing anything." I looked out the window, at the clapboard houses and tidy lawns that we sped by on our way out of the city. I lived in Inglewood and Simi Valley seemed a strange place to me, and an odd place for a man like Ben to live in. It was too quiet. Too boring. I thought he belonged someplace more interesting, with museums and culture. Turns out I was right. But I wouldn't find out about that side of him for a while yet. He only lived in my imagination.

I'd get home and my mother would be waiting on the sofa.

"Honey, you should not wear paint on your face," she'd say. "Good men won't want to talk to you that way."

"I only want one man to talk to me," I told her, finally. "And I don't know if he's good or not and I don't know if I care."

"Holy Jesus," she said.

Because my mother had a lot of sadness, I'd be the one making the family dinner most nights. I'd kick out of my heels and start cooking sopa de pata, which I spiced with curry and thickened with groundnuts. I chopped an onion and garlic and fried it in hot, popping grease. I stripped the soft meat off of cow feet and browned it to the color of tree bark. I sliced tripe into pale feathers, threw that in, too. In went the red curry. I tossed in the white yucca and a blessing of cilantro.

Juicy squares of red onion. A broken rib of celery. Long, cold pour of milk. Let it simmer for two hours, though three or four would be best.

Papi would come home and the house lit up. He'd stomp all around groaning about how good everything smelled. I'd run over to the pantry and pour him a bourbon. Sometimes, in my new state of mind, I'd sip from his glass when my mother wasn't looking. He'd pinch me on the cheek. We'd all sit down for the family meal, my mother looking at me suspicious over her plate, Papi eating the sopa in huge fast bites.

"This is fabuloso!" he'd say, his words long and drawn-out, like to make the compliment last longer.

[*Pauses. Drinks. Smokes.*]

After a month or so, I realized that I had to take control of the situation. Ben wasn't coming to me. But I was such an innocent. Lipstick couldn't change that. Neither could high heels or Nancy Wilson. How could I make him want me? Finally, I figured it out: I might be a bad flirt, and I sure couldn't type, but I could *cook*. So, one night, I made another sopa, though I barely spiced it, which caused my father to complain. After dinner, I wrapped some of it up—the cow foot meat, the yucca. I ladled broth into a cup. I brought it with me to work the next day. At noon, I walked over to Building 4143, where they kept the reactor. I'd learned by then that's where he worked. I didn't know exactly what he did. I still don't. I headed across the campus, passing the Rocketdyne pond, the one they said was contaminated. Birds and frogs splashed around in there, though they didn't make much noise, no croaking and cheeping. Weirdly silent animals. I could hear yelling from down by Black Canyon, where the protesters rallied. I felt the boom of the rockets blasting from Areas I–III. And the explosions from the burn pit, where the disposal team circled round, wearing white jumpsuits and gasmasks and dumping the sodium in the water. Still, even as hot as it was, it was pretty country up there, the hills covered with copper-colored grass and gray crows twirling through the air. When I passed the techs and the janitors and the guards, they greeted me with breezy *heys*, so I didn't feel scared at all. They weren't, so why would I be?

Clutching my dish of sopa, I walked into 4143. Didn't need a key, extra clearance, not anything. Just went in. I'd never been in there before. Seemed like a regular place. White men in suits and spectacles milled about, and men of color in overalls, but nobody wore ventilators or hazmat suits. I walked down the corridors and passed by rooms filled with machines. I found the offices. His door was open. I stood in the doorway and rapped my knuckles on the wood. He looked up.

I didn't say anything. I had a speech planned about how Kathleen told me he needed something typed. But my mouth went dry. He hulked behind his desk. Before I'd interrupted him, he'd been reading papers by the light let in through a window on the west wall. I noticed that he'd hung pictures almost everywhere. They were huge, framed, black-and-white photographs of the mountains around the lab site. Of course, he also had a whiteboard and walls full of books.

"Well, come in," he said, in a serious voice. But I could see a smile touching his lips.

I took a step forward, then another. I held up the sopa cup but didn't offer it to him. My heart beat wild. Then, I looked closer at the photographs. I'd never seen pictures like that before, not in person. Not ever. They showed the hills and the sky and the birds, the clouds. And, like I said, they were black-and-white. But the colors, or the shades, in the pictures struck me as special. The black resembled velvet, or deep space. The whites shone with different kinds of brightness, many shades of pale: snow, ivory, cream, vanilla, eggshell, and light gray.

"You like those?" he asked, still sitting at his desk.

"What are they?" I said.

"Shots from around here," he said. "It's just a hobby." He reached under his desk and opened a drawer. He brought out a camera, what I now know was a Leica IIIf, a screw-mount. He put it on his blotter. "I take them on my lunch breaks, sometimes. And I develop at home."

I didn't go look at the camera, because I felt too skittish to get close to him. I kept staring at the photos. They reminded me of drawings I sometimes made of Papi.

He let me look at his walls for a long time. He watched me. We both remained silent.

Finally, I walked to his desk and put the wrapped sopa next to the camera. He took off the brown paper. He smiled, then, for real. He opened up the cup and sniffed it.

"Oh, God," he said. He sniffed it again. "Is that cumin? Red pepper?"

I nodded, impressed he could tell. White people didn't eat things like that, then.

"My grandmother was from Port-au-Prince," he said, reading my expression.

"Oh," I exclaimed.

He seemed surprised. "You didn't know?"

I didn't know what I knew about him. I only shrugged, and felt so happy.

"Needs more spice," he said, while I watched him eat. After he finished the whole thing, he put down the cup and tilted his head at me, like he had the first time I'd seen him.

"I'm married," he said.

"I know," I said.

"To a good woman," he said. "And we have three grown sons."

I nodded. I didn't feel too well, except from being close to him. "All right," I said.

I did go back to see him again, though.

[*Drinks and shakes her head when asked a question.*]

No, I told you that I did not want to talk about that. About me and cancer. Hospitals. Lawsuits. Contamination.

Whatever happened to me, Ms. Rodriguez, is something that I will never talk about. And I'm not interested in it anymore, anyway. When you go through something like that, you need to learn how to forget. It's how a person stops herself from going crazy. From having a sad life, you know? I moved on from being sick.

I let you come here so that I could tell you about Ben. I don't know if I can make myself any clearer to you. If you keep coming back here, all you will hear about is him.

[JANUARY 11]

For all of that week I couldn't think of anything else but Ben. I dreamed of his eyes and his wide shoulders stretching his white shirt. I thought of the low tones of his voice. His long, strong hands touching his black-and-silver camera when he showed the Leica to me. And I thought about those pictures of his, the colors in them.

At home, I looked at my ink washes and thought they looked bad. I closed my eyes and visualized the photograph with the crows flying overhead. I had a small stock of white cotton paper and acrylic ink, and one brush. I tried to remake the picture as a drawing. I no longer painted as a regular practice. I was too tired, mostly, from working for the scientists and keeping dinner on the table. But I did my best with that sketch. Cross-hatching, light staining, and black slashes for the hills.

The next Wednesday I wrapped up some more sopa (spiced normally this time) and tucked my drawing into the typing manual I usually kept at my desk. At lunchtime I scurried past Kathleen, who gave me the stink-eye, and walked the hot, smoky path until I reached the open doorway of his office. He sat at his desk and raised his eyes when he sensed me there.

"Oh, hello there—what *is* your name, again?" he asked. "I realized the other day that I don't know it."

I walked in and closed the door, shocking myself.

"Elisa Oumarou."

"So," Ben said. "What I thought."

"My folks are from Cameroon and El Salvador," I said, softly, putting the wrapped cup on his desk and adjusting the typing manual under my arm. "And you?"

"Chicago," he said. "Then Cambridge, MIT."

"It must have been hard," I said.

"Wasn't easy." He put his hand on the cup but didn't open it. He hesitated, like he planned to say something about me leaving.

I saw a chair pushed to the side of the wall. I dragged it to his desk and sat down in it. I took out my drawing and pushed it across the surface of the desk.

"Ah," he said.

While he looked at the sketch, I examined his pictures again. I studied the black tones, which deepened into indigo, almost. The pearl shades. The gray. The dove. The shadow.

"I want to do what you do," I said.

"Photography, you mean," he said.

"Yes."

He traced my drawing with his finger. "You have a good, strong line, Elisa."

"A good, strong line," I repeated. I stood and approached the photograph with the crows. Like him, I traced the edges of the hillside with my fingertips against the glass. "Is that what you have?"

"What?"

"A strong line?"

He looked at me for a long time.

"Yes," he said.

[*Lights another cigarette.*]

When I left his office, I came back to Building 38 and went straight to the bathroom. I stood at the sink and frowned at my reflection in the mirror. I wore false lashes. Flakes of mica from the Moon Drops shimmered on my lips. Pale rose blush sat on top of my cheeks. And my hair—I'd spent two hours on it that morning, getting up at 4 A.M. just to make it set.

I didn't look like myself. I looked like another girl. And I decided at that moment that I didn't want paint on my face. Or to wear high heels so that I could barely walk. I wanted to be like those pictures of Ben's. Something better than the regular fake-up. Just those two talks with Ben made me see that.

I turned on the water faucet. At Santa Susana we drank purified water most of the time, but we washed in the water from the taps. I rinsed my face of all the makeup. The mascara made patterns like autumn leaves around my eyes. I got a paper towel and soaked it and scrubbed my mouth of the Moon Drops.

That night, I took down my hair and oiled it and put it back in my regular bun. I gave the shoes to my mother, who threw them away. She didn't understand, though; she thought I was coming back to Jesus.

[*Fingers her necklace and goes quiet for a while.*]

After I cleaned myself up, I looked like the person I'd been before meeting Ben. But I wasn't.

[JANUARY 12]

The next time I saw him, I brought my sopa as usual. He sat at his desk and started eating the stew with a plastic spoon right away, making noises and chuckling into the cup.

"I cannot get enough of this stuff," he said, chomping it down. I sat in his spare chair and looked at the pictures. I felt my soul sparkling and bursting inside me.

You can have as much as you want, I wanted to say.

He grinned at me over the sopa, rattling the spoon. When he finished, he patted his mouth with a paper towel I'd brought as a napkin. "I've got something for you," he said.

I sat straight up. "What?"

"It's just an old thing," he said. "Something I don't use anymore."

"What? What?"

He reached under his desk and brought out a camera. It was small, like his other one, but older and more scratched. He held it out and I snatched it.

"I don't know how to take pictures," I said.

He reached under his desk again and brought out a manual. "Here's a how-to."

"I'll need you to show me," I said, locking eyes with him. "I'll have to come by here more often."

He smiled with half his mouth. "Well, just for a few minutes I can show you, maybe."

We leaned against his desk while he taught me about the Leica. I still have it. A beautiful camera. He showed me the shutter speeds, the aperture, the focusing lever, the spools. Brought out a roll of film and taught me how to cut it.

I filled the camera and focused it on him. He looked bashful and uncertain, and so I lowered it.

"Why'd you start taking pictures?" I asked.

"I love beauty," he said, seriously. But then he blushed and smiled, so all the beautiful lines in his face stood out.

I raised the camera and took that shot of him.

"Ben?" somebody said, opening the door. One of his scientist friends, Dr. Herbert Müller. He had black glasses and a big belly, and I guess later won a Nobel Prize. He poked his head in and gawped when he saw me.

I flung the Leica over my arm, scooping up my manual and his cup.

"Well, let me know if you need anything else, Dr. Augustine," I said, and fled.

I started taking pictures then, all the time. It cost me money I didn't have. Ben helped me out, handing me three twenty-dollar bills during one of our lunches. I took the cash, and folded it into my pocket as if it were a million bucks. That weekend, I bought fixer, film, developing paper, and a black light bulb. At first, I'd take photos like he did, of mountains and birds. My father and I drove up to Baldwin Hills and I shot the rocks and the scrub, the red-tailed hawks and the small brown sparrows. Whatever I saw, a bushy mustard plant, clumps of wild radish, I snapped. And the black crows zipping through the clouds.

I liked to turn the camera on my father. That's something I'm grateful for, now that he's gone. He'd dawdle on the hills with me, wearing his tartan cap and his corduroy jacket with the green paisley handkerchief in the pocket. His face was so beautiful. I don't know if I realized that until I began to photograph him. If I'd really looked at him before as a person, not just felt him always there, a known quantity. He'd stand by an overlook, framed by the blue sky and smiling so wide his face burst forth in smile lines, like sunrays. He had dark freckles on his nose and below his eyes. Sometimes, I'd shoot his hands. He had long fingers, like you see in Imogen Cunningham's hand studies, Paul Strand's, Stieglitz's. Later, when I saw DeCarava's work—Roy DeCarava the photographer, who took portraits, deep faces, expressive gestures—I realized that I had an eye. But I didn't know that, yet. Not until Ben showed me what I could be.

"What are you trying to communicate here?" Ben would ask me, always during his Wednesday lunch hours, when he studied my work. I kept bringing him lunch, which he loved. He'd scoop into the food and then take a close look at my pictures. In the beginning, I'd only show him nature shots of mountains or birds. Oftentimes I overexposed the photos, or clouded them with fixer. He wouldn't ever criticize. He wanted to know what went on in my *mind*. "What were you thinking here?" "Why did you shoot from that angle?" "What do you want people to see in this image?" "What do you like about it?" "What do you hate about it?" No one had ever asked me so many questions before.

"I was just trying to make the kind of pictures you do," I said, one time.

"But you should do what only *you* can do," Ben said.

After that, I decided I would show him the pictures of my father. Up to then, I'd thought of them as simple snapshots, like those you find in a family album.

But when he peered at my photographs he began nodding right away. "Who is this?"

"My dad," I said, my heart pounding.

"It's your best work." He leaned toward me. "What were you thinking when you took it?"

"I don't know," I said.

"What do you mean, you don't know?" He raised his eyebrows. "Elisa, how do you think I got here from the South Side, to run the most sophisticated nuclear reactor in the nation? It wasn't just from being smart, or looking the way I do. I had to be clear about my ideas and believe in them."

"I don't have that," I said, and began crying like a fool.

"If you're going to do this, you need to know that *you* are important," he said, thumping his hand on the desk. "Your *vision* is important."

We stared at each other. I thought that maybe he would leap over his desk and take me in his arms. I trembled all over. His face opened, like a door. But he didn't make a move.

"You are important," he said again. "So tell me what you were thinking and feeling when you took this picture."

"That I love my dad," I wept.

"And that's what your work should have," he said. "Your emotion in it. Your life."

I soaked up his words like they were wine.

We sat there together for a while, me wanting him to hold me while whispering about my blessed "importance." Him wanting whatever he wanted. While crying, I peeped through my fingers and watched his soft mouth moving. I thought that maybe, while I was crying so hard, I could bend over, like from sobbing. He could see down my blouse to get a better idea of what to do. But he only reached into his pocket and pulled out a handkerchief. He gave it to me and waited until I stopped carrying on. "I think you should study the portraitists," he finally said, in a normal tone. He mentioned Cunningham and Stieglitz. He said I should get DeCarava's *The Sweet Flypaper of Life*.

"All right," I said, getting myself together and writing the title down.

The next Wednesday, I went to Ben's office with a cup of Ekwang stew with cocoyam and crayfish. I also brought a special photograph. A self-portrait. It showed me standing against a white-painted wall. I'd rented a tripod and taken it in my bedroom. I had a plain white shirt on, a scrubbed face. I didn't smile for the photograph. I didn't try to be pretty. Instead, I'd tried to make a picture that had my emotion and my life in it, the way he'd told me to.

He ate the stew, making grumbling noises of pleasure, but when I showed him the picture he went quiet. He wiped his hands carefully and rose from his chair to study the image in the natural light let in by his window. I stood next to him and looked at it, too.

"Why did you take this?" he asked, like he always did.

"I'm showing me trying to become myself," I said. "Trying to see myself."

"And what do you see?" he asked.

I hesitated. "That I'm a woman now, and not a girl anymore."

"Well, that's evident," he said, smiling.

"And that I'm a person who could be happy," I said.

"Happy about what?" he asked.

"Being alive," I stammered. "Maybe making pictures."

"That's good," he said.

"Maybe other things," I said.

We remained silent for a while longer.

"May I keep this?" he finally asked. "It shows a real gift."

"You can keep it," I whispered. I could smell the soap on his skin. I could hear his soft breathing. He didn't bend down toward me. He didn't reach for me. But he *looked* at me, with those eyes of his. Seeing me. Not even my father had ever seen me so clearly before, I think.

And that's when a knocking came at the door.

"Sweetheart?"

Ben's head jerked. A pretty, tiny, older white woman with dyed blond hair came into the office, smiling. She carried a paper bag in her small manicured hand. "You left your lunch, thought I'd just pop by and—"

Ben and I jumped apart, like criminals.

His wife's face faded when she saw me there.

"Darling?" she asked.

I started shaking, though I hadn't done anything yet. I walked fast over to the desk and began to clear up the cup and spoon and napkin.

"What are you doing?" she asked, her voice still soft, but edging higher.

"We work together," Ben said.

His wife glared at the picture of me in his hand. "You're—working?"

Ben looked old and mournful. He shook his head. He walked over to me while I still scrambled the lunch things together and handed me back the photograph. I smushed it under my armpit.

"I made a mistake, Wendy," he said, lowering his gaze to the ground. "But it's not like it seems."

The wife stared at me with her large blue eyes, with the wrinkles around them. She wore pink lipstick, which did not hide the lines and sags around her mouth. Yet her face seemed to catch on fire. "I'd like to speak with my husband alone, please," she said, in a controlled voice that did not match her expression.

I left, quick. I exited 4143. Walked, sweating, past the yellow smoke of the burn pits, the stink of the ponds, the commotion of the rockets. I returned to Building 38. Wiletta, Shauna, and Patricia ate their sandwiches on a sofa by the typing pool while Kathleen stood outside of her office and complained about their attention to detail in a loud voice.

"You miserable she-wolves should be able to produce a flawless business letter in under ten minutes, you hear me? Ten minutes," she gabbled on, but she shut up when I stalked past them. I could feel them following me with their eyes. By this time, they thought I was having an affair with Ben, especially since I'd grown more aloof on the rides to and from work because Kathleen sometimes made nasty jokes about homewreckers. I reached my desk and put Ben's cup and spoon beneath my chair. I laid down the picture I'd stuffed under my arm and tried to smooth out the creases I'd put there. But it was ruined.

The days passed. I couldn't sleep. At work, Ben didn't come by. I didn't go to Building 4143 that next Wednesday, or the Wednesday after. I'd see him walking to his car after work, while Kathleen and the other girls and I made our way to the bus in the parking lot. At home, I took photo after photo of myself, trying to come up with an image that he'd love so much that he'd know he had to keep teaching me. Those turned out to become a suite that I'd put in my first show. Three weeks after his wife stumbled in on us doing nothing, I tucked four of the photographs into a manila folder and trekked back to Building 4143, worried that I'd faint from nerves.

But when I knocked on his door, he didn't answer. I knocked again, and again, until I was practically pounding on the door and felt like one of those women who go crazy after a man and lose their judgment—I'd seen it before in the neighborhood, women falling all over themselves when their lovers leave them. I got control over myself quick enough, though, because Einsteins barreled down the hallways chattering in their number language, and Dr. Müller with the big belly stamped out of his office and yelled at me for making a ruckus. I bent down, slipped the pictures underneath Ben's door, and walked away.

That night, on Kathleen's bus, after Patricia and Wiletta and Shauna had been dropped off, I sat shotgun and stared dead-eyed through the windshield. Kathleen made a clucking noise.

"Come on, it's not that bad," she said.

"It is," I said. "You couldn't understand."

"I'll bet I could." She steered the bus by just touching two fingers to the wheel, like a maniac. "I'll tell you something, Elisa, though I hope you can keep it to yourself."

"I don't need to hear anything," I said.

"I had an affair with a married man, once. When he left me, it busted me in half." She reached over and patted me on the knee, which made her seem like an entirely different creature than the warthog who yelled at me at work. "But I got out of that hussy mentality and made myself get right. Had to move two states over, but I got past it in the end."

"We weren't having an affair," I said.

"Sure you weren't," she said.

"He was teaching me how to take pictures."

"They like to play their little games."

"It wasn't like that," I told her, my voice breaking.

"No need to get upset."

I put my face in my hands. "I don't know what we were doing."

She patted me again. "You're all right. I mean, you're a terrible typist, and the worst secretary in the whole building, but otherwise you're all right."

I started giggling, crying, and cursing her out at the same time.

"Let it out, baby," she said in her horrible loud voice, while screeching the bus around a corner. "Cry those ugly guts out."

Well, I did cry, and kept doing so—too much, maybe, considering that I hadn't even kissed him. When I realized that Ben would never again take me back into his office and ask me all of those questions, and look at my pictures, I cried nearly every night for the next four, five months, with my mother simultaneously praying over me and chastising me for being an unclean woman.

I quit Santa Susana after a year. That was in 1967, which was actually good timing, since the lab had a reactor accident two years later. Turns out that place wasn't as safe as I'd thought. There'd been a meltdown in 1959, and then another accident in 1964, so it had already been dangerous for a long time. There were toxins there, as you well know yourself, Ms. Rodriguez. The owners or the government didn't clean it up right. The water wasn't pure. The air wasn't safe. I don't know why the hell people stayed there, worked there, lived there. Maybe they were all like me, and didn't understand the risks. Because your boss, the government, never told us much. It let us stew in that misery.

But that's not why I left. During my last summer at the lab, on my days off, I'd sat around my bedroom in my old robe, taking pictures of myself that I couldn't afford to develop. I ran out of film and just lolled around, feeling like I'd died. My father tried to get me to walk around Baldwin Hills, but I wouldn't. My mother thought I'd lost my mind and I couldn't barely stand being in the house with her. Finally, I thought of what Kathleen had said about moving states and applied for a position as a salesclerk at Marshall Field's in Chicago. I got the job.

Everything seemed different once I moved here. I didn't stay at Field's for long. I made friends. I got out. Great city for a young gal. I took pictures with Ben's Leica and went to museums, galleries. Eventually, through people I met, I got a dream gig, assisting for John Tweedle. Oh, you should look him up if you don't know about him. He was the first African American photog working for a U.S. magazine, the *Chicago Daily News*. Also *Newsweek*, *Ebony*, *Playboy*. A prodigy. Photographed Dr. King, Coretta Scott King, Jesse Jackson, the rally at Soldier Field, the Chicago March.

I eventually forgot about Ben, except for feeling embarrassed about him every once in a while. This was 1971, '72. National Guardsmen were deployed to the University of Maryland, and we had the Emergency March, the Panthers, Vietnam. It was a time for being part of a movement, for feeling like you were with the people. My people were in photography. I did my work with John, keeping him supplied with film, his cameras in ready condition, snacks, transportation. I learned so much from him. I studied all the photographers Ben had mentioned to me, and more—DeCarava and Stieglitz, but also Capa, Avedon, Arbus, Frank, Karsh, Bourke-White, Doisneau. I partied with Ming

Smith, Daniel Dawson, Al Fennar. And I always had my Leica with me, too.

I rented a studio in Garfield Park, which had no heat or decoration except for camera equipment and a big bed. I took my lovers there. Charles Ulane, a redheaded poet that I'd picked up in Sadie's bar one night. And Lucille Winson, a Black model I met while doing a catalog shoot. But what interested me most were my pictures, and being clear about my ideas, and believing in them. And I did get clear, and I did believe in myself. After a few years, I built up enough of a name to get my gallery and could rent a bigger studio. Also, I managed to get health insurance, which I'd need plenty of starting in 1981.

[*Leaves room and is gone for a long while. I hear sounds of rustling and boxes moving, and the interviewee breathing hard and volubly. She rejects offers of help. Finally she returns with two envelopes. She motions me toward her dining table. She takes photographs out of the sleeves and spreads them before me. All of the photographs are 8 x 10 black-and-white images of people.*]

See that, the tension there? Even while she's smiling? That's Chicago, 1975, the anxiety.

This, a lovely girl, I remember her. Little pigtails.

Look at the contrast here. I was experimenting, it's almost an abstract.

Here, it's the moment right before their hands touch. Like Michelangelo, but real life.

[*Examines pictures for a long while, not talking, despite questions.*]

Of the breast and the bladder. But I won't tell you about that, like I said. Or why I think it happened. Or who should pay. You couldn't pay me enough, anyhow. For a long time, it took my womanhood away.

What I guess I will say is that when I was diagnosed, I remembered Ben again. You learn a lot about yourself when you go through an experience like that, getting sick. You're able to look back. You see when you were truly yourself with somebody, or when you were shamming. When you were really living, and when you were just pretending. Don't get me wrong, I've had some good friends, good, good people in my life. My father, for one. And Lucille, that model I took up with, she was a great girl. But when you get ill, you're looking for those moments that made this trip worth it—the trip here, to this planet. When you had hope. When you were really able to love.

And all of that happened to me with Ben. When I spoke with him, I could be myself, or at least wonder who "myself" was. I know I shouldn't have gone sniffing around him, with his having a wife and sons. When I got older, I felt ashamed of the way I'd behaved. But after I landed in the cancer ward, getting my medicine—what I'm saying is, I realized that it had always been Ben for me. Ben was the one who saw me. He knew how to ask me the simplest, most important things. And, by doing that, he taught me how to see.

What do you want? What are you trying to say? What are your dreams? Do you know that you are important? It's a form of love, looking at somebody's work, asking them about themselves and really caring. It's true love. And we didn't touch once, not one time.

I thought about that, after the surgery and the chemo. He was the one that I returned to when I had to put my body back together. His memory never left me after that. His questions have run through my whole life. They have kept me who I am. First when I was trying to become an artist, and then when I was trying to survive. And then, far later, when the internet came and I had to learn in that cold way that Dr. Ben Augustine died in 1973 of B-cell lymphoma, which he'd probably contracted from the reactor accidents in 1964 and 1969 that you did not protect him against, or the chemicals that you let lie in the ponds. Ms. Rodriguez, did he ever get his payout? Or did his widow? His sons? The way you've stumbled in here, without a clue in world as it seems to me, I will bet that they did not. But money doesn't matter anymore. What's left is my gratitude for having known him that little while.

Because I can still hear and see his questions, his voice, his eyes, his friendship, his gentleness, and it's a strength to me, even just this minute. Ben—my dear soulmate, for that's what he was—has been dead for coming on fifty years, but he's still helping me now, when I am an old woman and you government people come barging in here, trying to pry out of me my most private pains for your report. I know I invited you here, but forgive me, ma'am, it's true all the same. He is with me, and that love of his protects me while you ask me all your questions, and can't understand a single word I say. While you sit there never comprehending what you have done and pretend that listening to my story could ever make it right.

INTERVIEW WITH BARRY SCOTT

FEBRUARY 15–18, 2020

BURBANK, CALIFORNIA

[FEBRUARY 15]

You're asking the wrong question, kid. What happened to me back in the 1960s is just not that important. And you can see that I lived through it, though it didn't make me any prettier. What you should be worried about is yourself. What kind of people are you working for? Do you really know what you're involved in? Can you see the big picture? Those are the questions you should be asking.

I see I'm not getting through to you, so how about this: What's got a lump of butter for a brain and ten toes?

No, honey, it's a joke. What's got a lump of butter for a brain and ten toes?

The answer is, anybody who works for the government.

[*Laughs long and hard while clutching his belly.*]

You're so serious-looking for a girl that I'll tell you a little about it, though that's not why I finally answered your emails. The reason I contacted you folks is to tell you that I've been researching what happened down there, and what it all means. I know what you're really up to. Even if you don't.

I worked at Santa Susana from the 1960s to the '90s, with a long break in the '70s for treatment. I hydrided zirconium and uranium for the SNAPs. The SNAPs were the reactors, the Systems for Nuclear Auxiliary Power. The DoD wanted nuclear to power its new satellites, so the physicists came up with two choices: SNAPs, which run on fission, and radioisotope thermoelectric generators, which use decay. At Santa Susana we made the reactors. Another company, Glenn L. Martin Co. out of Baltimore, built the generators. They were our competitors for the military contract. I thought we were all the smartest guys you ever saw, working on the miracles of tomorrow. But it turned out that we were idiot brothers who worshipped together at the high altar of how-fucking-dumb-can-you-be.

I hydrided zirc and uranium, like I said. That created the fuel for the SNAPs. Zirconium's a white metal and uranium's a radioactive actinide that poor old Marie Curie knew was a stepping-stone to curing cancer. Back in 1965, I graduated with my degree in chemistry and was full to the brim with belief in the future. *I* thought I could cure the world of coal, the brimstone that killed my father and my two brothers out in Kentucky. I moved the wife from Lexington to Santa Susana so that I could spend my days heating metals in a hydrogen autoclave, which is sort of like a cooker. That's what hydriding means; don't worry if you never heard about it before. I had to explain it to my wife so many times.

[*Shakes his head, smiles.*]

We had some fine days out here in California, me and my girl Lou. She was, or maybe still is, a tall, sweet blonde with brown eyes and a soft voice. Every time I looked at her I couldn't believe how lucky I'd got. She and I met when I was in school. I tricked her into marrying me by pretending I was some hotshot with big plans. We were just all-of-the-way excited to move to So Cal. Me, because I thought that I was going to put Eastern Coal Corp out of business, and Lou because she'd read so much about the movie stars out here. She wanted to see the palm trees and the Chevrolets. And plus, at that time, she was in crazy in love with me. You sure as hell wouldn't know it now, but I was a Tab Hunter–type back then, all muscles and shiny teeth.

I'd come home from my day at the lab and she'd be waiting for me in the doorway, wearing a white dress, her hair down. Holding an ice-cold martini in her hand. It was a different time back then. Women didn't fuss about the things they holler over now. Lou liked taking care of me, she said. I'd flop down in the easy chair and she'd sit at my feet, asking me about my day. I can't tell you how beautiful that girl was, the tenderness of her cheeks, the yellow-rose color of her hair. I'd sip my drink and say, "Why, Lou, today we tested the NaK loops of the 8, and they seemed to work pretty well." Or, "Why, Lou, today they started testing the reflectors on the 10A, but they had some troubles with the retaining band." Things that didn't make a lick of sense to her, though I schooled her patiently. She'd nod, smiling with her chin propped on my knee and her eyes closed. She'd say, "That's so interesting, baby."

Can you imagine? Having a woman like that?

She begged me to have kids as quick as possible but I was a jackass about it. After my martini, we'd sit down to dinner, and I'd look at her across the dining table, which was set with her bridal china and the linens she'd ironed so carefully. I'd dig into my steak and say, "Darlin', I want you to myself just a bit longer. I'll take you to Hawaii and we'll go swimming in the blue water. Or we'll fly over to France and fandango in gay Paree." I knew that once we had a baby she'd love it more than me, and I couldn't bear the thought of it.

"But I love you so much I want your baby inside me now," she'd say, starting to cry.

"Oh, oh, oh," I'd tell her, laughing and snuggling her up. "It'll be just fine, you listen to hubby."

The problem with men is that they don't know two things: first, men don't know that women actually mean the things that they say. And second, men don't know that women are incapable of telling the whole truth, about how they can get to hate you as much as they love you. Women are a secret species. They keep the truth of themselves to themselves, but they sort of let you know, too, with little hints. And if you don't pick up on the mystery clues that they plant into their chatter about movie stars and stir into their icy martinis, then you're going to wind up a crazy old scarecrow with scars in the place where your face should be, eating cold hot dogs for dinner in assisted living—

[*Pause.*]

Why, aren't you a nifty one, Miss Rodriguez, getting me to chatter on like this? You sure know how to get a man talking. Though why you're taping me and writing all those notes into your book, I have no idea, when I thought you were here to take a report on radionuclide pollution at the lab and what happened to the people who worked there.

No, no. I told you, I don't want to talk about cancer, or go on about, what was that word you used? "Trauma?" Jesus wept.

I emailed you people to let you know that you are doing wrong, and about the big picture, and what I was saying about before.

Yeah, I think that's a good idea.

Yes, ma'am, thank you.

No, I'll call you.

[*Reacts as I get up.*]

Oh, oh, no. I'm sorry, I didn't know you had any physical troubles. Do you need help making your way out?

[FEBRUARY 16]

Don't you get yourself into such a bother about a grouch like me, Miss Rodriguez. I just needed to settle down after you had me recall everything about my dear departed wife. And I'm not done telling you about that big picture. Like I was trying to tell you yesterday. Because you're being played for a dimwit if you think that just because you work for some nice-sounding agency that you're on the side of right. You work for the system, sister. That puts you on the side of black hats. These villains have been with us for all of human history. Before they were your bosses, they were Manhattan Project men turning Marie Curie's discoveries into nuclear bombs, and before that, they were the German army turning good science into chemical weapons. They were the lords of Europe robbing the peasants with their Crusades and they were the Roman emperors courting and then killing Cicero.

I explained to you already that at Santa Susana, we made reactors, and Martin made the generators. It turns out that what we were actually doing at Santa Susana was showing the government that they should use the Martin products instead of ours. There was a big SNAP accident in 1964 before I got there, and then the one that caught me in '69. It's no surprise that the DoD decided to use generators instead of reactors to power the new satellites they were launching. Those were the Transit sats, which would one day be used to terrify all the people on God's green earth. But they weren't invented by evil men. Transits were born out of love for science. It all started when two kid physicists decided that they would eavesdrop on space and listen to what it whispered back to them. I'm talking about young William Guier and George Weiffenbach, two boys who were muddling through at APL—the Applied Physics Laboratory, out in Maryland.

The Soviets had just launched Sputnik in 1957. The Russki satellite was a feat not only of space innovation but also a stroke of public relations magic, because anybody could pick up the signal on a ham radio. People around the world were tuning into this marvel. Among them were Guier and Weiffenbach, who were weak-chinned, four-eyed APL pipsqueaks who spent their evenings and weekends listening in on Sputnik while it journeyed on its weeklong orbit.

Beep beep beep beep, they heard. *Beep beep beep beep*. The sound started loud and then it would get softer. Eventually the boys realized that they were hearing the Doppler effect. You know what I'm talking about. That's how sound or light waves increase in frequency the closer an observer moves toward a source, and then get weaker and fainter the farther they drift apart.

Guier and Weiffenbach did some rough estimates and found they could track the location of the satellite from figures derived from the Doppler shift. They didn't even know what they'd come across, at first, they were just full of the joy of being young men in the possession of secret knowledge. As I've heard the story, they rampaged through the lab, laughing like lunatics. They caught the eye of Dick Kershner, a pasty, bald, big-eared Ohioan and rocket wizard who was already in a cozy set-up with the DoD. Kershner grilled the kids on their findings and then asked them whether they could reverse the trick: Could they use the orbit parameters and Doppler stats of Sputnik to get hold of not only the satellite's location, but also the position of its observer? Guier and Weiffenbach thought about it for a minute, and then said yes, they could.

Kershner understood that these two young men could crack the world wide open. Since humans first thought to journey over the waters, we'd been resigned to the crudest, and most dangerous, forms of navigation. Ancient Polynesians tracked the travel patterns of birds to direct their crafts across the Indo-Pacific. The early Greek seafarers became experts in the dangerous arts of harnessing the stars. The medieval Chinese and Arab peoples invented the compass and astrolabe, which were used by Christopher Columbus when he sailed into the mysteries of the horizon. By the modern age, we were still groping in the dark. Oh, we invented the wireless and radio beacons, radar and LORAN, but we hadn't solved one of the toughest questions that man has always faced, even back in biblical times. As it says in Psalm

143, when King David asked God, show me the way I should go, for to you I lift up my soul.

When Guier and Weiffenbach showed Kershner their calculations, which fixed the exact location of the APL station by the lights of the Sputnik data, Kershner took another path than that advised by our Lord. He used their findings to create the first protocol for a satellite navigational system. And he brought it immediately to the military.

The navy used this science to develop the Transit satellites, which were powered by Martin's generators. They shot the goddam thing up on a Thor rocket and it was a cause of great hurrahs—even though it got destroyed not much long after, by one of those nuclear tests on the Johnston Atoll. But the part that's got to set your teeth on edge, Miss Rodriguez, is that all of this human greatness was bent, and twisted, and sickened into a plan of death. What I mean is, Guier and Weiffenbach did not use Christian Doppler's discovery to bring light into the world, but to offer guidance to those death-bearers, those ghoul-machines, those arrows of Satan, being the Polaris submarines. Those were the nuclear-powered boats, the ones that held ballistic missiles fixed with thermonuclear warheads that we planned on firing at the Soviet Union if they ever launched on us first. Mutual annihilation.

What I'm telling you is that the Transit satellites guided nuclear bombs and were powered by the nuclear tech invented by physicists and chemists just like me. But it shouldn't have ended that way. Moving from the Doppler shift to guided missiles designed for no other purpose than to end all life—well, that's obscene. Because the Doppler effect isn't just a means by which we can gauge radar or the speeds of liquids, or to measure stars and space. Doppler is sort of like a poem of life, if you think about it. *Beep beep beep beep.* The closer you get to the object, the higher its frequency burns. But the farther away you travel, the fainter it becomes.

[*Pause.*]

When I started at Santa Susana, my wife and I were as close together as petals on a flower, or puppies in their mama's womb. I heard her so clear. I know I did, truly. Those nights—when I'd come home, and she'd put her cheek on my thigh and close her eyes—were the best in my life. Her, asking me about my day. She had this skin, the color of—I don't know. White sheets and wine. A fresh peach. Pearls. She was all that. She was violets. She'd close her eyes and this expression on her face, it was love for me in there. That's what I saw. A peacefulness descended on her. And the way her mouth moved—her lips shook. I made her shy and full of heart.

She'd look up at me and wouldn't have to say a word. Brown eyes, she had. Has? Me, murmuring something. Nonsense love stuff. I lived my whole life in those minutes, in those seconds. She was with me and I was with her. I knew her. I thought I knew the whole of her. I didn't think that either of us would ever fade away.

[FEBRUARY 17]

My daddy and brothers were pick-and-shovel miners for Eastern Corp starting back in the 1940s, when they kicked up the coke used to build the anti-Boche tanks, and they bled true-blue coal till the day they lost their jobs to the new digging machines. When my father came home in the evenings, he'd grin down at me, his teeth bright in his stained face. My brothers would wash out back, pouring buckets from the well over their broad shoulders, the clear water running black. My mother hurried out after them with lemonade, yallering about how they'd better come to the dinner table clean as whistles. Pops stamped around the house singing the old mining songs. *When I was a boy said my daddy to me: stay out of the mines, take my warning, said he, or with dust you'll be choked and a pauper you'll be, broken down, down, down.*

"When you hit sixteen you'll be down there with us, son," he'd said, roughhousing me. "Won't you?" I was just a little bit then but he already knew I liked numbers, science. I think he was worried I'd wander off into a library and become something strange. Which I did.

"He ain't built for no mine," my brother Billy said. He was the older one, with the middle kid being Big Ken. "He's going to be more of a schoolteacher."

"He'll go to the circus," Kenny said.

"Hell no he ain't if I got anything to say about it," my father said, batting me around.

"I'll go down in them mines with you," I said. I loved them. I just loved them.

But they all lost their jobs to the new diggers. And then the moping started. My brothers took to drinking. And then Daddy got sick from the lead and the mercury. So.

[Nurse arrives to give subject pills, which he refuses to take.]
Where was I? Oh. My father dying.

If Daddy had lived just a while longer, Marie Curie might have saved his life, like she saved mine. I love those old pictures of Madame C, with her curly hair piled up akimbo, a tough look in her eyes. She was just a young whippet when she set on studying Becquerel's discovery, that uranium salts placed on a photographic plate covered with a piece of black paper made an impression, like a dark stain or a permanent shadow. Where did the energy come from? everyone wondered. Curie was one for knowing the answers to such questions. She stood in her cold garret, shivering, her hands in fingerless gloves and a shawl thrown over her bony shoulders. She stared down at her uranium salts, which looked like a handful of lemon-colored sand, while that demon's dust breathed invisible radioactivity onto her skin and into her lungs and seeped into her veins. Finally, Curie hit upon her method: she measured the air around the salts using an electrometer, a machine requiring an ionization chamber and a piece of quartz. Once she got her system rigged, she found that the uranium conducted electricity. She then understood that the energy emitted by the uranium was created by its atomic structure, a eureka that would later lead to the burning of innocent people in unnatural fires, as it was the first step toward figuring out that atoms were divisible.

Now old Curie was on the scent. She had to get herself some more uranium. But this precious element was difficult to obtain. Curie and her husband Pierre knew that uranium could be extracted from pitchblende, a velvet-black ore mostly found in Germany, and they began to scare up all the pitchblende they could get their hands on. What Curie didn't expect is that while she was digging inside of this stone, she'd find two new elements, polonium and radium—radium being that deadly, glowing substance like will o' wisps in fairy tales. Once Curie saw that green sprite dancing in her lab, she went crazy, and had to chase it past all care, past all reason. Radium, see, is like hen's teeth or a woman's love—as small as a mote in the eye of a newt that sleeps in the whiskers of the world's tiniest spider. Over the years, she got hold of tons of pitchblende and began to refine it by boiling it in a vat, standing over the hellish murk and stirring it with an iron rod, like a witch. When she reduced the mineral to a broth, she'd wash it with acid, alkaline salts, and water, over and over again until she refined and purified the stone down to a whisper of radium. At the end, she gathered together a few precious grains. She looked down at her hands—they were burned. She looked at her face in the mirror—it was scorched, too. And while any other person would have cursed herself, she somehow realized that her wounds proved that the energy in the radium could be used to heal people, and not just kill them.

You know what she said? Before she died on account of her ruined blood? *Nothing in life is to be feared, it is only to be understood. Now is the time to understand more, so that we may fear less.*

What a woman she was.

[*Looks out the window.*]

Back in the 1950s, when my daddy had cancer, radiotherapy wasn't what it is now. They didn't know how to use it right. He suffered during his treatments. His breath would get loud, then soft, and loud, then soft. His chest rose and fell like a wave in a storm. The truth is, sometimes it's best to leave well enough alone. A man should be able to die natural. But we can never know the best thing to do in that kind of situation.

I can still see it, how his mouth was open. His lips were dry. His eyes looked far away. He didn't seem like my pop anymore. No, I can't say how it really was. Some things can't be explained. I wish I had killed him myself, gentle, and without any fuss. I know he would have wanted it that way.

When it came to be my turn, after the accident at Santa Susana in 1969, I stood in a hospital hallway, remembered my father, and fell to the ground from the fear. Of what they would do to me with their chemicals. Lou had to pick me up from under my arms, crying and begging me to see the treatment through. That was before they explained that I couldn't have kids anymore. And before this. [*Gestures to face.*] All we wanted is for me to stay living one more day, we were that scared.

Madame Curie came to my rescue, and I don't blame her for my looks, or for Lou running away.

The part that really pains me is how, if you trace the actions of this remarkable lady, you see that she found out two important things. She discovered radium. But before that, she puzzled out that uranium emitted its rays because of its atomic structure, which led to the notion that uranium atoms weren't solid, that they could be split. By discovering a treatment for cancer she also opened the book on the bomb that would menace every living thing.

She was wrong, wasn't she? The truth is, the more we understand, the more we have to fear.

[FEBRUARY 18]

So I helped run the SNAPs at Santa Susana, which ran on nuclear fission. And what with our accidents, and the fuel damage, the DoD got scared off from reactor power. It decided in favor of the thermoelectric generators that Martin, Co., was making and used those to power the amazing Transit satellites. And what did we use those beautiful navigators for? The ones that were born in the minds of those kids at the APL? Like I said already, we used them to guide the Polaris submarines, which each held a thermonuclear warhead with eighty times the yield of "Little Boy." And we intended to use them on the Soviets in the event of a second strike.

They tested the Polaris once, back in 1962. On Christmas Island. In the Pacific. I have a whole file on it, somewhere, in storage. The sub they used was the *Ethan Allen*, named after the Revolutionary war hero, sociopath, and Vermonter. The *Ethan Allen* cruised into the dark open waters and launched its missile, which flew a thousand miles across the air. It detonated around five miles away from the people of the island. You can see it on YouTube today. The whole sky turns deadly bright. A white cloud erupts, then shoots its arms up into the heavens. Radioactive fallout spread across the skies and rained down onto the waters, onto the earth, onto the villages. It sank deep into the oceans.

There are many stories of people getting wrecked like me. You start researching what happened to the folks on Johnston Atoll, the Marshall Islands, Christmas, it'll make the hair stand straight up from your head. Brown-skinned mamas giving birth to strange-shaped babies that didn't have long to live. U.S. sailors scrubbing up plutonium on sandy beaches, and later dying bloody, or, if they were lucky, just being unable to father any young.

Some things are too awful to think about. You can't look at them for very long. Just as I can see that me talking about them right now is making you turn red and fidget, Miss Rodriguez. Because what you really want to know besides what happened to me, why

I lost everything, and how much I hurt, is whether, after all this time, I want to sue the government. I will say that in 1969, we were still testing the SNAPs at Santa Susana, and the reactor got too hot. I didn't know any of the particulars at the time. The heat melted the workings inside the core and the fuel elements were damaged. Radiation spread out into the lab, and I was one of the men on duty that day. I could see there was a problem because my film badge went black, but it's difficult to explain how brave we were. Which is to say, how out of our minds we were, not wearing protective gear, not running when we first heard the alarm. Because we thought we could live through it, for some reason. We couldn't understand the danger, even after Nagasaki. After Hiroshima. I think folks really didn't know the hazards until they read about the people in Chernobyl, Fukushima. Anyway, a couple years after the reactor burned down, the cancer reared up in me. Got into my skin and my innards. There were some months where Lou and me were scared I wouldn't make it. I had many operations. And when I finally came through it, I wasn't the same man.

Lou left me in 1974. That's all I really want to say about it. She took up with a doctor she met at church. It wasn't a big surprise, all you have to do is look at me to know that any young, beautiful girl with her whole life ahead of her would not want to be tied down by this. [*Gestures at left eye.*]

No, I don't want to talk about whose fault it was, or anything about compensation or lawsuits. Because it doesn't matter anymore. What matters is the big picture. What matters is the meaning of it all. I thought I could avenge my daddy and kill coal with my ideas, but I was just a boy being used by the powers-that-be. I hydrided the zirconium and the uranium for the fuel and then found myself on a gurney with a doctor mumbling apologies and my wife sobbing, and I wondered, why? Now, though, I have the answer. Because I've researched all about it. Out in storage, I've got files and files. It makes people smile at me strange when I tell them about it, and I know they think I probably wear a tinfoil hat at night and secretly believe in ETs. But it's because I've chased down the way the world works that I know about powerful men's manner of turning every wonderful thing into pure wickedness. About the Knights of the Crusades using Christ to slay the peasant. About the Germans using pesticides to make Sarin, which strangles men to death while they gulp air. About how a woman digs through a mountain of stone so that she can cure the world, never knowing that unholy forces will use her work to kill the children of the East. Or Benjamin Huntsman figuring how to use coke in steel-making, which led to tanks in World War II and the lead poisoning of gentle, harmless men. And about how Christian Doppler led to Guier and Weiffenbach, who led to Kershner, who led to Polaris, which led to detonating a star of wormwood over the clear blue Pacific, which led to the birth of unspeakable children on Christmas Island and the tainting of the oceans, the death of the creatures the Lord made to swim in the cold salt sea.

What we have to solve as a people is this question: How can good lead to only more good, and never evil? You can write that one up, child. Write that up in your little book.

[*Long pause*]

They have pretty fish there, out around Christmas Island. I saw a video of them on YouTube. My favorites are the butterfly fish. The swim in glittering schools, hugging close to coral reefs. They're about five inches long, just tiny ones.

They're shaped more like space ships, not butterflies. They have long, shining stripes of gold and indigo, black and pearl. They swim through the coral, patiently sifting the plankton and watching for enemies with their round black-button eyes. They sneak through the swaying flowers of the deep, poking into the pink buds with their long noses, waving their fins. The dark orange and deep green of their planet must be a wonder to them, which they delight in together as they sway in the currents, or move hard in chevrons and rapid bursts through hidey-holes when predators come stealing in. They seem to me like a family of fathers and sons, or husbands and wives, when I watch them drifting together past starfish, rocks, shells, and the sea-roses of coral. They move all as one, in a long swoop, like a woman's bright hair streaming in a breeze. I think they must feel the beat beat beat of their brothers' bodies in the water, and that's how they can tell when it's time to float easy or slice through the waves fast, when a killer approaches. Or maybe they can hear each other's fluttering, louder up close, softer as they get farther away. Listening to each other, they know they have to keep up, and that's how they help each other survive.

Sometimes I wonder about the butterfly fish that might have eaten a speck of cesium or strontium, which drifted down from the thunder in the sky in the days after the Polaris test. The shining stuff rained down through the blue. It flowed into the butterflies along with the plankton. On the tainted ones swam, at first, following their luckier brothers, following their wives. They glided past the cities of coral, the octopus, the shark, the red tide, all the time feeling the beat beat beat of their friends' moving bodies, which made codes in the water. Eventually, though, they'd find themselves weakening from the toxins. Slowing. Straggling. They'd see the school up ahead, getting farther from them every second. That beat would get fainter and fainter. The sickened butterfly fish would try to keep up. Then, finally, he wouldn't feel anything at all. No beat, no murmur, no code, no word of love. He would have fallen behind and found that, now, he was lost.

INTERVIEW WITH YAOXOCHITL SUDO

JANUARY 20, 2020
PALM SPRINGS, CALIFORNIA

I saw your email and am now hoping to register a complaint, Miss Rodriguez. I trust that no one from the department has spoken to you about me. If they have, please disregard what they've said. Unfortunately, the functionaries at your agency are disagreeable factotums with few of the virtues that most people aspire to maintain in order to ensure that this berserk jamboree we call civilization does not fall apart.

I am speaking of the official treatment of my inquiries. My many, many inquiries. My inquiries about Santa Susana, what transpired there, what the contaminants are, what the suspected etiologies are, what the cleanup plan is, and what the local and city and state and federal governments intend to do about this mess that they have made and refuse to remediate. Your colleagues, I am afraid to say, have obstructed me at every turn. The lost paperwork. The forwarded calls. The unanswered phones. The emails that receive no reply. I have sat in countless offices endeavoring to learn the facts. And every time I ask your associates a question, all I receive in return are rank platitudes. "I'll have my supervisor get back to you." "We are sorry, but we are not permitted to disclose that information." "Please fill out these forms in triplicate." "Should you like a return call, please leave your number and we will respond as soon as possible." As I learned through decades of hard experience, "as soon as possible" is a phrase that, when spoken by a government employee, possesses as much meaning as "have a nice day" might have when an asteroid is hurtling its lethal way toward planet earth.

I can see by the way that you are looking at me that you may have had communications with Dennis Ackerley. No, there is no need to

73

deny it. I hope that you do not credit anything he says. He is the person responsible for my tarnished reputation among your cohort and the one man alive whom I would like to see guillotined. I am only joking, of course. I know that I have the sort of face that makes my edgier efforts at mirth confusing to certain people, but, in truth, I am more interested in seeing him banned for life from any sort of bureaucratic position than in arranging for him to be disappeared. Even after all of this time, I check up on him every few months or so, and thus I know that he still retains his sinecure at the EPA's Southern California office. Where I assume that he is still setting the standard for the most sandwiches eaten and the least hours worked.

It all started in 1984. A portentous year. In my case, however, one is made to think less of George Orwell than of his predecessor, Franz Kafka. Kafka, whom I teach at the local city college, in my surprisingly unpopular class *Kafkas Fehler: Was du siehst ist was du kriegst*. It is true that in graduate school—Princeton—I possessed only a middling interest in *The Trial* or *The Castle*, being then a cheerfully radical postcolonial critic. But once I moved to Simi Valley, the author of these works became the passion of my life! Poor Franz understood that savages like Dennis Ackerley are trained in a dark magic that, with only a well-turned phrase, such as "how can I help you?" or "let's put a pin in that," can send credulous citizens like myself on mythic journeys the length and breadth of which would slay the most stalwart explorer even though they are conducted solely within the four feet between the reception area of the EPA's local toparchy and Mr. Ackerley's untidy office.

In 1984, I had a question. Mine was not a larger cosmic uncertainty about life and love and death and pain and suffering and turmoil and horror that is raised by the specter of the pixie dust of death that I imagine glistens in the air around Santa Susana since it was released in 1959. No, my concern at the time was about Item #4. Item #4 was the fourth item in Form 39682A1, the form otherwise known as "HAZARDOUS WASTE COMPLAINT," or HWC, the most relevant to my case of all of the many documents that the EPA invites the public to complete on puzzlements as various as where to recycle their toxic metals or how to transport electronic waste, but *not*, as it so happens, whether there have been deposited some nasty little stores of Cesium-137 in their backyards. Item #4 concerned "whom" against the HWC was being filed.

My question to Mr. Ackerley limned the delicate issue of whether my HWC needed to be filed against some shadowy "whom" or nobody at all. As this was the era before the helpful internet, I did not know yet if, indeed, radionuclides had been released into the area and I should be worried. Only then, if that were the case, would I be able to get to the secondary matter of "whom" amongst the manifold accountable scientists and nabobs and hacks and governors I should incriminate.

"I am not sure what to put here," I said to Mr. Ackerley that first day we met, when I sat in the dented metal chair he had positioned across from his paper-laden desk.

"You're supposed to put the name of the company you're complaining against," he said pleasantly, while folding his fingertips over his comfortable belly.

"Yes, but I do not yet know if there is anything to complain about," I said, rattling the paper at him. "Do you have a form for when a person is confused about whether lethal filth is *in fact* fluttering in the very air that their children breathe and invisibly attaching like barnacles to teddy bears and stirring itself into the family soup?"

"I don't understand the question," Mr. Ackerley said.

"It is just that *before* I may name a malefactor on this form I must know if some sort of malefaction has been committed."

Mr. Ackerley only blinked at me.

"There have been some reports on the television about a horrible accident that was supposed to have happened here in 1959 and I would like to know if they are true."

"I'm not privy to that information," Mr. Ackerley said.

"But you are a regional deputy supervisor of the EPA," I said, pointing at the nameplate on his messy desk. "If you do not know if there are toxic substances in the vicinity that need controlling, who does?"

"It sounds like maybe you have a police complaint," Mr. Ackerley said.

"My good man," I sputtered. "It is a simple question. Are we in danger?"

Mr. Ackerley looked around his office and fanned out his hands. "Everything seems fine to me."

"But that's the thing, isn't it?" I went on. "One never knows."

"Isn't that the truth," Mr. Ackerley said. "One never knows." He stood up. "Are you done with the form?"

"Are you going to address my concern?"

He smiled and took the paper back from me. "We'll get back to you as soon as possible, ma'am."

"Oh, as soon as possible," I said, mollified. "When is that, precisely?"

"Within the next week or so," he said.

"Next week," I repeated.

"Or month, maybe," he said.

"Next month," I said. "And you'll tell me whether there is a problem or not?"

"Yup," Mr. Ackerley said, and, just as I was explaining that I had written both my home and work number on line eight of the HWC, he muttered something about lunch and unceremoniously escorted me out his office door.

As it was not one of my teaching days, I went to my house. My son, Lawrence, soon arrived home in his full soccer regalia and began clamoring for dinner. I frisked around the kitchen assembling an elaborate nimono stew, his father's favorite. I stabbed at the onions and pummeled the shitakes and whacked at the taro root until my masterpiece filled the house with its perfume. I sat down at the table and delighted at the sight of Lawrence demolishing every last morsel on his plate and asking for more.

"What's wrong," Lawrence said, chewing.

"Nothing," I said.

"Mom," he said.

"I love you," I said.

"You're wigging out about something," he said.

"Do you want more milk?" I said.

"Yes," he said.

I rose from the table and fetched the milk carton from the refrigerator and came back to the living room and poured it for him.

Lawrence drained the glass and said, "You have a big vein sticking out of your forehead."

I waggled my fingers through my bangs so as to hide any evidence of my anxiety.

"Save room for dessert," I said, as I reached over to gently remove a mote of taro root from his glowing, beautiful cheek.

The whole next week I consulted our brand-new answering machine several times a day. I am a skeptic by nature and affiliation, but could not stop praying to God that Mr. Ackerley would reply to my query with a soothing response. "It was all cleaned up long ago," I imagined him saying, as he cited charts and diagrams confirming that the greatest health hazard in Simi Valley was its legions of city college students who remained uninterested in wielding the axe against the frozen sea within us despite the best efforts of their teachers. "You can rest easy," I dreamed of him telling me, while he quoted from scientific papers and exhaustive studies that established that the most perilous toxin in Simi Valley was its lack of bookstores and advanced culture.

But the call did not come. I examined my answering machine several times to ensure that it remained in good working order, mainly by calling my home phone from my college office and leaving myself abrupt messages that sounded increasingly agitated as the days wore on. After two weeks of this I decided to cut the Gordian knot by simply reaching out to Mr. Ackerley with a polite query, which led me to make a progressively harried series of voicemail messages that were later entered as evidence in my hearing, which I would rather not get into at this time.

He did not do as he said he would, in other words. Neither the next week nor the next month did he "circle back" to me. I, on the other hand, rang him thirty-eight times. I failed to reach him thirty-five times, though three times I did make contact, hearing his lazy and blighted voice saying "Ackerley, here" before descending into a muddled slur of vowels while I exclaimed in clear and precise syllables the nature of my call. I managed to get hold of three secretaries, a research science manager, an assistant deputy director, an acting deputy director, and a student intern named "Meg," the last of whom was a nice person and let me talk for a long while.

I thereafter began to visit the regional office of the EPA every day or two, and, as was protocol, I always made an appointment first. I would march into that mouse-brown building and encounter a Cerberus named Miss Molly Banner, who was a thin, fish-faced, huge-haired receptionist with a taste for dreadful plaid culottes and garish metallic belts.

"Help you?" she asked on the first few occasions that I manifested in the receiving area.

"May I have a copy of Form 39682A1?" I said.

As I spoke, I stood before Miss Banner's desk, but from that vantage I had a perfect view of Mr. Ackerley, whose office was only a few steps away. While I'd glower at Mr. Ackerley eating a hamburger or staring out of his window with a flaccid expression, Miss Banner would begin rifling through a file packed with white Xeroxes, becoming somewhat flummoxed. "One sec," she'd say.

"The Hazardous Waste Complaint," I'd say.

"Oh, right," she'd reply. "That one's . . . I think . . . in this binder."

The first few times, Miss Banner would hand me a document that was *not* an HWC but rather one that could allow me to become a registered sanitation engineer or to request to be contacted, though not necessarily helped, in ten business days should I be unable to communicate with the EPA in my primary language. After this little fracas, I would obtain eventually Form 39682A1 and write down, in the space provided in Item #4, the closest approximation of the identity of the entity I sought to complain against:

Whoever might have filled Simi Valley with radioactive waste and put my child in danger

The forces that are preventing me from learning the truth of whether Simi Valley is packed with radioactive effluences and consequently jeopardizing my child's health

The malevolent powers that are alleged to have set Simi Valley ablaze with nuclear waste and thus threatened the well-being of my fourteen-year-old son

"'Malevolent powers' aren't a recognized subject of complaint on this form, Mrs. Sudo," Mr. Ackerley said during one of these early visits. As he gazed at me sleepily over his pile of papers, a blush crept from his lower jowls up to his eyes, indicating that he was either in poor circulatory health or for some reason was becoming enraged.

"But you haven't answered my question and so I don't know who to put in Item #4," I said. I had slung around my shoulder a large purse, which was filled with documents I had Xeroxed at the local library after conducting inconclusive research concerning the environmental salubriousness of Simi Valley. I extracted my crinkling copies of articles taken from the *Los Angeles Times* and the Simi Valley *Acorn*, which recounted the triumphs of Ronald Reagan's presidency, Michael Jackson's hair catching on fire, the Winter Olympics in Sarajevo, and the

McMartin Preschool Trial, but contained only two brief items about a 1979 KNBC report on a nuclear meltdown that had occurred in the Santa Susana Field Laboratory in 1959. "As far as I can tell, there apparently have been no studies conducted on the local soils or waters, and so there is no way of knowing whether the news' hideous insinuations that this town is flaming with radioisotopes is true or not."

"We're still working on it," he said.

"And when will you have my answer?" I asked.

"As soon as—" he began.

I shook my finger at him. "Don't."

"Possible," Mr. Ackerley said, which prompted me to begin tossing my dossier of papers around the room.

The next time I arrived at the EPA, a stringy, twenty-something male guard with a huge Adam's apple had been stationed at the entrance door. In his octopus-like hand he carried a paper featuring a grainy and enlarged copy of my rather severe-looking driver's license photograph.

"Can't let you in," he said, pointing to the image.

"But that's not me, you beast," I said, trying to muscle my way past him. "You're going to make me late for my appointment with Mr. Ackerley, who I am hoping by this time might be able to answer my one very simple question."

"Sorry, ma'am, but I have orders."

"Can't you see that this photograph is of an entirely other person?" I ranted. In my driver's license portrait, I had my hair scraped back so that the enormous vein that always erupted during times of stress could be seen pulsing between my eyes. But I had changed my "look" since that picture had been taken. After a series of calamities in the early 1980s, I had glanced in the mirror and realized that I resembled a panicked harpy. I'd decided it would be nicer for my son to gaze upon a more pleasant visage, which is why I cut my bangs, so that they could hide my tell-tale forehead. This basic change in hairstyle proved enough to flummox the guard, who apparently was not much for discerning between non-white personages.

"Oh," the guard said, squinting at his paper. "Right. Sorry."

I rushed inside, only to be escorted back out by two bristly macho guards some fifteen minutes later.

Later that day, I taught a perfunctory class on *The Castle* to a lethargic cabal of philistines and then raced back to the house. I banged about for a bit in the kitchen and finally settled down enough to cook for Lawrence and myself a dinner of mole verde, which, as you might know, is a Oaxacan stew. I chopped up the pork shoulder and garlic and tomatillos, which were full of nourishing C and K vitamins, and just as my son came stomping in through the door, it was bubbling and tender on the stove.

"How was your day?" I asked, at table, while he spooned up the meal.

Lawrence shrugged. "OK, I guess."

I picked at the vegetables on my plate and looked at his gloomy face. "Darling, is that some sort of cherubic code for 'very bad?'"

"No," Lawrence said, eating all of the pork.

"All right," I said. I monitored him closely as he ate half a loaf of bread and drank a third glass of milk.

"It's a girl," he eventually said.

"Ah," I replied.

"She doesn't like me," he said.

"Of course she does," I said. "Everyone likes you."

"Mom," Lawrence said, and began laughing.

"Everyone likes you because you are the most lovable person in the world and you are perfect," I said.

Lawrence smiled into the soup, and my sore heart rang with happiness.

After the debacle at the EPA, I wasn't quite sure what to do. I considered for a brief moment assuming a variety of disguises that would allow me entrée past the agency's Soviet-level surveillance, but in the end settled for driving back to the building and sitting in its parking lot in my car. I brought along my husband's medical files, and the academic articles that I'd printed out on the nexus between radionuclide contamination and the disorders that may originate in a single B- or T-lymphocyte progenitor, with the idea that if I could just *explain* to Mr. Ackerley the most recent theories of causality then perhaps I could urge him to some more robust attitude of exigency on the question of whether we lived in a safe environment, or whether I should move my son out of the vicinity "as soon as possible."

At 4:45 P.M., Mr. Ackerley walked out of the EPA building. His face wore a mild scowl and he stomped his way across the parking lot, which ended on a tree-lined block containing a string of modest single-story homes on Moorpark Street. I gathered all of my files, debouched from my car, and commenced race-walking toward him.

"Mr. Ackerley!" I called out, flapping my manila folder at him.

"Oh, god," I heard him say.

"Mr. Ackerley!" I said again.

"Go away," he barked, walking quickly toward his own sedan.

"You must hear what I have to tell you!" I roared, and broke into a run.

Mr. Ackerley looked at me over his shoulder and I surmise that something about my darkly indigenous features gave him the wrong impression, as he began to hasten also, though he was not well equipped for his exertions.

Mr. Ackerley hurried up to his car but dropped his keys. Instead of retrieving them, he panicked and half-ran out of the parking lot, lumbering onto the street. He narrowly missed an oncoming vehicle but clambered onto the sidewalk opposite, then slowly jogged past the houses while attempting ineffective evasive maneuvers.

As people's curious and concerned faces appeared in their windows, I began crying. Mr. Ackerley skedaddled around a corner and then down another sidewalk, and, as I chased after him, he looked at me over his shoulder. He should have kept his gaze straight ahead, however, because the sidewalks around Moorpark are often cracked from tree roots and can be a trap for the unwary. Mr. Ackerley stumbled predictably over one of these fissures and crashed face-first onto the sidewalk, unfortunately breaking his nose.

"Ow, ow," he kept moaning, as I reached him.

"Are you all right?" I asked, bending down and examining his wounds.

Mr. Ackerley looked up at me from out of his bloodstained face and rolled his eyes.

"Why do you keep bothering me?" he gasped.

I sat on the ground next to him, gesticulating. The papers spilled out of my file and covered Mr. Ackerley's twitching frame like a shroud. I put my face in my hands.

"Because my husband died of cancer three years ago and I need to know why, as I have a son whom I would very much like to keep alive," I said.

The judge at my trial for misdemeanor assault was thankfully moved by the reasons for my pursuit of Mr. Ackerley. He saw things more from my perspective after I explained that my husband had contracted a rare carcinoma strongly associated with radiation exposure, and that I'd only wanted to get the facts on whether radiation did indeed linger in Simi Valley after the 1959 Santa Susana meltdown, as well as the 1964 and 1969 disasters. The court allowed me to describe at length my wonderful marriage to Edward Sudo, a scholarly and gentle expert in Franz Kafka whom I had met at Simi Valley City College, and who later became such a magnificent father to our son. The judge, himself a family man, was able to commiserate with me about the enormous, even paralyzing, anxieties that come with parenthood, and the duty of the government to respond to our reasonable inquiries about our safety with some measure of diligence. These factors aided me during the prosecution, and it also proved to my advantage that the California stalking laws had not yet been enacted. I was acquitted of all charges.

It turned out that I was not wrong to worry. In 1992, the California Department of Health Services issued a study finding a higher incidence of cancer among men living within close proximity to the lab. Also, in 2005 and 2006, the California Department of Toxic Substances Control analyzed soil samples in a nearby Dayton Canyon creek bed and found perchlorate, used in rocket fuel, in several locations. Percholates have caused cancer in animal studies.

At that point, however, Lawrence and I were long gone. Without adequate information on the safety of Simi Valley, I applied for and obtained a post at the College of the Desert, where I continue to teach English, composition, and, in honor of my husband and my son, my occasional and sparsely attended seminar on the art and life of Franz Kafka.

I realize, Miss Rodriguez, that it remains possible that the catastrophe that has wizened my life had no relation to radionuclides, or perchlorate, or any other space-age toxins. But really, it is sheer torture to remain in the dark about why your husband has died or whether your son's life could be cut short on account of some unseeable corruption. This anxiety seems to have overtaken me during that sorry period in the middle 1980s, and that is the only explanation I have for my admittedly unbalanced behavior with Mr. Ackerley. It does seem wrong to me, however, that we should have had to live in a place that is contaminated, and not to know what that means, and not to have anyone answer our questions, and to endure that fear. You see, I love my son a great deal. He himself has avoided the fate of his father, having grown up hale and hearty. Five years ago, he married a nice girl with whom he now has started a family. My precious Lawrence does not live in the past as I do, and thus does not know why I was so upset then, and remain today so devastated that when I saw your email I determined to relive our ordeal by telling you my story. But I am hoping that, woman of color to woman of color, you might understand?

INTERVIEW WITH CARRIE MASON

JULY I, 2019
SANTA ANA, CALIFORNIA

Do I think they "did" this to me? You work for the government, and so you probably see things in a certain way. You want to know if I can get a court to believe that they hurt me, that they owe me, so I can sue them and get some money. But the way I see it, you're asking a complicated question. Answering it requires an open mind.

Just think of Job, who lost everything only to have it returned to him through God's grace. Or, even better, think of the woman in Luke 13, who was infected by a spirit before being healed by Christ's touch. Why did she suffer? Whose fault was it? On one level, you have to believe that the future is God's plan, and there's a good reason for what happens. Sure, back when I was a wild young thing, I thought I was in control of my life. But I've since learned we must all bow down to a higher power. We've got to keep faith.

Still, as a child, I played in the water that came from the storm drains. When my younger sister Lila and I were kids, we lived in Bell Canyon, ten miles down from the lab. That's when we touched and swallowed the radioactive garbage those bastards left on the hill. Them exposing us to those chemicals was a wrong, wrong thing to do. But it's hard to understand exactly why that happened.

Lila and I liked to splash in the big rushing gulps of gutter water outside our house because we'd seen *From Here to Eternity*. That's an old show we'd watched on television in black-and-white with my mother. "Come here, girls," Mom had said when it was shown on Monday Night Movies, while lighting a More and pouring herself a glass of Chablis. This was, what, over thirty years ago. "I'm going to introduce you to Burt Lancaster," she told us.

Lila and I sat on the sofa with Mom, who smelled great, of alcohol and tobacco leaf. We watched Burt Lancaster chase Deborah Kerr up from the ocean and onto the beach. Deborah Kerr fell on the sand in that black bathing suit. Burt collapsed to his knees and kissed her passionately.

"Who-wee," my mother said, wriggling on the sofa.

My grandmother, Meena, didn't approve of sexy movies because she was a strict Methodist, as was my father. Grammy sat in an easy chair next to the sofa while we watched television. She smoked Mores, like Mom, but pursed her mouth and muttered Scripture. "And the woman was arrayed in purple and scarlet color, and decked with gold and precious stones and pearls, having a golden cup in her hand full of abominations and filthiness of her fornication." That's from Revelations 17, about the Whore of Babylon. I always liked that quote; it made me tingle and feel scared at the same time.

When Lila and I saw Deborah Kerr be the Whore of Babylon, we wanted to be the Whore of Babylon, too. So, after the fall rains, when the gutter waters got high, we put on our polka dot bikinis and swam around in the street.

"Kiss me, kiss me!" Lila said, twisting in the little river coming down the hill. Back then she was a crazy thing and liked to make me act like her beau. I'd grab her and pretend to kiss her on the mouth while she flailed her arms like Deborah Kerr/the Whore of Babylon. But one day, Grammy told Dad about our hijinks and he came running out of the house and beat us both with the back of his hand.

Later that night, my mother snuck into our room with a tray of chocolate chip cookies and milk and petted our heads while we cried. She lit another More and teased us until we stopped sobbing and ate the cookies.

"It's OK to be a little bad," she said, and winked at us.

We played in the local waters for probably ten, eleven years? From the ages of six to right before we graduated from high school? Not just the storm drains outside of our house. When we got older we spent time with the local boys around Simi Creek. The creek bed grew green from mold, but sometimes the rains filled it with blue water. We'd go wading in, then, while flirting with Teddy Fidler or Jason Green, who both played on the football team. They were handsome guys, with big muscles. Those two acted like they didn't give a damn whether Lila and I talked to them or what, which made us nuts about them.

Everybody hung out by the creek after school or at night in the summer. Somebody would bring a boom box and cigarettes and coolers and we'd party. Twenty or thirty kids showed up, dangling their feet into the dirty water and talking. We'd listen to Bon Jovi, Aerosmith, Mötley Crüe. I liked Taylor Dayne, though I suppose you don't know who that is. My favorite song was *Tell It to My Heart*. It was really good. *Tell it to my heart*, she sings. *Tell me I'm your only one.*

I'd drink the orange coolers and snuggle up to Jason Green, even if I really wanted Fidler. Lila liked him, though. The boys slung their arms around our throats so that their elbows stuck out around our chins. Like they'd wrangled a couple of calves. Lila and I both got drunker than pigs and stuck onto them. In my day, folks called girls like us drapes, because we draped all over the boys. We got loaded and draped on Jason and Fidler and it was fun.

Jason was tall, around six foot three, and Fidler stood shorter, about five eleven. Jason was a quarterback and Fidler was a running back. I liked Fidler better because he didn't have a temper. Once, Jason punched Mitchell Heller in the face when Mitchell rubbed his shoulder on my breasts at a party. I'd been too drunk to care, but Jason took offense and slammed his fist into Mitchell's mouth. Fidler jumped in between them with his arms spread out. "Chill! Chill!" he yelled. I crouched by the edge of the water and thought Jason was a moron and Fidler was a guy with his head screwed on straight. Meanwhile, Lila screamed and cried until Fidler released Jason from his headlock and hurried over to comfort her. Mitchell ran off and Jason sat up on the creek's shoulder and threw rocks at trees like he was the unhappiest kid in the world. I got so upset about the contrast between the two boys that I waded into the creek and dunked my head into it, swallowing some of the water. I didn't get out until Jason finally yelled at me to stop it, and what did I think I was doing, had I gone crazy. Lila didn't notice because she was too busy trying to tongue Fidler.

He was an idiot, but for all of my complaining about him, Jason was my first. He had thick, strong shoulders and kids followed him with their eyes when he entered a classroom or the cafeteria. And Fidler was Lila's first. My sister and I planned on losing our virginity on the same night, and that's what happened. Weeks before, in our bedroom, we made a sex to-do list with bullet points of where the deed would go down and what we would wear.

"I'm going to be in my red miniskirt and my purple ruffled blouse with the midriff and my hoops," Lila said, writing it all down in a notebook. "And Fidler's going to wear his green and yellow rugby shirt and his Tommy jeans."

"Who cares who wears what?" I'd said. "The issue is making sure it gets done."

"And you're going to wear your yellow wrap dress and your wedges," she said. "Though I don't care what Jason wears, just as long as he brings his van."

"We're not all going to do it in Jason's van," I said, angry that Lila got purple and scarlet decked with gold and precious stones and pearls, while I had to wear yellow and wedges.

"Yes, we are," Lila said. "Fidler's Ghia is too small and so it's going to have to be more of a double-date situation."

"Well, who's going to do it where?" I asked.

"You're going to do it in the front seat and Fidler and I will be in the back."

"But if it's Jason's van we should get the back and you and Fidler should be up in front," I said.

"No, it's better if you're in front because if you get scared you can honk the horn and I'll come to your rescue."

"Why don't you honk the horn if you get scared and I'll come to your rescue?" I said.

"Because you're more delicate and I have more upper body strength," she said.

"That's not the reason," I told her.

"It's the best plan," she said.

On the night in question, we all went out driving for a "date" in Jason's van. Once we parked, I did everything in my earthly power to maneuver Fidler and Lila to the front seat and Jason and me to the back seat. I said that I had lost my purse and that I needed to go to the back seat and look for it and Jason should help me find it and that Lila and Fidler should come to the front seat and talk there. When

Lila said my purse was by my feet in the front seat, I said then she and Fidler should come up to the front seat and Jason and I should go to the back seat because it was Jason's van and so he had priority. But Jason said he didn't care. Then I said that I lost my comb in the back seat and Lila said shut up and started mauling Fidler and Jason looked at me all puffed up and excited. I decided to just relax and figured that later I could have my revenge on Lila for having sex for the first time in the more comfortable back seat by stealing some of her clothes or some other retribution.

So I had sex with Jason in the front seat and Lila had sex with Fidler in the back seat.

Lila and I watched each other the whole time. I clambered onto Jason and she clambered onto Fidler. We all started kissing and there were slurping noises that sounded funny, I remember. But then Jason started mussing around with me and I jerked out my arms and hit the horn and it beeped.

"Do you need me to come to your rescue?" Lila said.

"No," I said.

"What?" Jason and Fidler said.

"Nothing," Lila and I said at the same time. We kept going at it. Lila and I eyeballed each other while the guys hiked up our skirts and we saw both guys' penises and it made the whole thing more interesting. I know I'm giving you a lot of details, Miss Rodriguez, but you said you wanted to know my story, and why I thought what happened to me happened, and this is part of that. We saw both boys' dicks and got revved up at watching each other being defiled, and that, I have to say, was more good-feeling than when the penises did finally go in because then it just hurt and we didn't know what the hell was going on.

Afterward, back at home, Lila and I laid on our beds and talked about it and we both felt exactly the same way. "That was gross but I'm glad it happened," Lila said. "Yeah," I agreed. "Now we're ready for anything." It was like before, when she'd made me pretend to kiss her on the mouth in the storm water. We had an intense connection, my sister and me, too intense, as if we had one body and shared it. And that's why I think that, about half a year later, we found out in the same month that we'd both got pregnant.

We were seventeen and eighteen years old then. The fathers were Jason and Fidler; they were still our boyfriends, off and on. Lila and

I put our heads together and agreed that maybe we could get them to marry us. A couple of girls in our class had already got humped and hitched. But Lila and I planned on ditching Jason and Fidler after we graduated because we aimed to go to a Christian college. Grammy Meena said that if we went to a holy school she'd pay for it. That's why we both got abortions, because we wanted a future, not to be tied down to these two guys.

Mom scheduled the procedures and didn't tell Dad anything. She said she'd had an abortion, too, when she was thirty, but it was her secret and now ours and we agreed to never say anything to anybody, though I guess I have just told you, which I shouldn't have done. Anyway, she told Dad that we were headed to a mother-and-daughters vacation to San Diego. We drove down to Balboa and went to the Planned Parenthood there. The weird thing was, even though Lila screamed and cried when something bad happened, like Jason hitting Mitchell, and I was weaker than her emotionally, during the abortion we both sat there, holding hands, and stayed calm. Our mother helped us. She told us that we shouldn't feel ashamed or sad, because we were taking care of ourselves. That maybe it would cramp some and bleed, but that wasn't as bad as ruining our futures. Lila and I drew strength from each other, too. In the clinic, in the waiting room, we looked deep into each other's eyes and I could feel her soul entering mine and I'm sure she could feel mine entering hers. Afterward, in the motel, we laid down next to each other and cried, but in a positive way, a healing way, I thought.

"You're all right," my mother said, holding us both. "You're going to be all right."

And, for a long time, we were.

After that we broke up with Jason and Fidler and went to a Christian college called Hass, in Orange County. I got there first, in 1991, and became a communications major. Lila came the following year, and she became a communications major, too. I loved it, because, though communications has a reputation as a lightweight subject, it's interesting and complicated. For example, we learned about interpersonal communication, and how it exists on a continuum. Interpersonal communication ranges from very impersonal to very personal. You have very impersonal communications, for example, with strangers or people you don't know very well. Like when a waiter takes your order at a restaurant, and they don't actually care whether you get the chicken or the fish, and you don't care what they think about you eating chicken or fish, that's very impersonal. Versus very personal. That's when you talk about your life with someone you love intensely and who loves you back intensely.

Those first years at college, I thought a lot about when my communications were impersonal and when they were personal. I realized that my communications had been very impersonal with Jason, which was strange, since I'd had sex with him many times. And when I came to think about it, they were also impersonal with Fidler, even though I had a secret crush on him and wanted to steal him away from Lila. Also, my communications had been moderately impersonal with my father, who was always off working at Santa Susana in one of the government-type labs that did the nuclear testing. And my grandmother, too, she and I were only moderately personal, as she tried to fill my head with ideas like the Whore of Babylon, which made me shut her off. I stayed pretty personal with my mother, though, especially during situations like when she helped us out with the abortions. But not even Mom compared with Lila, because my sister and I had extremely personal communications. When Lila came to Hass and we roomed together, we reached a new level of closeness. We wore each other's clothes and ate the same food in the cafeteria and took the same classes. Well, my junior year I took a class on the New Testament while Lila took a business class, but otherwise we kept to the same schedule: sleeping, waking, eating, studying, going to the movies, having fun, and partying together. We got so close we could read each other's minds. Like, Lila would be studying in bed and I could hear her get still, not breathing, and I'd know that she was off daydreaming about one of the boys on campus. I'd say, "You'd better get that homework done," and she'd stir and say, "I know." Or I'd be sitting in the library before a test and start sweating and panicking, and she wouldn't even look up at me from her reading, but she'd say, "Stop that." I'd say, "OK." And I would.

I had never been happier. For me, there was no being too close to Lila. We still competed and got angry with each other, though our fights usually had to do with needing a five-minute break from the togetherness. She slapped me once over a dress and I gave her an

Indian burn another time because she'd thrown up in my bed when she was drunk. But other than that we were like this. [*Crosses fingers.*]

All of that started to change, though, once I took that New Testament class and she took that business class. I learned about the Gospels while Lila learned about Nigel Thompson, a tall blond lacrosse player and math whiz who took the *Principles of Management* at the same time as her.

In my New Testament seminar, I enjoyed the Bible stories, most of all where they had women in them, like Mary Magdalene or the Virgin, or the unnamed lady in Luke 13 who can't walk right until Jesus's laying hands heal her. The lady in Luke 13 is like Job but she is female, so her situation made more sense to me. I still didn't believe in God. I don't know. All I can say is that I enjoyed the class and it made me think. But it did not convert me.

The person who was converted through her education was Lila. Lila converted to the church of Nigel Thompson. Nigel was an economics major and a BMOC. He wore super preppy clothes like baby blue Lacoste shirts with popped collars and deck shoes with no socks. That style looked dumb in the early 1990s but he was a die-hard Kennedy type, with his "lax & chill," his boat shoes, his sailing, his bro-ness, and his talking constantly about "internet relay chats," some early social media thing.

"There's a friend network developing in Canada and France that's going to be *massive*," he said the first time that I met him, in the quad outside of Wilkinson Hall. I'd been sitting under a tree studying for an upcoming quiz on the mysteries of the Trinity, waiting for Lila to show up so we could go have subs for lunch. She strolled up with Nigel, which is a strange name that makes it seem like he should be English but he's just from Arcadia. Lila had a look on her face that I'd never seen her get with Fidler but which reminded me of the time she and I played kissing like in *From Here to Eternity* while prancing in the high water flowing from the Santa Susana Field Lab. She pulled Nigel down to the grass and didn't even look at me the whole time but just sat there draping hard enough to pull a groin muscle with her eyes shooting rainbows and star dazzle.

"The network's being created by undernetters," Nigel went on, kicking off his deck shoes so that I could see the blond hair growing all over his big toes, "and once they make it less bandwidth consumptive and manage the channel chaos, it's going to *dominate*. The question will be how to crush the open knowledge morons and monetize the connections."

"I do not know what the hell you are talking about. Who are you?" I'd said.

"Hi, I'm Nigel," Nigel answered, grinning at me like a Crest commercial.

"You do too know who this is, Carrie," Lila said, petting his arm like it was a big needy cat that had been raised in a deprived environment and needed extra physical attention. "I told you about him before. I described him with a lot of detail."

"Well, I don't remember anything about that," I'd said. Of course, I did; she hadn't shut up about Nigel already for three weeks straight. "Let's you and me go for some subs."

"Subs aren't really good for you," Nigel said. "Let's go get veggie pockets."

"Yeah, OK," Lila said. "We'll go get veggie pockets."

"Veggie pockets are for squirrels," I said. "I want a loaded Italian chicken with jalapeño."

"So, you get chicken, and Nigel and I will get the veggie," Lila said.

"But we always get loaded Italians together on Thursdays," I said.

"I'm hungry," Nigel said, standing up and slipping back on his shoes, then immediately walking in the direction of the veggie pockets kiosk over by Wilson Field, while the subs were in a food court over by Henley Hall.

In the end, I had a veggie pocket because otherwise I would've had to walk alone to Henley Hall and then maybe not meet up with them again because they'd disappear into the wild with their mung beans and their lettuce fluff. I ate my pita filled with cucumber like it was the bitter herbs of the Jewish people that I knew about because sometimes in the New Testament class the Old, or First, Testament would come up as context.

After that, Lila began spending all of her time with Nigel, who rushed Delta Sigma Phi, the business fraternity on campus. For my part, I started to hang with the Delta Tau Deltas, who liked beer more than business. Lila and I still shared a dorm room and things seemed the same between us, what with me always stealing her clothes and her teasing me when I got nervous over a test, which happened less as time went on. But little things signaled the difference, proving without a doubt that we were moving from very personal communications to only moderate or sometimes, very impersonal, communications. Like that night when I wanted to crawl into bed with her after I'd had a nightmare about Dad and she'd gently but with no question shoved me out of her twin. She'd looked up at me from her pillow, with her yellow hair streaming over her face, and said, "We're too old for that now."

And another night I wanted to watch *The Simpsons* on our portable TV, the way we always had, with both of us lying on her bed or mine, with our legs tangled together, and our arms around each other, as we both ate from the same big bowl of popcorn. But Lila was dieting so she could have visible hipbones for Nigel and only ate three pieces of the corn. When I wrapped myself around her, she got stiff and said, "Nigel thinks that you and I have an unhealthy dynamic," which caused me to wrestle her until she hit me in the neck and ran out of the room.

Things were more personal with the Delta Tau Deltas, like Steve Hampshire and Larry O'Brien and Phillip Carr and Fernando Heygate. Hass College frats and sororities had houses mostly on Millbank Lane, and I became a Delta little sister, hanging out at the house all the time. About six or seven nights a week, I showed up around six o'clock, usually wearing a midriff and cut-offs, and started downing screwdrivers until I blacked out. I liked the first two drinks best, listening to Kriss Kross or Madonna or my favorite, Mariah Carey. My ultimate song was *I'll Be There*, which Mariah sang with Trey Lorenz, because secretly it reminded me of my sister and once I'd drank enough I'd hear it and sob. The boys listened to me talk about my problems while topping off my cocktails. I'd had sex with all of them, once two at a time, with Larry and Fernando, and it never felt nasty except with Steve Hampshire when he pulled on my hair too hard and didn't say sorry when I complained.

I liked to spread my body out on their hard bunk beds and lose all control. I found it pleasurable. The screwdrivers lifted up my spirit so it swelled and grew generous, and I laughed as I clung onto the guys. I felt their oily, sleek backs with my hands and gripped onto their hips and dug them deeper into me. I was a wildcat. The chains of my father and my grandmother released from my mind and the loneliness caused by my sister evaporated into the air. The next morning, I'd wake up and see the guys' taco wrappers and beer cans littered all around and it wouldn't seem as good. But I'd say *hey* to whatever boys wandered into the room, wrapping a sheet around me. Sometimes, they'd bring me a cup of coffee or even a donut for breakfast.

Meanwhile, my sister got more and more uptight and impersonal. My senior year, we used our dorm room only as a hub station, because Nigel rented an apartment on Plymouth Street and she stayed there every night almost. Whenever we met in our room, it felt awkward. She'd be dressed in a baby blue Polo dress, or khakis and a striped shirt, and I'd be in my cut-offs, and she'd give me the up and down. "You're falling into a pit," she said one time. "You're going to get yourself in trouble."

"Save me, then," I said, splayed out on my bed and looking up at her with a begging face.

For a second, I saw the old love there, when her mouth twisted down, the same way it had when she'd gripped onto me after our father had hit us. But she shook her head.

"Nigel says that I have to pick, and that I either choose the high path for myself or let you drag me down," she said.

"Whatever," I said, burying myself under the covers and not moving until I heard her leave.

The funny thing was, despite all of her judging of me, both of us got into jams, and almost at the same time. I guess we remained physically simpatico despite feeling emotionally so apart. I got pregnant in the winter quarter of my senior year and she got pregnant in the spring of her senior year.

I had another abortion, but Lila and Nigel got married. She had the baby.

[*Motions to me to pick up a framed photograph from a fireplace mantel. The picture shows a little boy with blond hair, about four years old.*]

My nephew, Arthur.

I graduated in 1995 and went into retail at Wet Seal, in the South Coast Plaza. Wet Seal's a women's clothing store, what they now call "fast fashion." We sold tube tops with ruching, distressed denim minis, sequined formals, gladiators, graphic Ts, maxis. I started with floor sales, on commission. I knew that a lot of our customers wanted to feel like I had when I'd spread out drunk and reckless on the Deltas' bunk beds, and I was an expert on how to dress for such an occasion. Almost every day, it seemed, a sad-looking gal with too much black eyeliner dragged in, pawing at the jackets, and I'd buttonhole her with a compliment on her piercing or her ink. Within twenty minutes, I'd be throwing bodycons at her from over the door of the dressing room. It didn't occur to me until I got into the church, years later, that I was the wardrobe designer for the daughters of the Whore of Babylon. I'd load up my customers with fake gold and false precious stones and synthetic pearls, so that they could get hammered at a frat with a Solo cup in their hand full of abominations and the filthiness of their fornication. Good times.

I made manager in '98 and stayed there until I had to file for SDI. I cleaned up my act. I stopped drinking. I woke up at 5 A.M. to get to the store and arrange the bags. I stayed until 9 or 10 P.M. doing the books. Thirteen girls worked under me, floor, cash register, stockroom, and they all had their own problems and sob stories. I took Mindy Greer to the hospital once for appendicitis. Sarah James called me panicked from a bad date in an Olive Garden in Anaheim, and I drove there and rescued her from a woman-beater who'd already left bruises on the top part of her arm. When I wasn't mother-henning the employees, I took the crappier merchandise home and stain-treated it and mended it and sold it for top dollar. I turned the O.C. Seal into one of the top money-makers in Southern California, and Maya Rooks, the tri-city's supervisor, twice awarded me commendations at our yearly company retreat.

I also had a boyfriend, Peter, who I dated for four years. Peter specialized in jewelry, timepieces. He managed a Tag Heuer two floors up from me at the Plaza. We mostly sat at home on the sofa in front of the television while he talked about watches. "The 2000 series was created in the early 1980s, not in the 2000s, like most customers think," he'd say, rubbing my feet, his own black Tag Heuer gripping onto his wrist like a giant tarantula. "The line was the first to include the six features that exemplify the TAG Heuer lifestyle."

"What's a Tag Heuer lifestyle, really," I'd say, giggling. "Knowing what time it is?"

"It's like a way of life," he'd say. "Because Tags are true sport watches, not like Rolexes or Cartier. They're very rugged."

"Isn't that something." I'd waggle my toes so he'd massage them harder.

Peter cooked spaghetti on Saturdays at his condo, which he shared with a tall Black guy named Jaime, his best friend since high school and the manager of the Plaza's Abercrombie & Fitch. Peter always set Jaime an extra place during Saturday spaghetti nights. While the three of us ate, I watched Peter and Jaime communicate in their mysterious way. Jaime could cock his head at Peter, or tense his lip, and that tiny sign sent messages across the dinner table, as if Jaime had thrown a paper airplane at Peter and Peter opened it up to see a poem that only he could read. Watching them being so brotherly made me remember my sister with a punch to the heart. When we'd been young, Lila could suck a tooth and I'd hear a secret symphony of complaints or a complicated four-part plan on how we would sneak out that night to go to the creek.

My sister was doing good. She and Nigel brought together their computer and communications smarts and started a PR company for social media. They had contracts with Google and Yahoo. They bought a big white house up above Montana Avenue in Santa Monica. As they got richer, they had three more children, Jenny, Susan, and Carrie, the last one obviously named after me so that I'd feel less awful over our breakup. I didn't see Lila that much anymore, except on Thanksgiving and Christmas. I'd bring Peter over to the house for holiday dinner, and my mother would be there. My father was dead by then. I'd eat turkey and talk about Wet Seal and Peter would sip his soup and talk about Tag Heuers while Lila and Nigel sent each other mystical silent telegrams of thoughts to each other, like Peter and Jaime did, and like Lila and I used to do.

Eventually I broke up with Peter because I realized that we did not share an intense love. By this time it was 2006. I nourished my spirituality by reading Eckhart Tolle and doing meditation and Asian cooking. I studied the books of Thich Nhat Hanh and tried to wish true happiness for my sister and my dead father and my grandmother, and eventually, after working hard on myself, I could do that. But I couldn't travel the whole road to enlightenment. I looked at my phone too often and dated too much, and still got caught up in meaningless sex. I worried about the accessories display at Wet Seal like it was a problem on par with world hunger. I couldn't keep my eye on my goal—I didn't even know what my goal *was*, except that it required me to know things I didn't know, so I could become a better person.

[*Looks down at the floor, and nods to herself.*]

I noticed my symptoms in the winter of 2011. I don't want to talk about what they were. I went to my doctor, who sent me to another doctor. I had a lot of tests. Finally, about a month after I first noticed a problem, I got a call from the oncologist while standing in my kitchen cooking Chinese chicken stir fry with water chestnuts. "It's ovarian," he said.

This was, I realize, twenty-eight years after I swam in that toxic water flowing down our street from the Santa Susana laboratory, but as soon as I got my diagnosis I knew that the filth those criminals sent into our neighborhood had made me sick. The reports on cancer clusters within a five-mile distance from the lab came out a while back, and I'd read about them in the paper. But because Lila and I were always healthy, I'd let myself forget all about it.

It spread. I had a hysterectomy and a radical mastectomy. I had chemotherapy. I took cisplatin and paclitaxel every three or four weeks. I had stomach pain. I threw up. I couldn't move my head. I couldn't move my legs or arms. I'd vomit if I moved my eyes. I'd lay there and think I might die from the medicine. But something was happening to me, even then. I'd be unable to move or do anything except for watch the light play on the painted wall of my bedroom and I'd think, the world is beautiful. The world is very, very, very beautiful.

My sister stopped working, hired an extra nanny, and took care of me. She bathed me and hauled me to the bathroom. I loved her face. She'd had Botox and fillers by then, but she still looked pretty. She didn't wear makeup when she nursed me. She looked like a saint. I'd reach up and touch her cheek, her mouth. I realized what a shit I'd been, to be jealous of her. "Please forgive me," I said. "For what?" she'd say. "For not being happy for you," I'd say. "Of course you're happy for me," she'd say, cleaning me up with a wet wipe or a towel.

No, we couldn't get back that closeness. Back to very personal communications. Back to *tell it to my heart, tell me I'm your only one*. We'd clench each other's hands and look into each other's eyes and love each other, but it wasn't the same. She belonged to Nigel, not to me.

At some point, I started to feel the call of God. In the depth of my sickness, I could feel God turning his face toward me. I remembered that New Testament class that I'd taken in college and how I'd liked the stories with the women in them—Mary Magdalene and the Virgin, and the unnamed lady in Luke 13 who is lame until Jesus heals her. How it goes is, on the Sabbath, Jesus was teaching, and a woman hurt by a spirit for eighteen years came to listen to what he had to say. She couldn't stand up straight, and it wore her down. Jesus saw her, stooped, in the crowd. He said, "Woman, come here." She shuffled over. Christ said, "Woman, you are set free from your infirmity." And he put his hands on her. All at once, she straightened up. "Praise God," she said. "Praise God."

I started to praise God. I felt the Lord. I felt the Lord coming in through the window in the form of the golden light that played in patterns on my bedroom wall, I felt the Lord in my sister's far-away face, I felt the Lord in my hollowed-out body, and I felt the Lord moving through my mind like a soft wind. Like a fall of rain. I felt Him.

I started reading religious books. Some of them weren't that great. One of them said that abortions give you cancer, that out-of-wedlock sex gives you cancer through the curse of HPV and AIDS, that cancer is the blight the holy Host sends to punish the wicked. But I didn't believe it. I didn't believe in the God of my Grammy, who hated the Whore of Babylon and was sure she was condemned to burn in the fiery flames of hell. My God loved the Whore of Babylon and all of her daughters, and he loved the jealous, stupid, heedless girl I had once been. Because God is love. God is love, and he wanted to love me, and *that's* why he sent me the cancer.

Yes, Miss Rodriguez, he sent me the cancer so I would know the truth about this life. That we are all condemned to die in suffering and that one terrible fact makes us all kin who must care for each other. He sent me the cancer so I could learn we should be gentle to one another, and love one another, as best as we can.

He didn't give it to my sister because she didn't need it. She had love in her life. She has it, because she moved away from the love I wanted to give her, a love that was too much for one sister to feel for another.

But God, he wanted all the love that I had to give him. Nothing from me could be too intense. I could embrace him, and I could cry to him, and I could beg him, and I could seduce him, and I could yell at him, and I could bother him, and I could talk nonsense to him, and I could need him, and it would still be all right.

And that's why, when you first showed up here to see if maybe I would sue the government, and wanted to know if I could prove that all of this shit is their doing—that's why I said that your question is complicated, because the reasons for our agonies are hidden from us, except in glimpses, like when I felt the call of God and realized that the path of blood and pain that he set me on would lead to my transcendence.

[*Pauses when asked a question.*]

No, you don't understand. I am not saying that God flew down from the sky and gave me cancer by laying hands on me in an evil way. That's the mystery of it all. Because other forces moved against me, and are responsible. You are asking me whether I think that the pollution from Santa Susana "caused" my cancer, and not only do I think it, but I know it, as sure as I know that you are sitting here before me. What the hell else do you think will happen to a young girl when she bathes in nuclear contamination for years? She will get very, very sick. And those men are at fault for making me ill. They must atone.

Yes, they must atone. Yes, I am interested in suing the government. No, I don't know how to "verify" my case. And I don't know what that is, a statute of limitations. All I can say is that this experience took many things from me. It has also been expensive. I lost my job, see. I want all that back.

I know that my sister didn't get sick, but that doesn't disprove what I am telling you. She didn't need to get it like I did. I know this is frustrating for you, Miss Rodriguez, you being a government person, and so confused about the world. You see things moving only in the direction of your intelligence.

But you need to understand that both things are true, at the same time. Santa Susana made it happen *and* God made it happen. The men at the lab hurt me, without giving me any warning. And God let the world work in a way that led to my being possessed by a spirit, so I could feel the woe which cleansed me of my confusion and my pride and, I am happy to say, set me on a journey that ended in the blessing of my remission, which I've been in for two whole years. And that's why, now, Miss Rodriguez, I am free of my sorrow over my sister. I learned to save up all my love for the Lord. Except for my money, my manager's position at Wet Seal, and those years, everything I lost has been returned to me, and so much more. God returned Job's seven sons and three daughters, didn't he? And I say to you, the only reason we don't know of all the miracles later bestowed upon the disabled lady in Luke 13, who was touched by Christ's mercy, is because the men who wrote the Bible didn't care enough to tell us her name or her story. But I can tell you what happened to me. What happened is, God's terrible love was given to me on a dark day and it filled my life with grace and tenderness. God's hard, hard love is the only reason that right now, this very second, I can stand up straight, with you as my witness, and say, "praise Him."

INTERVIEW WITH GREG WIŚNIEWSKI

I got into the business because I was good with tools. When I was fifteen, I was keen to get a motorcycle. A Kawasaki. My father had one, as he was a CHP officer for Los Angeles. That made me want one, too. I dreamed of blazing down the highway on my own bike. But my father said that before I could get one, I had to learn how to fix it. So, I'd fix his. I learned how to take it apart and put it back together again. We'd work on it together. After I figured out my way around the machine, he said I needed to make my own money to buy my ride, because he wasn't going to shell out. I went to work for the Kawasaki dealership. They gave me automotive mechanic training and I learned on the job.

At sixteen, I bought my KZ900 and it became my signature. Leather jacket, the whole thing. I had lots of girlfriends and raised plenty of hell until I met Terry. My wife. She's a hairdresser. She actually didn't care about the motorcycle, she just liked me, she said. Once we got together, she told me to get a better job. With better benefits. This was 1990. I wanted to go to the police academy, but I had heard from some guys at the dealership that Atomics International was looking for men. Technical stuff. It wasn't really clear what you would be doing. But they paid and they were hiring. I rode my bike up to Santa Susana and applied.

"I'll take whatever you got as long as I can work with my hands," I told the foreman. We sat in his office as I filled out the paperwork. He was a nice man, a Black gentleman, name of Henry Robertson. He was short, but strong. Built solid. With a big neck, and big shoulders.

"No problem if you haven't done work in nuclear yet," Henry said, nodding as he read my application. "We'll teach you up here."

"Learning on the job's fine with me," I said. "I've done that before."

Henry looked impressed. "And you'll be working with your hands, all right."

"Who'll be training me?" I asked.

Henry gave me a smile, with lots of teeth. "You're looking at him."

I felt excited. He seemed like he'd be a decent boss. My boss at Kawasaki was a yeller. But I got a positive feeling about Henry right off.

"Sounds good," I said.

Henry brought me to the Hot Lab in Building 20, in Area IV. Hot Lab's where the scientists had handled nuclear materials remotely before the Susana's nuke sector got shut down in 1988. Back then, if they wanted to check on the reactors' nuclear rods to see if they were busted, they'd look at them with robots in the Hot Lab. Or if they wanted to process isotopes, that'd be done there, too. Robots they used were the Waldos. They were master-slave manipulators. Named after a machine or a character in a short story by Robert Heinlein. I didn't read the story, but Henry told me about it. He said our skills were high tech and future-oriented. And they were, except that we also just did a lot of cleaning. The Waldo had a master arm, which we used in the operations cell, and it controlled the slave arm, which worked with the radioactive materials in the hot cell. The machine was like those little carnival claws in the grab-a-toy games we used to play at the arcade. But big. Anyhow, the operations cell and the hot cell were separated by thick concrete, so that the scientists didn't get exposed while they were handling the nuclear materials. It was safety first, Henry said, back then. Thing was, though, we were called in to do more dangerous decontamination work because there was radioactivity everywhere. Had been for thirty years. Atomics International was spending ten million dollars on the clean-up, the first big one they did. I got hazard pay. It was a high salary for somebody like me, and my wife was happy.

My job was taking apart the manipulators and sanitizing them. Repairing them if possible. The Waldos were going to be either disposed of as radioactive waste or fixed and reused or sold to another nuclear facility. We used TCE. Tons of TCE. Trichloroethylene. It's a halocarbon, a solvent. It'd been used to clean machinery since the

1920s and wasn't flagged as a cancer-causer until at least 1999, nine years after I started using it at AI.

I enjoyed my work. It was like a Star Wars version of fixing hogs. And Henry was a fine manager. Really, he was a teacher. He showed me how to disarticulate the encoders and motors, the gripper jaws, all that. He cared a lot about the people who worked under him. He was patient.

"You're doing a great job," he'd say, whenever I struggled with the Waldos' working arms, which were delicate. Far more complicated than anything on a motorcycle. "Don't rush," he'd go on, as I wrassled with the joints. "Nobody get hurt, that's rule number one."

Henry didn't like it if he saw us walking onto the floor only wearing our red-lines. That's what we called our jumpsuits. "Go get your respirator, for cripe's sake," he'd say. We had all kinds of gear. First, we had these white coveralls, protective suits, which had red trim at the neck and the cuffs. Why we called them red-lines. We had gloves, which were duct-taped on. We had duct-taped booties. Film badges. Dosimeters. Henry was worried about the red-lines not giving us enough of a shield against the radiation. We'd put them on and clean up the Waldos and get hot and sweaty, and after the day was done the clothes would get put into barrels and washed offsite. But after a certain point, if you waved your red-lines at a Geiger counter, they would go off. That's why Henry wanted to make sure we wore everything— our respirator, our booties, our gloves. Except, I was twenty-four years old. Sort of dumb. Sometimes I'd work without the breather because it made me feel like I was choking. Henry wouldn't hear of it. "Get back there and put on your damn mask," he'd say, muffled because he was already wearing one himself. I'd run back to the cabinet, do what he told me.

We decontaminated the Waldos with the TCE by either dunking parts into buckets filled with the stuff or slopping it on with a rag that was soaked through with it. At 6 P.M., we'd pour the TCE into barrels and that would get carted away, like our red-lines and gloves. I don't know exactly where they dumped it. I heard the chemicals got thrown in the ocean, and Henry said he'd seen some workmen pouring them into the dirt of the buffer zone of the lab site. That was nothing to do with him, though. If the TCE disposal had been his job, he would have done it tip-top.

"Dumbasses going to get us killed," he grumbled, about the guys polluting the place. He said it to me in private, once, over lunch. We'd started to eat together regularly. We talked about bikes and cars a lot, because Henry was into all of that, too. He talked some about science fiction, the Heinlein stuff, the Waldo story. We became friendly, even though he was thirty years older than I was. He was a dude. He'd tell dirty jokes and make fun of one of the lady supervisors at Santa Susana, but then he'd bring me muffins baked by his wife, Helen, and talk about her so respectfully. Once I brought him some ćwikła—this horseradish spread—as a joke, because I thought he wouldn't like it, and maybe poke fun at me like my wife did. But he was fine with it.

"Not bad," he said, spreading it on his sandwich. "Wiśniewski, you're Polish, right?"

"Granddad was from Kraków," I said.

"You get on with your grandpap?" he asked.

"Long time ago, when I was little," I said. "He was cool."

Henry took a bite of his sandwich. "How so?"

I shrugged.

"Right," Henry said. "It's all just family. That loving. Can't really come up with a word for it."

I watched him eat the sandwich and felt comfortable with him. I liked telling him about my grandfather. Dziadek and my mom hadn't got along, and Terry sometimes made jokes about me being part "Polack," you know. But Henry, he was interested.

"Pretty much," I agreed, about how there's no good word for describing how you love somebody.

So, like I say, I enjoyed my time there. And I didn't feel scared working in Area IV for the first year, because Henry had things under control. There were a couple of mistakes, though. One guy not wearing a respirator breathed in too much TCE and went crazy, because it makes you euphoric. Another guy cut himself with a gasket and had to be rushed to the hospital. Other slip-ups. In Area II there was an explosion, I heard, and a tech got burned bad. Another man in Area III got his hand crushed by a crane. But the worst accident happened to Henry, himself.

I was in there with him early on a Monday. We were at the lab before anybody else that morning, tearing apart Waldos. Our film badges were already black because the Waldos were covered in radio-activity. Henry was dismantling them with old-school tools, pliers. "These are the easiest to work with," he said. "The simplest ways are usually the best." To show me, he started disarticulating the slave arm so that its bolts stuck out, and they were sharp. After the demonstration, he turned to me, waved a hand around, saying, "'Slave arm' is a nasty way of putting it, don't you think? Ugly, if you ask me." He passed his hand over the bolts and they caught on his glove, and tore it all the way up to his elbow. He stopped talking and we both stared down at his exposed skin, immediately understanding what had happened. We ran to the washroom without saying a word.

We had showers in the back. Silkwood showers is what we joked they were, though it wasn't funny. Henry ripped off his ventilator and his red-lines and his gloves, but he did it in such a rush that he lost his balance and fell on the tiles. I worried that I could contaminate him and so I hauled out, with his clothes, straight into the disposal closet. I stripped off my protective gear and dumped our stuff in there. When I ran back into the shower stall he was struggling to get up. The fall had been bad. Blood came down his leg. I held him up and turned on the water. I scrubbed him with soap.

"Get it off me," he was yelling. He had his arm twined around my neck, so as to keep steady.

"You're OK, you're all right," I kept saying. Some of the guys started to wander in and after that it was a panic. They got us towels and bandages. A tech named Craig, one of our crew, helped me carry Henry to the locker room. I dried off Henry's cut and wrapped his shin while Henry sat hunched over and shook his head.

"Don't tell my wife," he kept saying. "She'll take it bad."

Let me admit it, I felt like crying, seeing him like that. Worrying about Helen when he should worry about himself. But my father had taught me to keep my lip stiff.

"No problem, Henry," I said.

Things went back to normal after that. Henry saw a doctor without telling his wife, and the doctor shrugged and said that people get exposed to lots of toxic stuff all the time and live through it OK. Cheered up, Henry returned to work. This was 1991. Not too many accidents after that. Another guy did get burned in Area II on account of a gasoline fire, but that didn't have anything to do with us.

Then came 1992. I can't say that was the greatest year here in Simi Valley.

There'd been the police brutality case, Rodney King. King got arrested, or whatever you want to call it, in March of '91. That same year, they held the trial against the four officers in the Simi Valley courthouse. Stacey Koon, Laurence Powell, Timothy Wind, and Theodore Briseno. All that time, we'd been watching the tape of Rodney King getting beat up, and you'd think that Henry and me would have talked about it. He did bring it up, curling his lip and saying, "Can you believe?" But I changed the subject, knowing it was better we didn't get into the details. Like I said, my dad was CHP. I'd grown up knowing what police officers dealt with on the job, and how they believed they had to protect themselves. After another couple tries, Henry could see that we weren't on the same page, but he was cool about it. We kept talking about pliers versus robots, or Helen's muffins, or Robert Heinlein, or the time I'd saved him, or office politics, or whatever.

Myself, I felt like the whole Rodney King thing had been blown out of proportion. I was glad that the prosecutor had moved the case to Simi Valley, because that's where the cops were. Lots of LAPD live here because of real estate not being insanely expensive and the politics. Our people support police officers, as I did. I knew about the danger of the life, the sacrifice. My father had come home many times, pale and quiet, because some drunk guy with a gun in his glove compartment reached for his weapon when Dad pulled him over. He had to subdue big, unpredictable men, sometimes. He'd told me the stories. About forcing their arms around their backs while they bucked like horses and my father would think he'd never see me or my mom again. He lived with that fear. And he didn't trust—he thought that certain people—he had some independent ideas, I'll say. That's how I grew up, with that perspective, you see. So, if Rodney King—I heard he had resisted arrest. It was said that there was a part of the tape that showed that, him resisting. I don't know, man. You believe what you believe.

There was the trial. It was a weird time. I could tell that Henry was tense about something, and I guessed it was that. As the months wore on he got a little sullen. One day, at lunch, Craig said he didn't think the trial was going to "come out good." But Henry shook his head. "If they don't convict, there'll be a fire around here," he said. "Because it's all on tape." Craig was worried that there was going to be a hung jury or an acquittal but Henry said he had to have faith that the trial would come out the way that he wanted it to. As for me, I hoped that the police officers would be exonerated. I wanted those men to be freed, all right. And I was as sure about my thoughts on the matter then as I am right now that in the day there's sunshine and at night there's stars.

Ever since the indictments, my dad had talked more and more about how if there was a guilty verdict then he and Mom were going to move to Nevada or Texas, some place more in line with their way of thinking. "Nobody respects the police these days," he said one night, over drinks, and started crying. "That's what hurts, the disrespect." After that, I got filled with anger about the Rodney King case. Because it was hurting my father. Terry didn't care one way or the other. But I started talking about it every night at dinner, like Dad did. I thought that the new political correctness had gone too far, and California was getting overtaken, and that Mexicans and Black people hated white people now.

"Whites will rule the world until the trumpet sounds, baby," Terry said to calm me down, laughing at me in her breezy way and drinking her glass of red wine.

[*Pauses, frowns.*]

I know you have a Spanish quality, Mrs. Rodriguez, and I hope you don't mind me laying all this out for you. I'm just trying to tell you the whole story.

The verdict came out on April 29. I still remember the date. A Wednesday. Craig, my friend at Santa Susana, he had a transistor that he listened to sometimes on breaks, and he told me what the jury had decided. He'd heard a report that there was a disturbance at the courthouse, on Alamo Street. Like a crowd coming together. I didn't see Henry at work that afternoon. I don't know where he was. But when I clocked off, I changed into my regular gear and went over to check out what was going on.

An ugly mob stood outside of the East County Courthouse. Some people had signs, pro and con. People were arguing with each other about the rightness of the verdicts. I stood on the side of the people who thought the acquittals were good. A woman on the other side started singing "We shall overcome," and it made me mad. I thought about my dad crying and saying, "the disrespect, the disrespect." I loved my pop. When another woman yelled at our side of the crowd that we were "racist pigs," I let her have it. Not physically, of course. I yelled back at her. I said, "You have no idea what you are talking about. The men in blue deserve your gratitude." Everybody started booing me and it made me yell some more. I said some not-great things. At some point, during the fuss, I looked around and saw Henry at the edge of the group with the civil rights people. He was looking at me with a grim and watchful expression.

"Hey," I said. "Hey, Henry."

But he didn't say hey back. He turned and walked away.

After that, it wasn't the same for me at work. Henry and I never talked about it, but when I invited him for lunch, he said no. "Busy," he told me, not meeting my eye. I knew what was up. I guess I hadn't realized what an important relationship that was to me, but now that he was cutting me off, because we'd had a difference of opinion, it made me sad, at first. I kept following him around, trying to make jokes that he didn't laugh at. And, finally, I got angry. I quit.

I went into the force, like Dad. I was twenty-seven at this point. Terry wasn't wild about my decision, because she was terrified about me getting shot, plus not having as good a salary. But the benefits were all right. I made detective. Did commercial crimes. I was in the Burglary Auto Theft section.

Terry came around to me being in the police. She settled into things, and we had two kids. Cheryl and Nina.

I thought about Henry a lot after I left. I wouldn't say I shifted over to his world philosophy after I joined the department. If anything, I believed more in the other direction, because that's what the job is, that belief system, about bad guys and good guys. In my opinion.

Three years passed. I was in touch, off and on, with some of the men from Santa Susana. Mostly Craig, the one with the transistor. He lived four blocks away from me in the Valley, so it was easy. I saw him when I gardened and he'd walk his dog by my house. In '97, we went out for drinks at Berrigan's. I think he liked hanging out at the cop bar, it made him feel tough. But that night, he had a couple beers and didn't ask me for any war stories. He seemed nervy and embarrassed.

"What?" I said.

"Henry's in the hospital," he said. "First Methodist."

I looked at him.

"He's got leukemia," Craig said.

I nodded, because there were other guys who'd got it from where we worked. We heard stories here and there about people getting blood and bladder cancer, other things. But Henry wasn't other guys. I felt like I'd been shot in the stomach. I didn't say anything, but it was like something was tearing at me. It surprised me, the intensity of it. I pressed my fists into my eyes and Craig got uncomfortable.

"I'm sure he'll be OK," he said, patting me on the arm.

I told Terry about it. It didn't faze her. "That's sad, but he's not a nice man," she said. "He blew you off, because of something to do with people neither of you ever met."

That didn't help me much. I felt strange. Sort of shaky, on the inside. I didn't know how I could help him. Henry probably wouldn't want to be bothered by me. I mean, people who are sick, they don't want to be bothered, right? Give him his privacy, I thought. This went on for about four months. I busied myself with investigating my cases and helping take care of the kids. But Henry stayed inside of me. I kept thinking about how I'd stripped him and washed him that time he'd fallen in the shower and we were so scared. How I had saved his life. But what's that thing the Chinese say? Once you save somebody's life then you're responsible for them for good?

I went to the hospital. I knew some orderlies and security guards from my days on the beat. I asked around, but Henry had been discharged around the same time Craig told me about him being sick. I couldn't get any other information on him.

I had his number, still. His land line. It was on an old directory I'd kept from Santa Susana. I called it and Helen picked up.

"Hey," I said. "I'm an old friend of Henry's, and I'm calling to see how everybody is. I heard about the bad news."

"What?" she asked. She sounded tired and harried, like she was doing a hundred things at the same time. "You're a who?"

"Friend of Henry's," I said. "From AI, the lab."

"Place killed him," she said.

"Oh," I said, holding my hand to my face. "Is Henry dead?"

"No," she said. She started sobbing. "I shouldn't have said that. He's here. He's alive."

"Can I get you anything?"

There was silence on the line for a while. Then she said, "I could use some groceries. I don't have the time to make the trip."

"Tell me what you need," I said. She gave me a list, and their address, because I'd never been to his house. I ran to the store and got the food and drinks and within an hour and a half, I was at their door.

Helen let me in. She was thin. But not a natural thin. She looked whittled, like she'd been worn down. I've seen that in some of the cases I've handled, with women who are dealing with too much. In policing, you'll see that kind of look where a lady's got a troubled kid doing drugs, or a drunk husband, something like that. But she was beat from taking care of Henry.

She stood in the kitchen and watched me like a sleepwalker while I put all the groceries away.

"What else can I do?" I asked.

She closed her eyes. "I need to take a nap. It'll only be fifteen minutes."

"OK," I said.

She walked down the hall and went into a spare room and closed the door. I was still in the kitchen, by myself, with no idea what I was doing there.

I washed the dishes in the sink. Went into the dining room and smoothed the tablecloth. I wandered into the living room and tidied up the magazines and books that had been spread out on the coffee table. After that, I tiptoed to the bathroom, and used it. When I came out, I heard Henry calling for Helen in a soft voice.

I went into his room.

I'm not going to say exactly how it was for him, because that's his business. But I hadn't understood what it meant to pass away. The physical process of it. He was awake, though. His mental outlook was fine. It was the physical that was the problem. I stood in the doorway and he peered up at me, and started, like he was scared of what he saw. He didn't recognize me. Maybe he thought I was an intruder.

"Henry," I said.

"Oh," he said, and then relaxed back down on his pillow.

I came over to his bed. His eyes shone up at me. He looked at me the old way, when he'd eaten my ćwikła or taught me how to dismantle the slave arms.

"Hi," I said.

"Hi," he said.

"I'm sorry," I said. I hadn't realized it until right then, how fucking sorry I was.

He knew exactly what I was talking about. "Yeah," he said, after a long silence. "I didn't like what you did."

"I'm sorry," I said again.

"Where's Helen?" he asked. "I need a bath."

"She's taking a nap."

"Good for her," he said, and shivered. That's when I saw how much he was sweating. Sweat poured down his head and throat, soaking his shirt.

"Are you hot?" I asked.

He said no. "It's the medicine."

His home care setup was complicated and involved a lot of tubes and parts. He couldn't get out of bed. Little comforts had been scattered here and there. On a nearby table, there was a bowl of water and some clean towels.

"I could pitch in," I said.

"Like that last time," he said, then started laughing and coughing.

"Looks like it didn't do any good," I said.

"Probably would've been dead within the year if you hadn't," he said.

I went over to the bowl and dipped one of the cloths in the water. I walked back to the bed and started wiping his face. Henry closed his eyes. I wiped his throat, and his right shoulder. I freshened his arms. His legs. His feet.

When I was done, he laid back, staring at the ceiling.

"Henry, I'm a fuckup," I said.

He shook his head.

"Do you forgive me?" I asked.

He was quiet again, for like five minutes.

"I'd like to be alone," he finally said, his voice hoarse. "I can't help you out."

"I'll help *you* out," I said.

"No, Greg," he told me. He wouldn't look at me.

I walked back out to the living room. I tidied the magazines again. I put away the remote control and dusted the coffee table with my sleeve. But the way I felt was, I suddenly didn't even know who I was. Like I was all blanked out. I can't explain it. It's the same as what Henry had said before, that there's no words for loving somebody in your family. Whatever I was feeling then, there's no word for it, except that it broke me down.

Helen took my calls every once in a while after that, and gave me updates. He died six months later. She let me go to the funeral. I think she knew all about me, and who I was, and what Henry heard me say at the courthouse.

My feelings about Henry got worse when he died. I could never relax. It was like I'd been poisoned. Like I hated myself. After a while, I got angry at him again, like I had been all those years ago, when I'd quit because he wouldn't have lunch with me after he'd seen me protesting. I kept thinking, why me? What'd I do? I went over there and bathed you, and that wasn't the first time. Why couldn't you just be nice? Why couldn't you help me out?

My wife was like, "This has got to stop." But what was happening was, I was changing on the inside and she couldn't really understand it.

About a year after he passed, I had a case involving this car theft ring, out of Burbank. A chop shop crew. We suspected about six African American gentlemen of working with a larger syndicate. They were alleged to specialize in Chevrolet Camaros. It was high-tech theft. They reprogrammed the Camaros' ECMs—engine-controlled modules—with their laptops, and that confused the car into thinking it didn't need a specific key. Actually, I don't know if it was six guys; that's what our CI said. Our confidential informant. One morning in 1998, winter, we got a no-knock warrant at a condo where half the crew was supposed to live. The CI said they had guns, and so I got a squad of seven men, and we went in armed to the hilt at five o'clock in the morning.

There was only one guy living there, about fifty years old. Black man. We couldn't find guns or even tech anywhere. We had the wrong address. As soon as we raided the house, the occupant started screaming and resisting. He jumped out of bed and slapped at the officers, who reverted to their training and subdued him to the ground. They used more force than was necessary, though it probably wasn't illegal, because police brutality's a high standard and there's a lot of immunity. What happened was, one officer named Jed Hauser hit the man on his shoulder and his hip with his baton, first when the guy was smacking him, and then when he was flat on the ground in his pajamas. Now, this should've been mother's milk to me. I'd seen way worse. This was non-lethal, a takedown, mostly ordinary protocol. Except, this time it seemed different. I wasn't thinking about Henry, exactly. It was more like I had that feeling again, like I didn't know who I was, like I was all blanked out. I felt like nobody. I ran over to Officer Hauser and tore the baton out of his hand and used it on him. I knocked Jed out and broke his jaw. I also injured the suspect when I swung the baton back and hit him accidentally in the head. The guy had a concussion and needed seven stitches.

It sure wasn't any hero story. It wasn't a Black Lives Matter. If I didn't like the degree of force, I should have exercised my authority as the lead officer and told Jed to stand down. But instead, I beat the shit out of him and hurt the arrestee.

After they fired me from the department, I was charged with aggravated assault and wound up serving eight months in county jail. My wife left me, and I lost custody, and my father carried his grief about me to his grave. So, that wasn't the best. I went back to fixing motor-cycles. Which is what I still do now.

I think I'm talking about myself too much, because I came here to tell you about Henry. I mean, Henry's dead. I wish he was alive. I'd have liked to make it up to him. It's taken me a long, long while, but I don't feel blanked out anymore when I think about what happened. You get blank because you know you're in the wrong, but without that wrong, you think, what are you going to hang your hat on? I did feel like nobody for a long time, though. I mean, I loved my dad and still do. But then you become friends with somebody, and see what I saw, and, I don't know, it can make you lose your way. And maybe that's not so bad.

It's all because of what happened at Santa Susana. The government put something unnatural there, something wicked, and because you people did that to us, I had to save Henry with my own hands. It's not a normal thing to do. It opened something up in me. Opened me up to another person. Because, what was I thinking to say that? "Police deserved your gratitude." And I haven't told you everything I did in the force. [*Long pause.*] I hurt people.

I can't ever make it right, but it's not about me, it's about Henry, and the kind of person he was. Telling me to put on my mask. Worrying about Helen. Talking to me about my grandad. Telling me about Waldos. That shame eats you. Well, so it goes. You just got to let it, and know you deserve it, and try to make sure that, when you get to see them, you don't wreck your children with the lessons that ruined you.

INTERVIEW WITH RUDY DIMATIBÁG

DECEMBER 9, 2019
MILL VALLEY, CALIFORNIA

There is no "why," Miss Rodriguez. There is only "how." From the clamor of our births to the silence of our deaths, all events arise through a calamitous process that is known by one word, a curious word, a word that signifies the lip print on the glass, the mutation of the cell, the dragon's flight, the unexpected touch of the hand, the brown bear of strength, and the life-blasting enigma of love. That word is "accident," Miss Rodriguez. "Accident."

Our poor planet flies through space on the wings of an accident, Miss Rodriguez.

I know this, because how else can I explain how my life has unfolded? I am the way I am because of an invisible wrinkle in my DNA as well as an intricacy of untraceable errors made by malevolent men working in a secret laboratory. And also for no reason at all. I am here, now, with all of my varieties of damage, because the galaxy is forged in a crucible of error. Human existence is nothing more than an alembic of astonishments and catastrophes.

As Exhibit 1 in support of my motion to suppress your misguided framing of my case, which insists that its most pressing issue is "why" I think this has happened to me, consider the following: Penny did not like me when we met. Penny. I am speaking of Penny Maher. I wrote to you about her in my email, Miss Rodriguez. This was in 1993. Penny and I both worked for Wilmer & Cutler, in Simi Valley. I was an appellate attorney, and she was a litigation associate in the property law division. Penny protected business owners from the incursion of state and federal regulation into the realm of private property rights, regulatory takings. Whereas I had a much more ecumenical practice: probate, copyright, patent, torts, constitutional law, and administrative law.

The first day I laid eyes on Penny she had just arrived at the office, fresh from Georgetown Law and a clerkship in the Central District. I had been at Wilmer & Cutler for five years, in the appellate section, as I have said. I grew up in Simi Valley and attended UC Irvine for my BA and UCLA for my JD. I could have gone to other schools, but I could not, at the same time: I could not leave Simi Valley. Since I was born, I had lived in the same house, my parents' house, the home of Timothy and Jasmine Dimatibág, a last name that means, interestingly enough, "cannot be harmed" in our native Tagalog. But from the very start, when I developed pulmonary squamous cell carcinoma at age three and then later, when my psychiatrist diagnosed me, my family and I realized that I, Rudy Dimatibág, could be harmed, indeed, quite possibly had been harmed even before the moment of my inception. So, I stayed at home with my parents all their lives. They both died of the same disaster that I have survived thus far, my mother in 1991 and my father in 1992.

I had been at Wilmer & Cutler for five years when I met Penny. This was in 1993. I see that I am repeating myself. A tendency that I will try to curb. It was in 1993, and I was alone. I am on the spectrum, as we all are. In my weakest moments, I am burdened by a circle of fear. Once I begin to speak with someone, I grow afraid that I'll get afraid, and then I am afraid the person I am speaking to will catch my fear as if it were a virus and my mind and my speech will lock into an unbreakable anxiety and my discussant will become so terrified that they run away.

My parents did everything they could to aid me. When I was in fifth grade, they discovered that if I took a book in hand, my fear would fold its wings, or crouch and hide somewhere deep inside me.

"Do your classwork, my boy," my father said, whenever I came home from school crying.

"Now, now, you'll be fine," my mother crooned, giving me a cup of hot tea or a glass of lemonade. "Do your assignment, my love."

They told me to read and write, so I would sit at our kitchen table and do my homework. And it did soothe me. I felt calmer, better. More in control.

That is why I could survive. At Wilmer & Cutler, in my office on the top floor, where there was the most limited noise, I could absorb a hundred years of precedent in a few hours and thereafter compose a brief on any legal question that will stand against the appellate products of the finest legal minds in the country. I have had the honor of appearing opposite Eric Holder, Neal Katyal, Theodore Olson. Not in oral argument, obviously. My arrangement with Wilmer & Cutler was that I never appear before the court personally. I tried to twice, and both times I suffered greatly afterward. But my briefs were satisfactory, and even with my considerable limitations, I made partner at the age of thirty-two.

I made partner the same year I met Penny. On that day I first saw her, she stood in the crowded fourth-floor conference room. Bill Wilmer introduced her to the attorneys and to the staff. It was after 6 P.M., during a cocktail reception. Outside the large office windows, night arrived with the harbinger of a dragon-colored sundown. The orange and cerulean shades offset Penny's beauty, which shone like a diamond. She was twenty-six years old. She had auburn hair. Auburn hair is red and brown, both. A soft, shining shade. Her hair was long and wavy then. It grew down her back and glimmered darkly. Her eyes were brown. Her face was round. Her mouth was thin. Her smile was like a tree. A beautiful tall tree branching delicately against the tangerine sky.

I stood at the back of the room. My partners liked me to make an appearance at events, but we had agreed that I would never have to display myself or speak before a crowd that included people I had not adjusted to. As a general rule, at merger announcements, celebrations of litigation victories, and similar affairs, I would stand near an exit, drinking only plain water and replying minimally to the badinage offered by my colleagues. I knew that my demeanor occasioned some smattering of gossip, most troublingly among the entering classes. Once, while in the bathroom, I heard a young trial associate named James Yearwood call me "Edward Scissorhands." At that time, I was not familiar with the reference. I now know that Edward Scissorhands is a title character in a Tim Burton film played by an actor named Johnny Depp and that poor Scissorhands is a traumatized mute with disabilities that turn out to be strengths. For a while I tried to persuade myself that James's nickname was a charming tribute to my complex character but admitted finally that the sobriquet had not been invented with friendly intentions.

There was Penny, with her auburn hair. She stood before the conference-room windows, which filled with the bright dusk. She drank a glass of champagne while Bill extolled her virtues in a loud voice. "Penny Maher graduated with distinction and, as a third-year, published an award-winning note in the *Georgetown Law Journal*. She clerked for the Honorable Clara Gellhorn in the Central District, which, as you all know, is one of the most competitive posts in our region. Help me welcome Penny to our firm: we are so happy to have you!" As the crowd clapped, Penny smiled in a shy, modest way and clutched her glass. She stood by James, a tall and thick-haired brute whom I had seen do fifty push-ups at one of our painful holiday parties. Every time James smiled at her, I noticed, she would blush from her hairline all the way down to her pale, long throat.

I stood at the back, by the exit, but did not leave even as the party ratcheted up in volume and vivacity. I stayed, because I wanted to keep looking at Penny. And, though I knew it was impossible, I wanted to make her blush like that, too.

My resting heart rate rose to an alarming level. Nonetheless, I took a step toward the front of the room, where Penny, James, and Bill stood. I pushed through the assembly of lawyers until I stood in front of Penny. Already, some associates and partners had turned to watch my unaccustomed venture into the social wilderness. Penny did not know I was breaking my own iron rules. She looked at me, beaming, while still holding her champagne glass. I said,

"Greetings. My name is Rudy Dimatibág, and I must chime in with Bill to say that we here at Wilmer & Cutler are all very happy that you have decided to join our firm. Your file impressed us with your breadth and range of interests as well as your remarkable letter of recommendation from Judge Gellhorn. We welcome you. We do welcome you. We welcome you into this beautiful evening with its night sky ablaze with gold and the most tender indigo blue. The world is a place of inscrutabilities that we must succumb to, yet we delight in making new friends with whom we might share the more durable blessings of our endurances, such as the amber of the clouds and the future with its shining silver question marks. The practice of law allows us to interrogate almost everything, including the cost of a human life and the tenacity of the heart's affections, yet, on a night such as this, when your smile like a tree grows its soft branches against the purple ink of the air, we are reminded that the poets allege that some gifts allotted to mankind are in saecula saeculorum, that is, lasting forever and ever, and we find ourselves enraptured with the possibility that, within this miserable fragment of existence which we are apportioned, grace could ever touch us, and let us know there is a reason, a motive, a purpose to being alive—"

Bill, James, and Penny had at this point moved abruptly to the opposite side of the room. There they began speaking to several litigation associates in the property department. During my soliloquy, Penny's face had grown flat and panicked before Bill and James tore her away from me. When she reached the property associates, she brightened up again, laughing and tossing her burgundy locks over her shoulder.

For my part, I had grown derailed at the very beginning of my speech, when I said, "I must chime in with Bill." At that moment, it seemed I stepped suddenly outside my body and proceeded to observe myself blathering about the wonders of the world to Penny, as if I were watching the third act in *Edward Scissorhands* when Edward attempts to socialize with the people in his neighborhood but only gets set upon by a bully. Every word I said to Penny arrived initially like a jewel encased in the luminosity of its own perfection, but then became a swift subject of meticulous and instantaneous second-guessing, and I attempted to repair the mounting destruction that I was causing with earnest phrases that, when subjected to review, were revealed as even more bizarre and inappropriate than their predecessors.

I was sweating. I looked down. Penny's quarter-full champagne coupe stood on a nearby table, with its delicate lip print on the rim. I took her glass and fled the conference room. I entered the elevator and hid in my top-floor office. I put Penny's coupe on my desk and looked at it. I picked it back up, drank its contents, and placed my lips to the print on the rim.

After that, I stayed in my office for many hours. I did not depart until after midnight, when I peeked out the window at the parking lot and felt assured that every other employee had left.

Penny and I spoke to each other only rarely after that for the next fifteen years. She installed herself in the property division and quickly made a name for herself in the area of regulatory takings, exactions in particular. She preferred to do her appeals herself, though at the beginning of her career Bill asked me to edit her arguments, which were consistently excellent. When I was first tasked with this work, I felt wild excitement, as I felt sure that I could impress Penny with my mastery of federal appellate law, doctrines that I intended to tutor her in during long, productive personal meetings. My aspirations, however, proved disappointed when I discovered that after my tragic first impression at the introductory cocktail fete, Bill had identified me as a possible litigation hazard. He explained to me carefully that Penny and I would only communicate through interoffice mail. I attempted to breach this chasm by praising Penny's work product with enthusiastic, smiley-face–drenched marginalia, but her briefs proved so impeccable I would have done so anyway, and she graduated quickly from needing my assistance. I thereafter gave up all hope and contented myself with loving her from afar.

During this period, I worked between sixteen and seventeen hours a day, seven days a week. I would wake in the morning and cook myself an enormous breakfast of omelet, French toast, asparagus in season, and black coffee. I ate this meal in the same kitchen where my parents had encouraged me to do my homework during my difficult youth, in our house that was seven short miles away from the fetid Santa Susana Field Laboratory. While they lived, our home had been decorated in shades of chocolate and orange, and had a battered old sofa that my father once liked to lounge on half-naked while watching baseball on television. Our ancestral seat had seemed to me a paradise of fond feeling and sanctuary, accented as it was by the tuneless ditties that my large, laughing mother had sung all day long, and the happy chatter of my father, who was a gifted gardener of the Sampaguita, know also by its Latin name of Jasminum sambac, which wove its perfume throughout the house like a spell cast by a beneficent fairy. After they died their horrible, violent, unforgivable deaths, deaths that I remain sure were spurred by the radionuclide contagion flowing downstream from the lab, I spent two years unable to do anything but work, writing appellate brief upon appellate brief until I developed a dangerous case of pneumonia. That was in 1995, and when my doctor took one look at my haggard face, he submitted me to a brief spate of inpatient care. Afterward, I concentrated on repairing what remained of my mental health until I felt well enough to refurbish the house and the garden, and embark upon my version of living again.

I had restored painstakingly the kitchen in which I ate my omelets and asparagus to its former glories. The walls glowed with fresh paint in a 1970s palette of fudge and sherbet; I'd mended the cracks in the little green backsplash tiles and regrouted them with obsessive accuracy; the melancholy fragrance of the Jasminum sambac floated in through the open, reglazed windows. After breakfast, I repaired to my sparkling pink bathroom, where I lathered myself into a soapy version of the abominable snowman. I would then rinse, towel, and climb into an iteration of my customary three-piece wool suit, which is charcoal gray, with a navy blue silk square in the pocket. I preferred oxblood leather captoes from Church's, and liked to dab myself with Vetiver by Guerlain.

Then I would go to the office.

On very lucky days, I caught glimpses of Penny in Wilmer & Cutler's hallways or elevators, and I was guaranteed to see her from my back-of-the-room vantage at our monthly meetings. Penny's beauty intensified at a rapid pace, transforming from that fragile brilliance into a fuller, burnished, red-lipped splendor that sent me into mild fits of tachycardia if I allowed my eyes to rest upon her for too long. It did not surprise me that the beastly James Yearwood began to pursue her with a combination of he-man ruthlessness and finesse that proved hatefully successful—for, in 1997, ten weeks after I witnessed James crushing a flushed and cooing Penny to his breast in the M section of our legal library and nine weeks after a local florist delivered an enormous bouquet of red roses to her office, Wilmer & Cutler sent out a congratulatory notice celebrating their engagement, a relationship, our managing partner took care to note, that had been approved and authenticated via their signing of a Human Resource waiver attesting to their mutual consent at the outset of their courtship.

Several days after the announcement, I found myself alone with Penny in the south elevator as I made my way up to the sixth floor. We both stepped in at the same time and took positions at opposite ends of the lift. At first, I made a show of glaring at the numbers over the doors. But then I could not resist. I peered at Penny from under my eyelashes and found that she was looking at me. Her russet hair flowed over her shoulders, and her strong, fur-brown eyes enveloped me in a warmth that reminded me of the radiance of my parents' beloved faces. My gaze locked with hers, and for a moment, I felt as if I would faint.

"Congratulations, Penny, I wish you every happiness," I stammered. "Happiness is a moth. A moth in a tree, a tree like your smile. Your smile is an oak tree with a white moth fluttering aloft its flowering branches. We cannot catch this moth in our nets. But it alights on some, a very lucky few. I wish it to alight on you. I wish you the moth, the butterfly, of love. The raven of bliss. The bear of tenderness. The deepest, closest, most secure peace in this terrible world. I wish you everything good. I wish you everything that you want."

Penny regarded me for a moment, and her soft, thin mouth flickered.

"Oh, Rudy," she said, her voice catching. "Thank you."

We remained looking at one another for two or three seconds that seemed to stretch as long as my life thus far. The door opened. She got out. I closed my eyes. Tears flowed down my cheeks as the elevator whirred upward again. I spent the rest of the day unable to read or write. I only stared out my office window, pressing my handkerchief to my face while the words "Edward Scissorhands" sang madly in the back of my head.

Penny married James seven months later.

The years churned forward. Except for a depressive episode that resulted in a two-month in-patient stay in 2002, I remained in place. I ensconced myself at my desk, before my computer, whose screen glowed with legal ciphers that I cracked like a codebreaker. The same crystal cup sat by my elbow. Well-meaning paralegals dithered in my doorway with thick sheaves of papers and then vanished, leaving me to redo their research. My dark hair silvered at the temples, then seemed to blanch of color overnight. During Wilmer & Cutler's periodic festivities, I assumed my customary place at the back of the room. I hovered by the exit during the monthly meetings. My heart beat, and beat, though no longer threatened to explode. When I turned forty-six, my doctor introduced a new medication into my regimen, and, for the first time, my fear shrank from a tornado into a mere blizzard. I attempted to share small talk with the parking-lot attendant and even traded a few jokey moments with Bill and the trepidatious paralegals.

As often as not during these conversations, I would observe myself and then observe myself observing myself, until my mutterings about the weather whirligigged into rhizomatic and recursive perorations that treated subjects as various as the current phase of the moon, the sublime patterns of the clouds, how heartache is caused by an irritation of the vagus nerve, the burden of proof in antitrust actions, the rapturous loneliness of hermits, the color red, the color brown, the color auburn, the wonderment of smiling trees . . . but even as my interlocutors stiffened and stared, I realized that these outbursts of mine were sometimes quite lovely. I could share this new appreciation for my own poetry only with myself, but even that was good. I saw that the clouds, the moon, heartbreak, auburn, the burden, and the hermit were all weakly linked by a fragile fortuity, which itself was a message, teaching us that the gorgeous world is an assemblage of paper cards that can be destroyed by a single breath.

Penny appeared to be doing well. I saw her in the conference room, in the elevator. We barely spoke. She thrived, for a while. Her wine-dark hair glimmered in the hallway like the ocean at dawn. For the initial seven years of their marriage, she and James drove to work together in a mint-green Mercedes, and smiled at each other in a secret way during meetings. Both she and James made partner, she two years after he did. She strode through the office at first like a goddess, then like a warrior, as she grew older. There were no children. Her face grew slender and paler. Her smile came a little slower than before. Then one green Mercedes became two Mercedes, the green and now a blue, as she and James developed schedules so hectic they could no longer commute together. The secret glances between husband and wife grew rarer. One evening, in the library, I saw James buttonholing a first-year female associate with long lemon-colored hair who blushed the color of a burst vein and laughed far too loudly at his jokes. Whenever I chanced to pass Penny's office, I saw her bent over her desk, her table lamp stroking her face with silver, as if she were a girl in a painting by de La Tour. Her thin mouth no longer branched like a tree. But she remained perfect. She was perfect to me.

After another year passed, James and the lemon-haired associate could sometimes be seen standing close together in the commons room while getting coffee or affecting to select snacks. Their shoulders touched. The girl had blue eyes, which looked up at James, as large and lustrous as mirrors that reflected back a man of power and animal sexuality. The truth was, of course, more banal. James had developed a paunch; he had lost half his hair. But he loved the way he looked in the glass that girl held up, and after some more months eked by, Penny dissolved into tears at one of our monthly meetings. Six weeks later, in 2008, James was discharged for sexual harassment and Penny left the firm.

I wished her well, in my heart and in a letter, to which she never replied. Even after she disappeared, I continued to drink from the crystal coupe that she had clutched on the first day that we met.

I realized that my health might have suffered a blow in 2015, when I first perceived a pallor in my face and a tightness of breath. I made an appointment with my doctor and submitted to a round of tests that took three weeks to complete. My physician returned with a diagnosis announcing the return of my childhood ailment. I took disability leave from the office and was subjected to a surgery similar to the ones I had endured as a toddler and those my parents had barely survived before their own protracted deaths. My procedure, now, was successful. Then it came time for my treatments.

I lay in my room at City of Hope and received my infusions. At first, I was too weak to do anything but look out the window at a view of a nearby park, where mists drifted through cypress trees. But later, I could read—appellate court opinions, mostly, on new developments in copyright and administrative law. My prognosis, they said, was not that bad, and I responded well to the protocol. One of the doctors asked me if I had ever been exposed to radiation. I said I did not think so. She shrugged and allowed that the causes of cancer remained complex and, in most cases, unexplained. But her question struck me, and inspired a bout of research, during which I discovered the history of the Santa Susana Lab, and the dark work that Atomics International and Rocketdyne once did within fifteen minutes' proximity to my parents' home. It's then that I developed my own theories.

I remained in the hospital for a great while, but after the first month and a half grew able to ramble the halls with the aid of a walker and a mobile IV. The doctors encouraged this exercise, which helped me avoid pneumonia and manage my intense depression. I passed other patients' rooms and saw them lying there, staring, alone. I talked with them. Unless they were in pain, they did not mind the way I am. Or, possibly, on account of advances in psychiatric medicine, I am not exactly that way anymore. In any event, I listened to them, did errands for them. I brought an elderly man named Walter Adastik a daily cup of chamomile tea. I offered a lady named Esmeralda Muñoz copies of *Star*, *People*, *Us Weekly*, and the *National Enquirer*, all of which I later subscribed to for her, to her great delight. I would pass by new admits and bring them Jell-O and ice pops, as I had learned where the nurses stored these treats in the hospital galley. Sometimes, if a patient was in distress, I would sit next to them and try to share their unhappiness.

After two months in the hospital, right before my discharge, I passed by room 311 and saw a new patient, a woman, lying in her bed. It was Penny.

My Penny. I squeezed my eyes shut and opened them again. Yes, it was her. She was very pale. Very thin. She had lost her auburn hair. But I knew her immediately upon sight. I stood in the doorway, unable to speak.

She turned and saw me, in my paper robe. She recognized me, too.

"Rudy," she said.

I entered her room with my IV and sat in the chair by her bed.

"Why are you here?" she whispered, closing her eyes.

"Lung," I managed to say. "And you?"

"Skin," she said.

I remained there, by her side, for an hour, and we did not speak. She drifted. Nurses came in, came out. They knew me. I explained that we were friends who had worked at the same law firm, and they did not make me leave. She slept. As evening came, the heavens outside her window brightened, the way they had on that first night I saw her.

"Penny," I said.

Still with her eyes closed, she reached out, and I grasped her hand.

"The sky was made only for you, Penny," I said. "You are a diamond as bright as a blue cloud, as flawless as the tangerine wind. You are as precious as the Sampaguita jasmine. Your eyes are the most tender shade of brown bear. You are as strong as a bear, Penny. You have the strength of a thousand sunsets in your body and your mind. You have the heart of a dragon that flies through the orange air, out of this room, into the world, into the world that needs you, and where you will return."

She laughed softly, and now her smile was like a tree again.

"You always had the most beautiful way of talking," she said.

The world was created and is unmade by accidents, Miss Rodriguez. As I have discovered through my research, a long time ago, scientists made a plethora of mistakes in the Santa Susana Field Laboratory, where they tried to create a bequest for humanity in the form of nuclear reactors and formidable rockets, but they mostly only succeeded in spilling great quantities of radionuclides and trichloroethylene into the earth, where they have festered and spread all of these years.

Not everyone in Simi Valley grew sick. A contingency in my DNA and that of my parents, or perhaps some unknown combination of events that led us to be more exposed than most, made us vulnerable to the toxins in ways others were not. You will ask me how I am able to be so certain about the causal connection between Santa Susana and the fates of my parents, Penny, and me, and to that I may point only to the known lethal qualities of these chemicals and the ancient and simple principle of res ipsa loquitur. No, I never smoked. I myself joined an ongoing suit against Boeing, but have learned that the vagaries of record-keeping at Santa Susana have imperiled the strength of that cause of action. As to the possibility of winning a case against the government, I rejected that path on account of the discretionary function exception of the Federal Tort Claims Act and the fact that so many of the players in this comedy were not government employees but rather independent contractors. Nevertheless, even if I ascribe the pain that my family has endured to arbitrary vicissitudes, that does not deny that the men who envenomed Simi Valley are deeply responsible, as responsible as God would be for our maladies, if he existed. Which he does not.

For there is no "why," as I have said, Miss Rodriguez. There is only "how." There are no Elysian Fields and no grand plan written on the orange and indigo sky by a holy governor with evil or pure motivations. And yet, while we mortals must do the work of finding fault in the absence of a rationale, the empty heavens do not deprive the world of meaning. Penny and I have been married for three years, and we live today far away from Simi Valley, here in the Marin forest, where there are no nuclear ghosts. Our prospects look good, if not in saecula saeculorum. Up to six years for me. A chance of a full lifetime for her. That itself has meaning. It means everything. And our meaning was made from the raw materials of that which is haphazard and unforeseen.

You must realize that a random series of mishaps caused me to be like this, or how I used to be, or how I still am, which is able to speak only in nervous circles. This idiosyncrasy of mine was a piece of very bad "luck" for a long time, luck that was augmented by a further amalgam of causalities, including the heart-stopping deaths of my parents. But this bundle of flukes also flowered into other possibilities, such as the discovery that a book could gentle my fear and that school was my refuge and that I was a good lawyer. This in turn led me to inhabit an Edward Scissorhands–like existence at Wilmer & Cutler for thirty years, an existence that was brightened for a time by auburn hair and a tree-smile. And then a combination of further hazards pushed me into my future. They have made me complete. They have brought me my wife. What are all of these incidentals? These balls knocking and flying across the green baize of a cosmic billiards table? They are disparate and uncountable, and add up to my life. They include: mad scientists with a Promethean plan, a family who could not live up to their name, a man who could do fifty push-ups, an awkward conversation about moths in an elevator, the second failure of my lungs, the day I saw Penny in the hospital, the moment she gave me her hand, and then, those priceless, terrifying seconds when I spoke to her of jasmine and dragons, of diamonds and bears, and she could hear me, and love me, and understand.

INTERVIEW WITH SIMON GRAHAM

NOVEMBER 11–12, 2019
SIMI VALLEY, CALIFORNIA

[NOVEMBER 11]

I guess what's the most difficult thing is how unreal it seems. Like, they wouldn't put us in this kind of danger, would they? That's what I keep thinking. But then I remember the fire and the rains, and I read the studies about the laboratory, and I think, yes, they did, and I'm not being crazy. That's why I answered the government email checking up on us. I think that's what happened and I want you to tell me the truth.

On the morning of the fire, I only thought, I have to get my daughter and my father out of here. I figured that afterward, when the firefighters put the blaze out, we'd be safe. I'm talking about the Woolsey Fire. We'd had a lot of drought here, we still do, and so fires weren't new in this area. They are getting worse, though. I never saw a fire like Woolsey.

I was here, in my apartment, when it happened. Getting ready for my shift. I hadn't even showered yet. It was two-fifteen, two-thirty. I get up late because I'm the night manager where I work. I lay in bed, drinking coffee. It seemed as normal as a day could be. Until I opened the drapes. The sky wasn't right. The color of it was wrong. It was orange. Orange and brass-colored, and the light tilted strange.

I've lived here all of my life, and I knew our sky shouldn't look that way.

I grew up on Sinaloa Road, down the hill from Santa Susana. My mother left my dad and me when I was ten. She had long blond hair, curly. She was devil-may-care. Mom would laugh at Dad when he got mad and dimples would show in her cheeks. "Eat my shorts!" she'd yell, with her hands on her hips, while my father cussed her out for not keeping house. "Talk to my bright red fanny!" He was a lot to handle and she took off. After that, the light went out of everything. "Clean up this place, it's a pigsty," my dad would yell about my room, grabbing me hard at the nape of my neck. He worked as the cook and manager at the Reagan Country Café, at the Ronald Reagan Library, off the 118. He wanted me to do well in school and go to college, but back then I just couldn't. I had a lot of anger in me and I expressed it by acting out. In the end, I wound up making a bad mistake.

It happened in 2001. I was fifteen and a sophomore at Monroe High. Didn't have any friends except for a couple of scammers in school, Vincent and Gene, who were seniors and taught me all I knew about heisting. I'd ditch to go thieving with them, and later we'd get high at the beach and pick up girls. At Bolsa Chica I met a freshman named Jill from Wilson and had sex with her in the dunes. Which is maybe TMI. I'm only saying that Jill was shy and saw me as cool because I bragged about boosting cars by breaking their ignition locks with screwdrivers, and bogarting junk from CVS by wearing a big coat with pockets. She had glasses and was chubby and would do anything I told her to, like things she wasn't too experienced with. Nothing anybody else didn't do. She was just really young and got upset once, I guess. She later said I took advantage. But she exaggerated. Because, I was young, too. And she was teasing me and I got a little overexcited, maybe. Anyway, I was starting to honestly like her when the bad thing happened.

Around Christmastime, I somehow managed to lift a late model Silverado from the Macy's parking lot. I'd done it alone, whereas before I'd always stood by and watched Vincent and Gene TWOC cars and gone along for the ride. I called Jill and told her to get ready for the beach. Even though I could barely drive that thing, I managed to pick her up from her school. We jammed over to the CVS to get tequila. I parked in the lot by the entrance, and told her to wait in the truck while I "did a little shopping." She'd been stiff and not talking to me before, except right then she got nervous and chattery. "I don't want anything, let's just go." But I hustled to the store, moving past an old homeless guy laying down by the front doors. Once in, I went straight for the liquor area, which I usually never did because that aisle's got heavy surveillance.

Didn't take thirty seconds for a security guard to start tracking me. As soon as I slid the Jose Cuervo into my pocket he lunged at me and I ran. I booked out of the CVS, past the homeless guy, and when I slammed myself inside of the Silverado Jill curled up on the front seat with her face in her knees.

I gunned the gas. Backed up fast and jerked the car into drive. I screeched around the parking lot. Hit the old homeless man. Jill screamed. She ran out of the car and I don't know where she went.

I hurt him bad. He curled up and didn't move. I got out and checked to see if he was alive. His face didn't look good. His eyes stared at me like he was blind, though he wasn't. I tried to get away, but the police came and got hold of me pretty quick.

The old man passed away six months after the accident, of a combination of causes, including me hitting him. My public defender told me the D.A. would have trouble convincing the jury that I killed him. It'd been too long between the accident and his lungs failing, and he had other problems because of alcohol and drugs. I was charged with felony hit and run, reckless driving, grand auto theft, shoplifting, and resisting arrest, but not murder.

They tried me in juvenile court. I got convicted and sent to juvenile detention. I had trouble processing it. My father stopped talking to me until he found out about Evie. The counselors didn't give up on me, though, and tried to get me to confront what I'd done. This one lady, Shayla, was nice. She'd speak to me in a gentle voice about the old man and Jill. "You need to take a hard look at what you've done," she'd say. I didn't want to hear the first thing about it.

I saw things in a weird way. Even when the homeless guy died, I didn't consider myself a killer. I liked how the prosecutor figured it, that there was too long a period between my hitting him and his passing away for anybody to think me a murderer. But then I'd remember the way the old man looked when my car hit him. I'd be lying in my bunk and he'd appear. I'd see his blind eyes. I'd shoo him away, but he always came back after me like a ghost.

I blamed everything on Vincent and Gene. I told Shayla, "The reason I'm in here is because of those assholes who taught me how to pop cars in the first place." Shayla wore silk and cotton scarves around her neck and she talked with her hands. She'd wave her fingers at me and say, "That's twisted reasoning, Simon. You need to think straight and take responsibility before you can change."

I was messed up. It didn't help things with my father that Jill had gotten pregnant. I didn't know until after I'd been in detention for four months. Jill wouldn't talk to me or visit me because she'd developed all these theories about how I didn't respect girls who were minorities. Because, Jill's Black, which I don't know if I said. Anyway, while I was inside, she had the baby, even though her parents wanted her to go to college. I'm sure they also didn't want to have any grandchildren from me because they figured my genes would ruin a kid. My father had my phone and when her mom called me he'd picked up and she told him that he could either have it or Jill would give it up for adoption.

"Of course I'll take the baby," my father said, though he had no idea how he'd get the money to raise her.

I got out when I was eighteen. They didn't try me as an adult for any of it and I was let go.

I moved back home. Dad wanted me to take care of Evie so he didn't have to pay for daycare anymore. She was beautiful. She had huge brown eyes and dimples in her cheeks. She also had a lot of tantrums, nothing unusual for a child of that age. But I was still a teenager. Wanted to go out and have fun. My father yelled at me all the time about how I didn't keep the house tidy, and that meant I didn't respect myself or my daughter or him. Eventually, I split, and I think he was relieved.

I worked during the days at Rite Aid and partied at night. I went through a tough time. Sometimes I'd have dreams about the man I hit with the car and that bothered me. And he'd still appear in my mind during the day. I'd be doing any random thing, like watching baseball, and I'd see him standing there, staring at me.

Once a week, I'd go to my father's house and hang out with Evie, but Dad said he didn't like the example I set. I was like, "What am

I doing wrong now?" I smoked pot then, but he couldn't tell. He couldn't put his finger on it. He said, "There's something about you that's not right."

It wasn't until I turned twenty-eight that I could admit my father had a point. It happened on Thanksgiving in 2013. I went over to Dad's for dinner. Evie was eleven years old. She had her hair done up in a million long beautiful braids, and her eyes looked up at me, huge and shining. She helped my father set the table and serve the turkey and the vegetables. I sat at the table, drinking a beer. Dad told her in a soft way that she hadn't put the utensils down in the right order. She put her hands on her hips and smiled at him, so that the dimples showed in her cheeks. "I think I did it perfect!" she said, and they laughed together. In that moment, the light came back into the world.

When I saw how Evie had that brightness inside of her, my heart opened up like it'd been cut by a knife. I fell in love with my daughter, my first real fatherly love. And I loved Dad, too, for how wonderfully he raised her.

I started crying and had to go to the bathroom to get myself together before I could return to the table and finish eating dinner with them.

That night I thought about what Shayla had said so many years before, about me having twisted thinking and how I had to take responsibility before I could change. I decided I wanted to be with my family, my father and my daughter. I wanted to have a right to sit with them at the dinner table, to be a part of their lives.

Sitting in the busted easy chair of my filthy apartment, I took a long look at myself. I'd hit the homeless guy with my car and never said a goddamn word of sorry. His eyes had been open, shocked. He couldn't speak. His mouth had sagged from the side of his face. I took that inside of me after all those years. For the first time, I knew why I had an empty place in my soul and a mind crammed full of messed-up thoughts.

Over the next few weeks I tracked down the old man's family. Even though he was homeless, kind of a lost cause I guess, he still had a sister who loved him. She put up a memorial webpage when he'd died. His name was Mr. William Robertson. I called his people and attempted to apologize, though they hung up on me.

Accepting responsibility for the wrongs I'd committed didn't make me immediately better. It caused me a great deal of pain, of depression. But that pain made me feel things again, like I had before my mother left. I came back to my family. I told my daughter how sorry I was that I hadn't been a good father. Told my dad that he was right, that there was something wrong with me, and I wanted him to help me fix it. By then, Evie had softened him up some. He put his hand on my shoulder and said everything would be OK.

I got myself together. I became the night manager at Rite Aid. I tried to live at Dad's place again but he got snappy, so I got another apartment, here. Learned how to clean a house and bought a new twin bed for the spare room. I got Storm bedding—Storm, from the X-Men—so that my daughter liked to stay over. Did my daughter's laundry. Bought a Camry minivan because of its safety ratings. Learned how to cook. I'd go over to the house and make Dad and Evie dinner.

My daughter's seventeen now, and she wants to go to college and become a pharmacist. Her mom works as a pharmacist, over at Cedars in L.A., and they see each other three times a week after Jill got a new coparenting arrangement with my dad in '07. Even though Jill won't talk to me much because she's still mad about how she thinks I didn't treat her right when we were younger, she and my dad get along great. They're like best friends now. But I like to think Evie also got the idea of going into pharmacology from seeing where I work, at the Rite Aid, because we have lady pharmacists there. On a few occasions I brought her to the shop on Bring Your Daughter to Work Day. Evie bounced up to the woman pharmacists behind the counter, asking them intelligent questions while they talked about the five drug schedules or contraindications. In the middle of all those half-dead adults she glowed like a candle and chattered like a ladybug.

Knowing about how hard I worked to get my daughter back in my life, Miss Rodriguez, you might understand how terrified I felt when it seemed that the fire would take her away from me again.

I looked out the window and saw the sky turn orange. That's a fire color, here. The winds blew rough, too. The palm trees jerked back and forth. I knew that wind and fire together spelled trouble. Right away, I looked at my phone, but didn't find any warnings. I called Dad.

"What," he said.

"Where's Evie?" I said, pulling on my clothes. I couldn't smell anything yet.

"Basketball."

My daughter's on the team and practiced after school. I mentally mapped the route to the court while checking my phone again. I saw news that Woolsey had started up at Santa Susana earlier in the day, but the feeds tangled up and I couldn't figure what was going on yet.

"Something's weird in the air," I texted Evie. "I'm coming to get you."

I yanked on sweats and grabbed my wallet. Jammed out of the house and got into the minivan. Headed over to Dad's. It's only two blocks away. Dad stood out on the front lawn in his jeans and his white shirt. He squinted upwards while his hair flapped crazy on account of the Santa Anas blasting overhead.

I rolled down the passenger's window and yelled, "Get in."

Dad climbed into the van. I drove toward the school. We could hear fire sirens, already. The radio station just had music, but then one of the announcers said, "There's an evacuation alert for Simi Valley and Conejo Valley." My heart started pounding out of my chest and my father went white. A few cars zipped down the street. I sped onto Yosemite and pulled up by the school's court, peering through its chain link fence. The girls stood around in their uniforms looking confused. The wind blew dust into their faces and they held up their hands. The coach talked to somebody on the phone and tried to corral them, but everything seemed disorganized and slow.

"Evie," I yelled. "Evie, Evie."

Evie was squinting up at the orange air just like her grandpa had been doing when I'd picked him up. She snapped her head when she heard my voice. The sky turned very bizarre, then. A bright flash of light appeared, as if the sun had just come out, except that the sun hung in another part of the sky already. Her grandpa and I both screamed out of the window like insane people. The girls stared at us; some of them had scared faces and some of them laughed.

Evie sprinted off the court. Dad opened the back door and she got inside, pressing her face up to the back window. "Dad, maybe we should get my friends."

"No," my father and I both said as I drove off.

The smoke started. It was like a gray storm rolled into town, with spots of too-bright gold. You could smell the acid and the char in the air. I put up the windows. The fire seemed far away but close, too. Cars booked down the street fast. I got onto the 118. Evie wouldn't talk to me because I wouldn't save her girlfriends. She sobbed about how they would get burned alive. But I made her check the roads on my phone and she said that it looked OK in the San Fernando Valley, so I headed there. Traffic jammed the 118. The world got dark and spooky. The fire blazed on the horizon like something unnatural. Like a special effect in a movie. Evie called her mom, and Jill was hysterical, and so she got hysterical, too. I was shaking and sweating and it took over an hour to get to the Valley, about half an hour longer than usual.

I went to Ventura Boulevard, which was only a little smoky. I took us to a diner. It was business as usual in there. It was like people in the San Fernando Valley didn't know we had a problem in Simi Valley. Meanwhile, the fire jumped freeways and headed west, and would burn everything in its path to the ocean. The three of us would have to stay in a motel for the next week and they temporarily shut Evie's school.

In the diner, I didn't know if I'd overreacted or what. Later, I wouldn't think so. Dad ordered steak and eggs and coffee and I did the same. Evie kept crying and didn't want anything, so I got her steak and eggs, too, and an orange juice.

After a while of her being mad, she looked up at me. Her face crumpled.

"Oh, Dad," she said. "You came and got me."

"Of course he did," my father said.

I never felt so happy in my life.

Finally, we got back home. The air smelled bitter. It rained ash for days and days. Big flakes of it, like snowflakes, but disgusting. I'd come out to my car and find piles of gray crap on the windshield. I had to shake it out of my head and slap it off of my shoulders and arms. Can't say I liked the idea of my daughter breathing all that garbage into her lungs.

"Wear a T-shirt over your face," I told her the day after we got home. I'd gone over early for breakfast while she got ready for school.

She looked in the mirror and put on lip gloss. "Yeah, OK."

"Leave her alone," Dad would say. "You and me lived through a dozen fires in our day and we were just fine."

We fought about it, and Evie went out without wearing a mask or anything. Not that I was wearing a mask either. But she's my kid.

Still, the air cleared with the winds. I felt like we'd missed a bullet. It didn't even occur to me to ask where the fire had started. I read something in the paper about it getting triggered by a fallen power line in an Edison station, and the article mentioned the Santa Susana Field Laboratory, which used to be around here. But that seemed less important than the fact that I'd gotten us out in time and we still had places to live.

At work, though, there's this pharmacist named Nedina Baker. She's older, talks a lot. Negative outlook on life. Doesn't trust the government too much. "State says tap water's safe but it's a lie," is the kind of thing she says. She drinks filtered, only. "Full of forever chemicals. Perfluoroalkyls and polyfluoroalkyls." She showed me a webpage on it, once, and wrote out the names for me. Nedina bugged her eyes out while yammering about how the chemicals never leave your body and they cause cancer and high blood pressure. But I didn't go for that kind of paranoia. I didn't pay much attention to Nedina about the forever chemicals. And I didn't mind her when she told me, a week or so after the fire, that Woolsey had set loose radioactive junk into the air.

"It's all from a secret lab they used to have in Santa Susana," she said, while filling an order of Prometrium. "It got closed in the 1990s, but it's been lousy with radionuclides since the 1950s. There was an actual nuclear meltdown there, just up the hill. And it makes you think about Chernobyl, right? In 2015? The wildfires there released the nuclear waste spilled in '86. They've got crazy-looking plants in the Exclusion Zone. Two-headed rabbits, pink coyotes." I didn't know what the hell she was talking about. "And it's the same here, except nobody says anything. The government doesn't want you to know."

I laughed. "OK, whatever."

"Don't get like that." She shook her head. "It's real."

"Look out the window," I said. Not that we could see out the window from the pharmacy. "It's all blue skies. Those winds blew everything away."

"The damage is already done," she said. "People living here were exposed in the hours and days after the fire."

I ignored her and did my work. I didn't think about pink coyotes. Or about my daughter getting hurt by radioactivity when she'd been on the basketball court looking at the sky. My concern was making enough money. After the fire, I went back to planning how I might get another raise so that I could sock more away for Evie's college. I think I already said that Evie wants to become a pharmacist. Jill says it's her good influence, but she and her family believe that I'm trash and I could never have any positive input in my daughter's life. I think Evie wants to do pharmacology when she grows up partly because she's seen me working with Nedina at the Rite Aid. Nedina was very friendly with Evie those times they met, and Evie was impressed to see her in her white coat, so like I said, I believe she got the idea from that, because I took her to see the pharmacy on Bring Your Daughter to Work Day.

[*Pauses, passes his hand over his eyes.*]

There's a good program at USC and we've been looking at that. But it's expensive. I just need to make some more money to afford it. Because I want Evie to have everything that she needs out of this life. I want her to grow up, and go to school, and never worry, and be a pharmacist, and be happy, and very healthy, and make friends, and—

[*Interviewee stops talking. He holds up his hand over his face. Interview stopped for the day.*]

[NOVEMBER 12]

We were talking about the fire, and what came after. Like, when I started to have the realization that maybe we had a problem. I mean, I'm not sure if there's a problem, but I'm scared that there is. That my daughter will have a problem. And that's why I agreed to talk to you, so that you will tell me if you people screwed up and I should get my kid the hell out of here.

The fire came and then the wind blew the smoke away. Things seemed fine. After that, we saw heavy rains in December of 2018 because of El Niño. In the mornings, I'd step outside and couldn't make out the car in the driveway. The rain fell that thick. Just white walls of water. The gutter water turned into rivers, roaring down the street. It lasted for days and days.

Evie loved it. "We have a drought," she said, looking through the window and watching it come down. "It's good for the environment."

I said that to Nedina later in the afternoon, at work. I thought the rain would make her happy because she's always going on about how terrible everything is.

"This weather's a pain but at least it's clearing everything away," I said, leaning against the prescription counter.

Nedina shook her head while studying a Vicodin scrip. "You've got to be joking, right?"

"The rain," I said. "It's good for the environment."

"Haven't you listened to a word I told you?" Nedina said, her eyes bugging.

"It perks up the air quality, or whatever. I thought you'd be jumping up and down with joy."

"The rain *washes it down*," she hissed at me. "It washes it from the hillside and into town. The radium, the uranium. The thorium. What didn't get spread into the air from the fire is covering us now with the water."

"Why on earth do you think the government would let that happen and not say anything?" I said. I liked Nedina enough, but I lost my temper.

"People don't like to admit when they're in the wrong," she said.

"Sure they do," I said.

She shook her head. "Not when it costs them."

That night, Evie arrived home from basketball practice a little late. Dad and I had been making dinner, meatloaf, at his house. I came out to the living room when I heard her walking through the door and saw her soaking wet.

"Car splashed the gutter water all over me when I was waiting for the bus," Evie laughed, squeezing out her hair. The rain dripped down her face and her arms and legs and her sneakers and her dress.

I looked at her and felt nervous.

"Go take a shower," I said.

"I'll just towel off," she said.

"Go take a shower, now," I said.

"Lordy," she said, pretending to get mad. "Fine!" She stomped in a big, clownish way off to the bathroom.

Dad came out from the kitchen, wiping his hands on a towel. "What are you two fussing over?"

"You ever hear anything about a nuclear lab up in Santa Susana?" I asked.

Dad bunched up his face at me. "What you going on about?"

"A nuke lab," I said. "Up the hill?"

He shrugged. "Used to be one. They shut it down in the '90s or something."

"And they had an accident?"

"Yeah, I don't know," he said. "Million years ago. So what?"

"Was it dangerous?"

"Maybe for the guys working there," Dad said.

"Could it be dangerous for Evie?"

"Simon," he said. "What's dangerous for Evie is boys and getting kidnapped."

"She's not going to get kidnapped, I told you to stop worrying about that," I said. He's always scared that Evie's so beautiful that boys are going to kidnap her and take her to the desert and have their way with her.

"Well, then stop wasting time and come help me with the potatoes," Dad said.

He turned around and went back to the kitchen. I followed him and finished the gratin. Didn't mention Santa Susana again. But all through dinner I looked at my daughter while Nedina's voice buzzed in my ear. *The rain washes it down, the radium, the uranium.*

I didn't know if I was catching her crazy, or what.

I started researching it. Nedina helped me. She told me all about Santa Susana. About how they had a nuclear and rocket factory there, and the accidents that happened in 1959 and 1964 and 1969. She told me about radionuclides and what they do to the human body. She explained about how Rocketdyne workers used trichloroethylene to clean off the grease on heavy machinery and it might have given some of them kidney sickness. She said they dumped it all into the ground and it's still there. She said it was a conspiracy on the part of the Defense Department to experiment on citizens, like in the 1949 "Green Run" radiation experiments, and how Alaskans were exposed to radiation, and that government doctors in Memphis fed premature babies radio-active iodine, and she talked about the Tuskegee syphilis study, which I'd never heard of, and the use of LSD on prisoners, and then she also talked a lot about John F. Kennedy and Marilyn Monroe and the mob.

"If it's so bad, why do you live here?" I asked her once.

She cackled at me. "I don't live here, I live in Rancho Cucamonga. I have my own well and I test it every month."

I can't say that talking to Nedina so much about this stuff did my mind any favors and I'm still not sure how much of it is real.

But I can't believe that I lived here in Simi Valley all my life and never knew that there'd been a nuclear meltdown five minutes from where I live and that it'd never been cleaned up properly. Once I started look-ing it up on Google, I found a lot of sources and they seem reliable. Studies showing how people living within a couple miles of the lab had more problems with their thyroids and bladders and stomachs—I can't remember all of it. And there's blogs and articles and community groups. How did I not know?

I asked my dad how he could have set up house here and he shrugged. "There's problems everywhere and this place is full of good people. It's safer than most."

Even with Evie being Black, he doesn't like other Black people that much, and I guess he'd rather live in Simi Valley next to a nuclear reac-tor dump than somewhere else where his neighbor maybe wouldn't be white.

But I'll say, sometimes I think about all the things that Nedina told me and I get scared.

The reason I get scared is I know how people can do evil and still think of themselves as good. Because if the government let radioactive waste sit up there for sixty years without cleaning it up, and exposed people to that danger without admitting it was so, that would be evil, wouldn't it? It sure would, Miss Rodriguez. You might know that, too, seeing as you came all the way out here to talk to me about it. I can see from your face that you do.

It's easy to think that the government would never do an evil thing to another American and that you'd have to be crazy to say otherwise. But then, I think about myself. I hit that old homeless guy. He lay there with his blind-looking eyes, his mouth hanging down from his face, and I erased it from my head as much as I could. I always think about how Shayla said that I had twisted reasoning and needed to take responsibility. I could only do that because my daughter's love made me a better person. The government doesn't love people, though. It doesn't have the same incentive that I do to own up to what it's done.

It's true that if Jill heard me saying this to you right now, she'd go nuts, like she does sometimes. She'd be sure to let you know that I'm just another cliché of a man. "What he did to me was way worse than accidentally hitting somebody with a car," she'd yell. "But he'd never confess that to our daughter." To that, I'd tell her my love for Evie has changed me, and that Jill should not forget that I was the one who got our kid out of the fire. I would tell Jill that if she's looking for a bad guy, she should be looking at you, the government, who told us that everything was all right, even while you knew we were living next to radiation all this time.

INTERVIEW WITH MONICA RAMÍREZ

JANUARY 6, 2020
MONTEBELLO, CALIFORNIA

When we got to the old Rocketdyne lab to do the Woolsey job, Brenda took one look at the fire behavior and said it wasn't normal. She and I got out of the truck and scoped the hills. Gold flames shot up to the sky and burst like firecrackers under the Santa Anas. The area had a huge fuel load—brush, weeds, the whole shebang. Plus the drought. Southeast wind moving about twenty-five to thirty miles. The stage shifted from growth to fully developed faster than I ever saw before.

"It's a doozy," Brenda said, fitting her mask on and grabbing her Pulaski. She pressed her lips together tight. She was focused, ready. We got ready to charge orange mountains of fire. Thing looked like a red monster jumping around the hills, hunting for somebody to kill. I'd never fought one like that, and she knew it. She gave me a long gander and then winked.

"I'm fine, Captain," I said.

"I know you are." She hitched up her gear and yelled at the men, "Dig a line." They couldn't hear her that well through the PPE, but we all knew what she was saying.

We stood aways back on the east side of the hill and the smoke and gases shot away from us. We all wore SCBAs—breathing apparatuses—but the bottles are small and you've got to refill them with the air tenders. You're just not totally protected by the hazmats. For one thing, you still absorb everything through your suit. We'd been briefed on the pollution from the lab. The toxins in the ground. But at the time, I didn't think of that. I focused on fighting the biggest fire I ever worked. I was excited, to tell you the truth. I grinned at Brenda, and then we both hauled up our Pulaskis and started cutting the brush clear alongside our brothers.

Brenda stayed in front, swinging the 'laski. A Pulaski's a combo hoe and axe that tears away the vegetation in the area, so you starve the fire of its fuel. Thing can get heavy after using it for a while, but she swung it like it was a golf club. *Cack! Cack! Cack!* She whacked the soil, using her big arms and bending her knees, using the form she'd taught me when I first showed up at the station. The guys fell in behind her, following her cues. I bushwhacked right behind her, breathing so hard that my mask got fogged and I could barely see. Sweat poured down my face and my body. I heaved up my chopper with a kind of joy and brought it down hard enough to split the earth. I had always wanted to be on the job. That's what we call it, firefighting. *On the job.* Cause firefighting is the best job. It's the only job.

Brenda and I smashed the hell out of the mesa and the men tried to keep up. Every once in a while she looked back over her shoulder to check on me and I shrugged her off, even though I liked it. Meanwhile, the flames kept getting taller and redder and hotter. The copters charged ahead and dumped water on the far hills. The wind blasted into us so that we had to dig our feet in. When I looked up, I saw the sky turn black.

The reason I'm talking to you, Reyna, is because Brenda is a special person and I just want you to know what we were up against that day. She fought out there for a long time. Brenda has backed me every step of this journey when others wouldn't, and she says everything's OK. But I've heard some things and have to say, I'm worried.

[*Interviewee's mouth twitches and she goes silent. I get her a cup of coffee and it's a few minutes before we resume.*]

Brenda made me believe I could do the work, but my family didn't want me to be a firefighter. "No," my dad said. "No," my mom said. "No," my uncles said, and my aunts. I wanted to be one, though, ever since my family's home caught on fire, in Montebello. I was twelve. It started in the kitchen. Maybe my dad did it accidentally, but he never said. When the house filled with smoke, we called 911 and, ten minutes later, a team of toughs roared up in a truck scream-ing with sirens. They had a huge ladder and powerful hoses that crushed the fire slashing through our house with long, white ropes of water. When they put the flames out, one of the firefighters came out to the street where I waited with my parents, shivering. The guy looked like an astronaut in his big hat. He wrapped me up in a silver Mylar blanket. Another firefighter patted my mom's shoulder while she cried. My father even hugged one of the men, who seemed used to such displays and hugged him right back. My family wasn't a very touchy or emotional sort with strangers but the firefighters were special.

I held that dream of firefighting inside of me after that. I didn't know women had to fight harder to get into the club. The only prob-lem seemed to be my parents. And, later, my husband. They wanted me to go to college and become a P.E. teacher like my mother. First my family gave me grief about it, and then, when I turned eighteen and started dating Miguel, he turned out to be dead set against the idea just the same as them.

"No wife of mine is going to run into houses on fire," Miguel said, when we'd been together a year. Miguel is a line cook at the Four Seasons and he fell in love with me because I reminded him of the women in the olden days, back in Mexico. "A classical beauty, is what you are," he liked to tell me. "Like a Diego Rivera painting." It was funny him saying that because I'd been a wrestler in high school, one of the first girls on the team, getting the shit kicked out of me by males all the time. But Miguel is a sweet person and that made me want to stick by his side. I'd told him plenty about my dream and, when we first started seeing each other, he acted like it was an interesting idea. He even seemed supportive, like about the wrestling. But firefighting turned out to be different from wrestling where he was concerned. Once he decided on us being married, he changed. Didn't want to hear anything about it. "Do you know how dangerous that is?" he said. "Do you know you could get killed doing something like that?" "Do you want to leave me a widower?"

"No," I said, to the last question, but who the hell doesn't know that firefighting's dangerous? Part of the appeal. Anyway, we got mar-ried when I turned nineteen. I got my degree and started work on my teaching credential. He seemed happy. But I wasn't.

When I was twenty-one, I studied for my master's in teaching at UCLA. But one night, after a couple of drinks, and Miguel went to bed, I started to feel sad about my lost dream. I looked up information on the LAFD on the web. That's how I found out about the hiring process, which was intense. I learned I'd have to become an EMT and take a CPAT, a physical ability test. The CPAT would be fine, I knew, but to become an EMT you had to sit a course and the exams, and only then could you apply to the department. Which itself required seven stages of tests and interviews and a whole rigmarole.

The next day, I told Miguel that I planned on signing up. He didn't look that surprised. I think he knew that him trying to control me wouldn't work forever. I'd lettered in wrestling. He was aware of who I am. But he was desperate for me to change my mind.

"Preciosa, come on now," he kept saying. "If you love me, please don't make me frightened like this. And what about having a baby? How are you going to take care of a child when you're getting burned to pieces?"

I told him I loved him, which I do. But I wouldn't be budged.

"I'm doing it," I said.

[*Shrugs.*]

I don't know, maybe I was selfish.

Training at the academy tested me hard, I won't soft-pedal it. This was in 2014, at the Drill Tower in Elysian Park. I was the only woman in a class of seventy recruits. Over half were white. The men didn't haze me too outright because there'd been a scandal years before. Civil rights lawsuits and millions of dollars awarded to a Black lesbian woman whose superiors put her in unsafe situations, and a Black man made to eat dog food. And men had filmed women failing at the drills and played the tapes as entertainment at their parties. They spliced together the scenes of the women struggling and called the movie the *Female Follies*. Now all that's part of the LAFD lore. The "bad old days." Well, I got there after the "bad old days," but there are other ways, less obvious ways, for hard-hearted people to make you feel unwelcome, and I got some of that. Like, when it came time for me to throw the ladder against a building—it's one of the training drills, and the hardest, I think—some of the men would line up with their arms crossed against their chests and just watch, silent and smiling. But I got that ladder up there, even though it was hundreds of pounds. I finished the seventeen weeks and qualified.

After I got my notice that I passed, I felt proud. But when Miguel and my family came to the ceremony, they all looked upset as they sat in the audience. I felt angry at them when the chief handed me my certificate. Kind of ruined it. My husband and I had conflict off-and-on through the process, while he tried to convince me to go back to my teaching credential. "I'll buy you a new car," he'd say. "I'll get a better job." "I'll take you on a vacation, whatever you want." He didn't come off mean about it. Still, with him seeing things that way, I couldn't come home and complain about being the only woman, or some males watching me and smiling with their arms crossed over their chests. And I sure couldn't say anything to the rest of my folks, either, as every time I brought up the department they clasped their hands and moaned about how I would die in a fire. So, I felt good about myself, but I started to get a hard shell on me. I was alone. Until I met Brenda.

Brenda's a real Red Adair of the department, one of the reasons why she made it to the top. She won't let anybody else take the risks she does, but she guns hard. Too hard, I think, during the Woolsey Fire. She's always been that way. Born for it, more than me. She came up during the "bad old days." She's Black, like the firefighters who sued, but she didn't ever complain about anything publicly. She actually never talks about any of it. "Ancient history," she'd say, shrugging, whenever I brought it up. She does her job. Better than anybody else. That's what she had to do to become captain of Station 585. That's in Little Tokyo.

First day I met her, I showed up to the station in a group of four rookies, the rest of them dudes I knew from the academy. Some of them were dicks, some weren't. This was three years ago, at the orientation. She stood in front of us with her legs apart and her arms crossed behind her. Her eyes didn't rest on me longer than any of the others. She said, "You are here to serve the greatest fire department in the world, in the greatest city in the world, and you earned that honor. Know that there is no secret to success but hard work, perseverance, and learning from every single one of your failures, of which there surely will be some. But you are here because you have shown yourselves to be warriors: honorable, trustworthy, and tough as nails. Remain so always, men and woman of Station 585. And remember this: Iron sharpens iron."

That night, I was on duty and so was she. For dinner, an old-timer named Hank cooked us burritos and we sat around the table, laughing and making small talk. I sat next to a fighter named Chip, who took the chair next to Brenda. A guy named Russ, who I didn't like from the academy, pulled up on my other side. Russ was one of the gadgets who watched me quiet and smiling while I threw up the ladders. I ate my food and tried to seem normal. I felt scared and happy, but also anxious about Miguel, who'd shut off his phone that night. He didn't understand why I couldn't sleep in my own house. During the meal, I watched Brenda as she chatted with the guys and ate her dinner, casual and comfortable, while talking shop about a long-ago fire in Hidden Hills.

"Big one," she said, waving her fork in the air while all the men listened. "Air Ops got shut down because of turbulence. Loads of propane popping, and when I ran into the apartment complex I saw—"

"What was the drawdown on the job last week?" Russ asked Chip, cutting Brenda off in the middle of her story.

Chip sucked his teeth and didn't say a word. The rest of the men hushed down too. Russ was asking a show-off question about a recent fight in Torrance, and how many resources that station had decided to go down to before requesting mutual aid. Brenda kept talking over Russ, about Hidden Hills and the propane, while you could feel the men create a force field around her, showing him that she was boss and they respected her. I tried to send her my own force field, too, just on principle, but I couldn't tell if it worked. She didn't need it, anyway. When Brenda finished her story, she looked over at Russ and raised an eyebrow.

"It was fifty percent, buddy," she said.

"Oh, that's good," Russ said, kind of quiet.

"Mm hmm," she said.

Later, at bedtime, she and I got ready in the women's quarters. We showered and got into fresh clothes and sat on our bunks. On the table next to her bed, Brenda had put a framed picture of her wife, Serena, and their two kids, Molly and Dash. I hadn't brought a picture of Miguel, but I would after that. Brenda stretched out her legs and cracked her feet, and then leaned toward me, putting her elbows on her knees. She met my eyes, with a kind and serious expression.

"You are very welcome here," she said.

That's when I knew that everything I had gone through was worth it.

Still, I've been through my rough patches since I joined the department.

"You can't run around half-cocked, Monica!" Brenda once told me, or yelled, more like. "For Christ's sake, this job isn't a suicide mission."

I'd made a mistake that day. A year ago, we answered a fully involved house fire here in Montebello, and got called in late as drawdown because the local stations fought a body shop explosion on the other side of the neighborhood. Fully involved means that there's flames shooting all through the structure. I got carried away in the attack because Montebello's my town. Also, because, honestly, Brenda's my role model, and I wanted to be like her. In 2011, she extracted eight victims from a gasoline tank fire in Tujunga on her own steam. In 2014, during budget cuts, when she had only three-quarters of a force to work with, she led a team of six men to handle the southern section of the Colby fire, in the San Gabriel Mountains, and achieved 98 percent containment even though it cost her a week in the hospital from the smoke inhalation. Woman's a legend.

I'm going to be a legend, too, I'd thought. I don't know, Miguel and I had separated by then and I was in a bad headspace. When we arrived on the scene, the Montebello house had fists of fire punching through the roof and a giant halo made of sulfur and tar-black smoke. I worked outside, next to Russ. We got the pipes—the hoses—stretched and injected the foam. Brenda stood to the side with the family, getting the details, and Russ called out, "Anybody in there?"

"One, been in there for an hour," Brenda yelled back, in a tone that meant, *risks aren't worth the men*. "Hold back till I give the order."

"Poor bastard," Russ said.

I didn't like his tone when he said that, like he didn't understand the situation in Montebello, where we sometimes have unsafe housing, with lots of fire hazards, and it's just unacceptable. Made me mad. Anyway, I ignored Brenda's DL command that we do a defensive operation instead of an offensive attack, and ran inside.

House was all lit up. Fire's beautiful, you know. The smoke poured into the air like ink getting spilled onto a star. Spangles of flame glittered in the fumes. I yelled through my mask, but no one could have heard me over the crashing sound of the southern part of the house collapsing. I moved from what had been the foyer and toward the pile of debris that might have been a bedroom. Most deaths occur in the bedroom because people get choked in their beds. The roof split open above me, but I ran to that pile of flaming wood, looking for any sign of life. I couldn't see anything for the smoke. I pushed through the fumes and through the debris, while the flames chewed at me like I was tinder. Hot rubies circled around my arms and shot at my legs. I pushed myself farther into it, grunting, boiling, mostly blind—until, all at once, I felt hands grabbing my waist and throwing me down the hall. Brenda yanked me out of the house so hard I ripped a tendon in my right shoulder. Turned out that the person in the house, a grandmother, had been in another bedroom toward the back and was for sure already dead. Brenda slammed me out of the front door and dragged me onto the front lawn. I laid there on the grass, gasping like a jackass while Russ looked on, talking out of the side of his mouth to Chip. Brenda demerited me and sent me to the medic, who threw a sling on me and sent me home.

Brenda and I didn't speak for three weeks, and I felt so mad at her for embarrassing me in front of the men.

"What the hell," I finally said, when I'd come back on duty and it was just her and me in the women's bunks, and she started yelling at me about suicide missions. "You dug out eight vics in Tujunga in a Level II hazmat," I said. "You smashed Colby with six men. You think that wasn't kamikaze?"

She sniffed and looked at me, squinting, like to say, *you really that dumb?*

"I had to do that, and you don't," she finally said.

"Why?" I asked.

Brenda shook her head at me, clucking. But she smiled and reached over, giving me a tough little goose on the thigh. She started laughing and I knew things between us would be OK.

"Because I cut the path you're walking, baby," she said.

Come Woolsey, I thought I'd learned my way around a blaze. Montebello wasn't the worst situation I've found myself in at the LAFD. Fires here get worse every year, it seems, and I've picked up a lot of knowledge in a short amount of time. But Brenda was right about the fire behavior at Santa Susana. It was crazy, unnatural.

After we cut the line with the Pulaskis, Woolsey exploded. The flames rushed up to us faster than a pride of lions. Dozers sliced paths ahead, but neither those breaks, nor the ones we'd made, slowed it down. We clicked on our bottles and ran back to the truck, stumbling over that hilly and uneven terrain. I stretched a line and shot foam into a southward-trending wall of fire. Our crew numbered twelve, but after a few minutes I couldn't see anybody but Brenda. We gripped our pipes and sprayed. The foam entered the fire and disappeared. Like the fire ate it. The flames ran around tall, screaming at us. Hillside turned into black, melted coal. Sparks fluttered from the sky, covering my mask like fireflies. I wasn't thinking about toxins, yet. Brenda shouted. I got confused and didn't know what was going on. I tripped on one of the rocks. I think I fell. The black came and moved inside of me. It got hot. Hot like your blood's cooking. Brenda looked back at me and her face changed. Then I lost it. I was gone. I passed out.

I don't know when I woke up. Twenty minutes later? Brenda got on the horn and Russ and Cliff trucked me to an EMT. When I came to, I lay in an ambulance. I guess I lost consciousness again, because I woke up a day later in the hospital, with oxygen and IVs. I couldn't get any information. My parents fussed over me, so angry. "I told you, I told you." My mother's face had gone gray and I felt bad. I felt guilty.

The doctors came in and wanted to do blood tests. That's when they started scaring me with the nuclear stuff. I knew about the possibility of pollutants, but they said there'd been a meltdown in the area we staged the attack, at that lab site where they used to run rockets and reactors. Said it was possibly radioactive. An endocrinologist showed up and threw around a bunch of medical terms, numbers, words for science things I only had half a clue about. The upshot was, toxins fouled the incident scene and the docs feared the fire had let them loose and contaminated me.

Now, toxins, that's part of the job. All of us in the department know that we're cutting our life years down. We'll lose like a decade, they say. It's not because of getting burned up. It's on account of the chemicals that we get exposed to from house and chemical fires. The household plastics and synthetics, that's what gets you. The benzene in furniture wax. The hydrogen cyanide in fabrics. And the foam's toxic, the PPE's toxic. It's all toxic. We know it. We live with it.

But this was something else.

"Nuclear waste," the doctor said.

"What the hell are you talking about?" I said.

"Place where you collapsed is dangerous," he told me. "Santa Susana used to be famous for generating nuclear power. But there were some accidents in the 1960s and it was never cleaned up."

"So, what, I'm going get sick?" I asked.

He looked at my results and shrugged. "Good thing you weren't out there for too long."

"What's too long?" I asked.

"It's all too long," he said.

My parents made such a business about cancer on hearing that. I could only think of Brenda. The drugs made it hard to read my phone, but I called the station about fifteen times and finally got hold of Russ.

"Where's Chief?" I asked.

"Hey, chickie, how you holding up?"

"Where is she?" I pressed him.

Russ hesitated for a second. I could hear the television in the background. Sounds of clattering in the kitchen, a radio.

"She's still out there, Monica," he finally said.

Brenda took out four separate teams and worked the job for three days. Obviously she switched out bottles, but there's no escaping breathing some unfiltered air and getting exposed through your suit. Suit's not made to guard against radiation.

Chief Terrazas later gave Brenda a commendation. It's a gold plaque that says, *To Brenda Willard, for Exceptional Performance in the Course of Duty*. Brenda wanted to bring it to her house and put it on her fireplace, but the boys and I insisted that we hang it up at the station, so that we can always remember what kind of captain we work for.

It's been two years since Woolsey, and Brenda seems fine. She got burned and treated for smoke, but there hasn't been anything strange going on with her. Her medicals have come back normal, except for her blood pressure. My tests are normal, too.

Last week, Brenda and I were on duty and bunking together like usual. She'd put her picture up of Serena, Molly, and Dash. She laid back in her bunk, in her khakis and tank top. She doesn't shave her armpits and she has this nice little fluff. I don't know. She looks good. She looks pretty.

"Nice and cozy, in the firehouse, where we belong," she said, burrowing into her covers, and laughing, with a shiny face.

I'm in love with her, which is probably no mystery to you, hearing how I've been going on. I love her, and I'm never going to say a word about it because she's married with two kids.

But, Reyna, ever since that fire, and hearing that business from the doctors, I'm worried about her. That's why I emailed you that I wanted to ask you some questions. Now, I've always followed Brenda's lead. She's been in the force for twenty-five years, and she is a hero, and she is my captain, and she knows best. Except, what I want to know is, did I let her down? Should I have pulled her out of the field like she pulled me out of that house? I'm asking you if it is true what they say about Santa Susana, and there being nuclear garbage that never got cleaned up. That radioactivity. It's just haunting me, the idea of it. I can't rest. So, I want you to tell me, straight: Could she have gotten hurt, and we just don't know it yet?

INTERVIEW WITH VIOLA SINGER

MAY 30, 2020
NEW YORK CITY, VIA ZOOM

I always wanted to play Hamlet. That's why I became an actress. After I saw Richard Burton starring in the Gielgud production at the Lunt-Fontanne Theatre in 1964, I could not get that character out of my mind. Most women actors want to play Lady Macbeth. And, of course, I wanted to play Lady Macbeth, too. But Hamlet, that was the real prize. There's no better role for an actor on earth than the dreary and deadly prince.

The reason I burned to play the poor Dane was because Burton got it all wrong and I knew, even at eighteen years old, that I, a girl, could do far better. Burton was delectable, I'll admit, as he stalked about the stage gassing on about whether to be or not to be. It was not his *oomph*, precisely, that was the problem. All roles require a soupçon of minge. Yet Hamlet was not suited by Burton's caveman sex appeal. Burton stormed around the stage barking about bodkins and all you wanted to do was let him paddle you with his big hard hand. And that's not Hamlet, is it? Hamlet needs a languorous, nervous, tetchy sensuality, as if he would stop all that talking and squirming if Horatio would finally get the picture and take him to bed.

It's not as if a man couldn't do it. Olivier. Rylance. Whishaw, that upstart, certainly. But Hamlet is an especially female role. Sarah Siddons was the first to don the unbraced doublet, then Bernhardt. Hamlet is a woman's part because he can't decide what to do, and as long as we have to get our hearts broken by all of these men, well, we can't decide what to do, either.

So, Hamlet seemed perfect for me, as I was a girl who had lost her father and was well aware how confusing that could be.

[*Disappears from the screen while fiddling with something.*]

Can you hear me on this thing? It's so inhuman, conversing like this. When will this bloody business end?

I ached to get out of Simi Valley. I moved to New York as soon as I could. After my father's funeral, my mother begged me to stay, but I couldn't take it. You know how brutal young people are. I wanted to fly! That's why we become artists, to be able to do something with our memories. You make your grief into a piece of art and then you can just give it away. Not for very much money, usually.

I went to New York. I've been here for fifty-seven years, when I wasn't in London. Live on Jane Street. Rent-controlled apartment. It once was perfect heaven, though after the 1980s and Giuliani and Bloomberg the soul went out. Back then, the place crawled with folk musicians, so there was an awful lot of warbling. I loved the gay scene, the writers. In the early 1970s you could still see James Baldwin on the corner, smoking his cigarettes. Norman Mailer plumed about after he had stabbed his wife. Warhol wafted through the streets like a madman. My people were the theater freaks—Cindy Bradzillian, Lou Floyd, Madame Q. You wouldn't by chance have heard of them, would you? Or, on the off chance, even, of me? I had my moment in the sun, you might have come across my name once or twice . . . No, no problem at all. That's how it goes. But, Lord, that crew. They were perverts, all of them. Oh, my god. How I loved them to death! So many nights did I stay up until 3 A.M. at an Off Off Broadway insane asylum where Madame or Lou floated about the stage naked and dripping in honey or setting themselves on fire. Endless days and nights of sex and love and art and acting and lunacy. Greenwich Village.

That's where I got my start, Greenwich's Off Off Broadway. Ya Basta, the famous theater. The great Ellen Sweetzer founded it. In '76 I was cast in an Ionesco knock-off called *The Plaid Pig*, which was about how a senator with a taste for Burberry is turned into a honking swine while eating a breakfast of pork chops and stewed pears. He goes into such shock at his new beastliness that he begins to wear his raincoat inside-out and dashes around his apartment quoting the preamble to the United States Constitution while his wife goes slowly mad. The fourth act ends in a denouement where the little missus

takes off all of her clothes, kills her grunting husband with a bread-
knife, covers herself in blood, runs for Congress, and wins. I played
the wife. I still remember the lines.

Should I turn you into crackling, or are you a truffle pig?
Very cheeky.

What? Oh. The thing you emailed us all about. Yes. See, when
I wrote you back, I was in a nostalgic, sad mood. There's no men
around here that you can get your hands on. And I haven't seen anyone, really, for a week. It's the worst. The paper keeps screaming
about people over sixty-five getting it and, then, poof. I thought, well,
I have the time, I'm a little lonely. I'll talk to this girl about my father,
you know, finally come to terms, give you government people a good
piece of my mind. See if there's any money in it, which I know there's
not. I looked up that thing, the statute of limitations for the lawsuits.
I found that the deadlines have long passed. And my father didn't
qualify for that other program, either.

He's why I wanted to play Hamlet, is what I was saying before.
Daddy. Because Hamlet's tragedy is that he can't forget Big Hamlet
becoming The Ghost, or becoming Nothing, which is the puzzle and
the genius of the play. That's why he's such a mess. And I could relate.
Even back then, when I was rubbing fake blood all over my tits, I
could never really get past it. When you watch someone you love die
like that, it's just utterly . . . you know . . . just so awfully . . .

[*Pauses, adjusts her scarves.*]

But they had no interest in putting Hamlet on Off Off Broadway.
Not my group, anyway. Even if you set Shakespeare on Mars the Bard
wasn't sufficiently avant for Rob Link or Joe Chaikin. Molière, on the
other hand, sometimes. Mostly, we put on Doric Wilson, Genet. *The
Maids.* And Edgar, Edgar Gutiérrez, the writer-director. The Mexican!
He was the wildest one of them all, though he believed in the Method.
The Method, dear. Stanislavski? Strasberg? It's an acting system. It's
absolutely horrid. One must find the motivation for the character
through psychology, one's past experience. You have to dig deep and
give birth to yourself through your psychic vagina. Lots of screaming,
so much sobbing. One delves back into memories of pain and joy and
then gives them as gifts to the role. You remember not the emotion
itself but the context in which it was created—the color of the sky
on the day your father died, let's say. The temperature of the air. The

birds that sang in the trees. The scents of perfume or rubbing alcohol. The feel of skin-on-skin. And then the feelings come rushing in and you have a nervous fucking breakdown.

Edgar wrote a one-act for me called *Messalina*, about the Roman Emperor Claudius's wife. She was an infamous nymphomaniac. Had a sex competition with a Roman prostitute and won with a grand total of twenty-five swains in one night. The preparation for that one was easy as my emotional recall system amounted to pretty much just remembering what I'd done the night before. I had to get in touch with my beast-side, Edgar said. My animal nature. I didn't tell him that my animal nature was already in fine working order. You have to let directors believe that they are really corrupting you if you want to keep them in proper pique. Edgar would dress me up in these gorgeous gowns from Halston, which he got from a boyfriend who dressed Bianca Jagger, and we'd swan into Studio 54 and start with the cocaine. Oh, my god. Rubell knew everybody and I had my pick. I fucked [redacted], and [redacted], [redacted], and [redacted], the last one in a bacchanalia at a mansion where I ate too much pecan pie and got sick.

Messalina had barely any dialogue. It was more like a silent movie. We communicated with our bodies and our eyes. And it was very sympathetic to the protagonist. I played her as a feminist getting in touch with the forbidden. Trying to become unshackled by these men, homophobic man-society. I refused to actually have sex so we fitted me with a prosthetic and I went at it. It was fifty sports on the stage wearing nothing but Christmas tinsel. I was covered in gold body paint and my co-star, Shelly Danzinger, who later had the bad taste to accept a regular role on *Dallas*, wore a furry bear suit, which was much worse than the body paint because the costume got so wet and hot. It was disgusting and perfect. Edgar supported me, so much. He listened to me, and held me, while I cried over the process. "You are a woman of deep reserves," he would try to convince me. He would say that even though it wasn't true at all and everyone else in the city knew that I wasn't anything but a perfect flibbertigibbet. He insisted that I could be a serious actor. That I shouldn't play Messalina for the prurient value. I took his direction and determined to play her as very dark, very Judith Anderson. He wanted me to think about my childhood but of course I wouldn't do that. Secretly, I abandoned the

Method and instead just did a lot of shrieking. "You can do it, Viola," Edgar would say, holding my harness. "My little lollipop, my precious jewel. The flower of New York theater."

Edgar believed that somewhere in my shallows I was a real artist. I will say that with his help, I emerged from my chrysalis as a sexual monster who maintained a perfect command of her dialogue rhythms. I also got bronchitis, and the attention of Harold Connolly, the son of the peer and industrialist Sir Harold Connolly Sr. Junior was a bit of a Dashing Dan with his foulard and brilliantine and money, money, money, it was said. He sat there glittering in the first row on our last night and I acted so hard that my prosthesis flew across the room. In 1972, Harold had infamously directed Beckett's *Happy Days* as a rogue action, as it was staged secretly in the basement of the Old Vic until the management faffed things by calling the law. Inigo Triste had been in the role of Winnie. Instead of being buried in a pile of earth or sand she was covered in a huge mound of tennis balls that went rolling everywhere and kept getting dumped back on her head by Willie and thrown about the room by the audience. It was supposed to be a metaphor *on top* of the metaphor. It got mixed but really quite blazing reviews and I'd heard the rumor that Harold intended to best that triumph by directing a very sort of Vorticist *Hamlet* in the West End.

After Harold caught me in *Messalina*, he took me to dinner at La Grenouille and I told him that I wanted to play his *Hamlet*'s lead. He wouldn't have anything to do with that idea even though I was thirty-one by this point, and as lovely as a tulip. I had Warren Beatty trying to get in bed with me but I wouldn't because *please*. I was more for a man like Rip Torn or De Niro. Jesus Christ, De Niro. I was, in other words, a hot tomato. But Harold wanted me to play Gertrude. Absolutely not, I said. You must be joking. How fucking old do you think I look? If not the Dane himself then obviously Ophelia. Harold laughed and allowed that it might be interesting to stage an Ophelia who does not flower-drown herself in the river because of Polonius, but rather because of her subtextually fading fertility. I told him to strangle himself to death, then jumped at the part. It was in London. I'd never been yet, except with Haji once, but we stayed at the Connaught and never saw the light of day.

Harold promised to refund the cost for my ticket and I packed my panties and flew to Heathrow. For four days I lounged at the May

Fair, smoking every cigarette in sight and waiting for him to come and collect me. But Harold had run off to Egypt with Quentin Crisp and a six-foot-tall modern dancer called She, like the Rider Haggard heroine. It turned out that while Harold's father was very rich, he was not.

I smoked hash in Chelsea until I was hired for *All Creatures Great and Small*, which was a BBC vehicle about an English country veterinarian named Dr. James Herriot who dewily euthanizes innumerable heifers and is an absolute snore. My role as Clementine Taylor-Gibbon, a morally reprobate femme fatale and goat owner who finds herself fishily out of water in the Yorkshire Dales, was supposed to be a one-off, but it went so well that they devised a small quasi-adulterous love interest C plot and extended me for two seasons. The British barely pay anything at all but it was a living. I sleep-walked through Thatcher's Britain until they fired me and I moved back to Greenwich in 1982. I'd been gone for so long that the New York I knew was already vanished. I'd been subleasing to a boy ballet dancer and so at least was able to return to my old apartment and try to help my friends.

AIDS had hit, see. I did a lot of nursing. Me and so many others. It was the end of the world. Different than this, right now, with everyone screaming about the new virus. The focus was on gay men, so the government didn't care. Edgar died. Michael Bennett. Later, Leigh Bowery. Geniuses. I took care of Edgar. I bathed him and fed him and held him, as he had held me when he'd told me that I could be an artist and pull off that dark reading of *Messalina*. I wanted to help him in the same way, though it was impossible. [*Voice cracks.*] I can see you're too young to really understand. What their dying meant, what was lost.

[*Pauses, cocks her head.*]

Is that the sound of a baby crying? Is it yours?

Of course. Certainly. A baby, how lovely. [*Dabs her face with a handkerchief.*] Actually, I'd like to freshen up a bit myself.

[*I momentarily leave to attend to personal business.*]

What you do is identify the emotional state that your character will embody and then you remember a time when you had that emotion, too. Say, love. Is love an emotion? In acting it is. In acting, in art, everything is emotion. So, let's say you want to remember a time you felt deep, deep love. Perfect love. First, you have to close your eyes. It's called emotional recall. Sense memory. Close your eyes, come on. There you go.

Remember the time that you felt that love. Who were you with? You don't need to tell me if you don't want. Where were you? The bedroom. *Who* were you? A child. Yes. What was it like in there? What color was your room? Pink, white. What were you wearing? Try to remember. A striped dress. What was the other person wearing? A long blue dress with feathers. Bare feet. Could you smell anything? Ah, L'Heure Bleue. So delicate and sweet. Cigarette smoke. White wine.

And what did she say? Something about angels singing.

And how did you feel?

You felt . . . tell me.

You felt . . . say it.

Oh, dear, darling.

Darling, darling.

It's all right. It's all right. Go ahead and cry. We all do. It's perfectly all right.

[*The remainder of this portion of the interview is redacted for space and relevance.*]

So you see that acting is a madwoman's profession, because you have to go through that. The Method, though, is dangerous for the mind. I only pretended to do it in *Messalina* and I certainly never went there for *All Creatures Great and Small*, even when my character was jilted at the altar by a strapping farmhand named Sven, or in *AMC* when I was playing the clown stalker. It just wasn't worth it. But then, when I appeared in *Hamlet* finally and had to play a person in deep, deep mourning, I reconsidered. Only for *Hamlet* would I have risked such a thing. Because the memory, it can tear you down. It can tear you down until there's nothing left. So one must be careful in the remembering.

My father's name was Maury Singer. He worked at the Santa Susana Field Laboratory. He was a janitor. Part-time. Only about twenty hours a week or so. His other job was as a line cook at restaurants—Louie's,

Cole's, the Tam O'Shanter in L.A. Or whatever came along. He did drywalling, gardening. My mother, Marla, was a waitress and a house-cleaner. She had been a beauty contestant in 1950s Burbank, but then she fell in love with my father and let him ruin her life, she said. She and I didn't get along.

My father was a man capable of giving love. He wasn't a frivolous person like I turned out to be. I had or I suppose still have three sisters as well but *blech* I don't want to talk about them. I loved my daddy. He was short and fat and ugly and nice. He had terrible teeth. He would listen to me, very intently. I chattered to him about all of my plans of being a beauty queen like Mother, and whatever I rattled on about, he would act as if I were the most fascinating person in the world.

"Of course you'll be a beauty queen," he said. "You're my beauty queen, right now."

He liked to sing me that song, "Sweet Sue."

Every star above, baby,
Knows the one I love:
Sweet Sue—just you!

And that's what he'd call me. "Sweet Sue," he'd say, kissing me on the head and hugging me when he came home after work while my hideous sisters bitched and seethed at how I was his favorite.

It's a story like every other person's story. Every other person who has ever loved someone. Sounds like nothing when you tell it out loud, but it's everything to you. And that's what an actor remembers, the everything. What's beyond language. Because an actor must rise above the words of the script to deliver that which is truly human.

The lab Daddy worked for had a nuclear reactor; it was not eight minutes away from where we lived. And there was some sort of problem, there. I never really figured it out. I did read the news reports. There had been an enormous blunder in the 1950s but they hadn't fixed it. As you know. An actual nuclear meltdown. How was that possible? In the heartland of California? Sorry—not to say that it would be less horrible if it had occurred somewhere else. Edgar's death taught me about that.

But there was real nuclear waste there. And other chemicals. Tox-ics. They threw the men who worked at the lab at that horror and just let them live with the consequences, without any sufficient warnings. I never saw my father wear any protective gear.

And in the 1960s, evidently, there were other meltdowns. Who on earth was in charge of that thing? I remember how one night, very late, Daddy came home and was moody. It was unlike him. He went to the bathroom immediately and took a shower and then carried his clothes out to the garbage and threw them away.

"What's going on?" my mother asked. She, my three sisters, and I had come out of our bedrooms, rubbing our eyes and complaining. My mother was upset that he binned his clothes. "What are you doing?"

"There was an accident," my father said. His face was shut. That's the best word for it. Usually, his face was open to us, like an outstretched hand. Plain and good and without mystery. But now it was tied into a knot. He took out a cigarette and started smoking.

"What do you mean, an accident?" my mother said.

He said it was a fuel breakage, or something. It let out radioactivity into the laboratory. My father's supervisor told him to clean the walls and the floors with soap and water. They needed to decontaminate. It took hours. He hadn't understood, at first. It was only when he looked at the scientists and how scared they seemed that he began to get nervous. One of them had run out of the room as if the building were on fire. Daddy had worried about that on his drive home, and that's why he'd showered and gotten rid of his clothes.

"Daddy." I'd come up to him and tried to give him a hug. He shook his head and moved away from me.

"Don't," he said.

He got sick less than a year later. Throat.

His hospital room was white. His gown was blue. I was wearing a brown dress. My mother wore a flower print. My sisters were so horrified, they had ceased bathing. They all had greasy hair and faces that hung down like rags. As did I. Smell of antiseptic. Nurses. No window. Artificial light. Sounds of machines.

The cruelty of it.

He couldn't say "Sweet Sue." He had bandages, all kinds of gear around his neck.

He mouthed it, though. I could read his lips.

I left home after we buried him. I wanted to forget. Off to New York, I went. I buried myself in beauty. Because that's what experimental theater was. Pure, pure beauty. Beauty and not remembering what had happened to you. Becoming someone else entirely. I mean, I wasn't born a Viola. My parents named me Martha.

I ran off to Manhattan and met Edgar and pretended that I was an actor. And then I ran off to London and then I came back and then Edgar was sick and I took care of him. But it was very strange, because when I took care of Edgar, I also took care of my father. The past caught up with me. I was taking care of Edgar and my father at the same time.

I'm not making sense. What I am telling you is that I loved Edgar Gutiérrez. Edgar was a passionate person. He would sing opera. He would cook crêpes. And when he had directed me, he held me in his hands like I was a turtledove.

"I want you to feel what you want to feel," he had said, as I sobbed in rehearsals for *Messalina*. "And I want you to feel more than that."

"I can't," I'd say.

"You are a woman of deep reserves," he told me, over and over.

When I was nursing Edgar, I finally found my deep reserves. I bathed him, I gave him water. I gave him medicine. I fed him. We held hands. He called me "my little jewel" and "my lollipop" like before. We laughed. I brought him flowers.

At the same time, though, while I was with Edgar, I was also with my father. Time merged. It didn't exist anymore.

Edgar's room was painted pale blue, and he had Piranesi prints on the walls. He had an authentic pink Fortuny lamp. I spritzed Chanel No. 5 everywhere. There were other scents. I played him Chopin. The nocturnes. A slight and melancholy music. We watched musicals on television. I'd be in the room, wiping and kissing his face, and we'd be listening to *Babes on Broadway*.

But I was also in the white room with my father and my sisters and my mother. I saw the blue gown. The brown dress. The flower print. No window. Nurses. Sweet Sue.

It's a relief when they die. But I went crazy. There was a long time when I would find myself stranded in a supermarket, or on the street, unsure about where and when I was. The past kept leaking in and it made me confused.

Anyway, too few cared. Not Reagan, he wouldn't even say the words out loud. "HIV." "AIDS." "Gay." I became so angry I thought that I'd die, too.

After Edgar, I tried to pull the same trick as when my father passed away. I made an effort to "move on." This was now 1989. I was forty-three. Experimental theater was in shambles. No work. I had lost twenty-five pounds and I looked like an old witch. I found Haji, who was still alive on the Lower East Side, and she told me how to get myself back into fighting condition. I ate cheese, nuts, bread, milk, chicken, salads, and lots of water. No alcohol. That's all anyone wanted, was to drink. But it ruins the skin. Soon, thank God, my face and tits returned. You might not believe me, but a woman can still come back at forty-three.

Edgar left me fifty thousand dollars. I bought myself a Fürstenberg and dyed my hair. Soon, I was going to parties again, but I was now angling for TV. I was too old for prime-time network shows, but soaps discriminated a little less. I wore my Fürstenberg to a party on a Benetti at the New York Yacht Club, where I buttonholed ABC's Brandon Stoddard and ultimately wangled that into a recurring bit part on *All My Children*.

I played Pippa, the girlfriend of Eric Kane, who is the father of the lead character Erica Kane, played by the terrifying Susan Lucci. Erica Kane is a goddess and dark beauty with a daddy complex because her black-eyed, brooding, and very dashing father Eric left her and her mother when she was a child in order to find vast success in Hollywood as a director. Eric's desertion gives Erica her motivation and her hero's journey, which is to overcome her fear of abandonment by dominating all the bitches in Pine Valley, as les monstres sacrés are wont to do. For most of the series, Erica mentions her père here and there in sparkling-eyed monologues, but in the late '80s, Stephen Schenkel decided to spice up the incest factor by reintroducing Eric in a primary role, even though he had been reputedly killed in a car accident five years earlier. One day, Erica is sharpening her nails on Jackson Montgomery, who is the brother of her sixth *and* seventh husband, Travis Montgomery, and Jackson lets it slip that he heard a whisper that Eric had faked his own death. Erica promptly has an early midlife crisis and wanders off in search of her father, only to find him installed in a Midwestern clown college and embroiled in a sadomasochistic affair with Pippa, whose specialty is in creepy clowning as opposed to the more classic Tramp type that Eric is studying. Erica persuades Eric to leave Pippa and come back with her to Pine Valley, but Pippa has her own abandonment issues, as her father had died in a Bulgarian train wreck when she was eight years old, which created a sort of Pippa-Erica *mise en abyme* of Electra neurosis. Pippa has a psychotic break and begins to stalk Eric and Erica through Pine Valley while wearing her creepy makeup. The whole thing was humiliating for me personally, of course, except that when you are an actor you can't think of that. Pippa begins a vengeful affair with Travis, prompting a heroic catfight between her and Erica, wherein Erica throws Pippa off an eleventh-floor hotel balcony, but not before Pippa makes an impassioned speech about her true and undying love for Eric, whom she accidentally calls by her father's name just before she plummets to her death.

I got depressed again after Pippa was killed off because even if it was trash, *AMC* was a fabulous gig and gave me health insurance. The soap people were a lovely crew and they had welcomed me with open arms. I was so realistic about my prospects that as long as they kept me employed, I'd been perfectly happy to defer to Lucci, who has a reputation as a wonderful person and is so and you would never hear me say a word otherwise. I suppose it could be said also that it was difficult for me to accept that I was no longer the bright star of *Messalina*. And that when I looked in the mirror I no longer saw the sexy beast whom Edgar always said was a jewel and a lollipop who had such deep reserves and etcetera. And then I did begin drinking again a little because without the commotion of the set I had some time to think about him dying and my father also dying.

Thank God, then Harold Connolly, that bastard who had left me stranded at the May Fair twelve years earlier, inherited four million dollars after his father carked it. Harold had grown tired of caravanning around Egypt with Quentin and She. He had, moreover, heard that my last season on *AMC* had been very impressive, as he explained on the phone, having called me in early 1991. "I understand that you were able to play a clown bitch very convincingly, which could have been no small trick, and that tells me that you haven't lost your touch, my dear," he said. "Of course I haven't," I replied, stuffing my face into a pillow because I was crying. "Darling," he said. "Come to London. I can make good this time, I swear. I'm putting on *Hamlet* again, for real, actually I'm producing it and Stevie Merchant is directing. I'm sorry that I can't offer you Hamlet or Ophelia, but I do want you to play Gertrude. I think you would be perfect."

I lay in bed wearing a huge muumuu, covered in the three repellant Persian cats that I had just saved from the SPCA, and musing on which of pills or razors would make for the most stylish exit.

"All right," I said.

I no longer wanted to play Hamlet, in any case. Gertrude was now the only part for me. She's a real, grown woman, with that unhealable wound you get when you're older. I understood her in a way that had been beyond me before I took care of Edgar, when I held him and bathed him and tried to feed him while the memories of my father's death crawled back into my mind like a snake. Because, do you really think that Gertrude can't see The Ghost? Of course she can. And she *can't*, at the same time. Gertrude marries her husband's murderous brother and feasts on the funeral baked meats at her wedding because time split and merged for her in the same way that it did for me.

It was Munger Carr as Hamlet, Betheny Weaver as Ophelia, Yidris Hamacheck as Claudius, Timothy Redding as Horatio, and Karl Teacher as Polonius. We premiered on March 30, 1993. Packed crowd. I walked out onto the stage in a halo of light. I remembered everything, my dad, Edgar, and what Edgar had tried to teach me about the Method so many years before. I didn't notice the audience or the other actors. Instead, I saw the brown dress, and the flower print, and the way my father's eye had wept blood in his last days. I saw the Fortuny lamp and Edgar's shaking hand. I felt that old sadness that had thrashed within me when I was a young girl at my father's deathbed, at Edgar's deathbed. I romanced my son and new husband with that ugly insanity that you feel when a loved one is dying and no one will hear you or help you. While Hamlet raged in my boudoir, The Ghost entered stage right and buried me with his stone look. I couldn't breathe and was blind. I clung onto Hamlet and acted as if I didn't feel, that I didn't grieve. I would not see The Ghost, even though he was screaming right at me.

Alas, how is't with you, that you do bend your eye on vacancy? I asked the Prince, my heart shattering as I pretended that my dead beloved didn't exist.

It was really quite a performance, if I might say so myself.

[*Wipes her eyes, then makes a dramatic, dismissive gesture with her hand.*]

I won an Olivier. And later, when we brought the act to New York, I won a Tony.

INTERVIEW WITH MYSELF

JUNE 5, 2020
SAN FRANCISCO, CALIFORNIA

I don't believe in ghosts, but one time I did second-guess my certainty that life ends at death. If ghosts do exist despite all probabilities, I don't think they arrive in a Shakespearean array of bloodstains and belligerent speeches. I admit that human recall can be terrifying, even deadly. But, after my one, uncanny, experience, I concluded that if ghosts are real, then they're more accommodating than our memories. Spirits are gentle, with delicate manners. Even if they're in despair, they don't want to intrude. They'd only like to know they haven't been forgotten. Yet they understand if you turn your eyes away and refuse to see them, pretending they don't exist.

I was haunted, once. What that means precisely I can't say. It happened during the winter of 2015. I was twenty-seven years old. Farid and I began the evening with a lavish meal at Paolo's, where I dined on lasagna and he ordered the steak. We shared a bottle of Pinot. The candlelight filled the restaurant with a soft pollen color. His face shone like amber. I wore a long black skirt and a pure white cotton blouse with a high collar. My hair up. No makeup. No jewelry. No scent. I pretended to taste my wine as my pulse quaked.

"You're beautiful," he said.

Bitter distractions such as ghosts didn't enter my mind. I felt alive, a warmth spreading from my stomach to my chest. I cut carefully into my food. The mushrooms were round, dark, slippery. My fork chased them all around the plate. I felt short of breath and slightly faint.

"We should slow down," I said.

He'd barely even touched me yet.

Earlier that year, I met Farid on a website that catered to singles. I found it an odd mechanism for discovering a potential mate. I'd posted a photograph of myself standing by my apartment's north-facing window. The photos of me wearing an enthusiastic smile all looked fraught, so I offered one where I stared plainly at the camera, attempting to give my prospective male or female lovers candid data about my appearance. I didn't submit a lengthy essay about myself. I said that I worked for the Environmental Protection Agency and had never been married. "I am seeking someone with whom I might share my life," I wrote.

I had few takers. Other women on the website seemed less interested in avoiding sentences that end in prepositions than in displaying photos of themselves doing miraculous things like windsailing, attending galas in glamorous gowns, and racing in marathons. Their smiles radiated from my screens, lovely and sexual. In my photograph, I rested my hands against my bodice in a tentative gesture, so I looked like Emily Dickinson. I found some suitors' responses brusque or even crass. But I didn't delete my profile. I checked it every few weeks, and went out on two dates, with two different people, neither of whom were enthralled by my personality or physique.

After three months, Farid contacted me.

"I'm a high school teacher," he said. "I'm divorced."

"What do you like to do?" I asked.

"Read," he said.

"We should meet," I wrote back.

For our first date, we decided to connect at a bookstore, City Lights. His suggestion. We'd discover each other in the classics section. I wandered through the stacks and found Farid standing next to the Penguin translations. He wore a splendid gray suit and gleaming black shoes. He'd shaved his head. He was five-eight, a good seven inches taller than I am. I knew already that he was thirty-nine years old, twelve years older than me. He held a black-and-white paperback. He turned and smiled.

"Madam," he said.

I laughed.

We stood there, shyly, until I inquired after the book he'd selected.

"I teach American history and also the ancients." He mentioned a local private high school. He handed me the paperback, a copy of *Gilgamesh*.

"It's a love story," he said. "Also a sad story, about the land of the dead."

"I've never read it," I said.

"I'd buy it for you," he said, looking at the shelves. "But maybe I should pick something more cheerful. Say, Sappho." He furrowed his brow. "Though I'm not sure she's so happy, either."

"I don't think she was," I said.

"Yes, she wrote of love, also," he said, smiling at me in a gentle way. He plucked a Sappho from a stack and placed it on top of the *Gilgamesh*. "I'll buy you both."

We began to see each other, usually on the weekends because of our busy schedules. Farid invited me for outings, which we took in the Presidio. We moved through nature paths and admired the thick pines and the aggressive eucalyptus. We faced the bay and breathed in the freshness of the ozone and the tang of salt.

"My father taught at Damascus University before the war," Farid said, taking my hand to steady me while we attempted to clamber over the park's boulders. "Ancient philosophy. Plato, Aristotle, Cicero. And Damascius, Apollonius."

"My mother worked as a janitor," I said.

"Well, after his career at university ended, my father became a janitor, too," Farid said.

We shared a knowing, cheerful look. The air was gold and green. We walked without talking for a while, listening to the wind in the trees.

"You're special, Reyna," Farid said.

I loved to look at him. He had dark eyes, like deep water.

I began to read the classics when I had time, in lieu of the nihilist Austrians and unhappy Russians who usually occupy my evenings.

I reread Sophocles's *Oedipus Rex*. And I studied the playwright's story of Antigone, who couldn't overcome her grief over the death of her brother, Polynices. I learned of the tragedian Nikolaus of Damascus, whose work is now almost entirely lost, and who wrote about the Romans' history of civil unrest. These readings led to other books. I learned about the contemporary war in Syria, the use of sarin and mustard gases, and the long-term impacts of those toxins, which resemble those created by the American weapons of the 1950s.

"Let's not talk of that," Farid said, softly. "We have a chance to be happy now."

Farid led me away from those topics, to Sappho, whom I'd read as a child with only limited comprehension:

but my tongue is frozen in silence;
instantly a delicate flame runs beneath my skin.

As I sit here at my desk writing about Farid, I'm alert to the strange silence of the night. I can't find it easy to concentrate.

"Do you need me?" I call out.

"No," comes the answer. "We're fine."

I sit back down and look at this screen. It's quiet. She's sleeping. I still have a few moments to write this ghost story for you, Regional Supervisor.

Farid quoted Sappho to me, as I've said. Her poetry explained why I sometimes stammered when he turned toward me, and the thin bright heat that possessed me. But he didn't press a physical relationship. He watched my signs. We attended plays and ballets, sitting straight-backed in our seats, our elbows brushing together. We continued our peregrinations, making trips to Angel Island, where we visited the Nike Missile site that Bell Labs built during the Cold War.

Farid would thread my arm through his and squeeze it lightly against his ribs. He took my hand in his own broad, warm one. One day, after we'd known each other for three weeks, we went to Point Reyes and, despite the difficulty I sometimes have with walking, I managed to reach a huge cathedral made of live oaks. The light dappled down and I raised my face, closing my eyes.

"The world is better because you're in it," Farid said, removing a leaf from my hair.

I felt a rapid fluttering under my ribs. I was frightened of him, in a way, but also at ease. I loved that curious sensation.

We sat in a theater in the Castro watching Joan Fontaine in *Jane Eyre*. I didn't pay much attention to the movie, with its distressing and all-too-real phantoms. At work, I labored hard on a brief about a Superfund site in Oxnard, whose lagoons had been tainted by an ammonia contaminant that endangered a small, white-breasted bird called the snowy plover. Farid also put in long hours, as his school was in the middle of testing season and he had to consult with his students after classes.

But in the theater we both gleamed with energy. I stole glances at his face, which the movie screen's glow tinted silver. He had a long, strong nose and a broad mouth. His cheekbones rose high and almost sharp. His hand lingered on the armrest between us. I placed my hand on his and watched his eyes grow warm. He stroked my knuckles with his thumb. My throat tightened as I sensed the teetering instability that signals the first, wild stage of love.

Later, I'd ask him how he knew to wait. He chuckled into my neck and said, "I wanted you to feel swept away."

Two nights after we saw *Jane Eyre*, he took me to that dinner at Paolo's. I was in a state of confusion. I hadn't slept from thinking of him. I looked terrible, with shadows under my eyes. I told him we should slow down, and he grinned at me.

"If you like," he said, as I attempted to spear my mushrooms with my fork.

I drank my glass of wine. Farid reached over and lightly touched my arm.

"No, never mind that," I said, my mind whirling.

"Never mind what?" he asked.

"I don't want to slow down."

"We can do anything you want," he said. He lifted my hand and kissed it.

I watched his lips touch my skin. "Let's go to your apartment," I said.

I'd taken other lovers. After my childhood medical crisis, and my mother's death, I'd managed to obtain some degree of control over my body, and didn't permit my disabilities to steal from me the pleasures I'd read about in the novels of Jean Rhys and the poems of Pablo Neruda. Still, when I entered Farid's foyer, it felt as if I'd never been with anyone else. I reached his living room, trembling. I still wore my heavy wool coat. I looked around at his spare and elegant furniture. He stood next to me and put his hand on my shoulder.

"Would you like another wine? A glass of water?"

I turned and held his face in my hands. I kissed him.

He kissed me back, gently at first. Then he grew warm and agile. He put his tongue inside of my mouth. I closed my eyes. He moved his hands through my hair. He moved his hands down my breasts and my hips.

My body became something fast, rushing.

He stepped back. "Reyna."

I kissed him again. He led me to his bedroom. I couldn't talk, didn't want to. He unbuttoned my shirt. He held my body against his. He slipped off my garments, they fell to the floor. He removed his own clothes with hasty gestures. I stripped off my shoes, my stockings. Laughing, we crawled into his large bed, with its cold sheets. I laid back and he looked at me. I put my hand over my stomach.

He removed it and kissed my scars. I felt like I was falling and falling.

"Yes," I said.

Later that night, I rested my arm on his shoulder, feeling it rise and lower. Soon, we'd grow to become easy sleepers, addicted to each other's warmth and the sound of our mingled breath. Except that night, that first night, I remained restless and partially awake. Close to morning, in a state of half-dreaming, something happened that I still can't explain.

I lay my head on the pillow. I twined my body around Farid's firm, wide back. I slept, or believed that I did. But I opened my eyes.

I'd learned not to think of my mother too much since her death five years before. I knew those memories hurt and weakened me. And I certainly didn't consider myself a mystic. In my work with the agency, I grew impressed only with those causes of sorrow that could be remediated, like the presence of trichloroethylene on military bases or the thorium degrading the suburbs. I didn't believe in the underworld or its phantasms.

Yet, at that moment, I felt my mother walk into the room and stand behind me.

She possessed the space like a vibration. I detected a disturbance in the air. She walked through the veil and summoned me back to her. It was the same as when I'd been a child, distracted with a book or magazine, and sensed her before realizing fully that she was there. As I lay next to Farid, I could picture her at the doorway, gazing at me with her large eyes. I saw her blue dress with the feathers, her long hair. Her unsmiling mouth. She was calm but sad. She didn't call out to me or clamor for my attention. She only waited there, patiently. I thought that she wanted to tell me that she loved me, that she was happy for me, and that she was lonely.

In the dark, I kept my eyes on the round rise of Farid's shoulder. My heart juddered and my breath came in shallow waves.

"No," I whispered.

I felt her vanish. When I looked behind me, I saw nothing there.

III. CONCLUSION

As I sit in my office, writing this report, it's turned late. The clock's struck 1 A.M. And someone's crying.

I'm exhausted and nearly done writing this account of Santa Susana's community impacts, Regional Supervisor. As I review these pages, the boulevards of San Francisco teem with protesters, while many other people cower and fret behind closed doors.

The cries grow louder.

I rise from my desk and go to the second bedroom, where we've installed a crib.

Farid's already there, ministering to our new charge. I stand next to him and look down. A tiny, furious face glares up at us. It's gorgeous and incandescent with rage.

There's a baby in our apartment.

It's June 2020. Heather's brown eyes follow me as I wander around the kitchen. She's six months old. She splays, wriggling, in her infant seat. Her hands grip onto me. Her tiny nails slice my skin. When she cries, her cheeks turn bright brown, and her tears splash onto my throat and mouth as I hold her, not too tightly.

"You're all right, sweetheart," Farid says, bending down to kiss her feathery head.

Heather doesn't belong to Farid and me. She's only been with us for a few weeks.

I stroke her black hair and look over at my laptop, which perches on the kitchen table. On the open screen, I see this draft of my report, which has shone at me like a beacon or a migraine for the past year and a half.

As Farid feeds Heather her bottle I move over to my computer and begin to write, furiously.

Time moves in a loop. After my mother died, I grew so busy with work that she dove under the surface of the world, only to reemerge after the Woolsey Fire. I don't know if it's good or bad, but she now seems to be receding again.

Time doesn't just circle in the mind. I write this as a pandemic and several atrocities rage across the United States. Each is caused in part by a welter of unhearing and lies that seem as if they play on repeat in America.

A few months into the lockdown, in the wake of reports that George Floyd, Breonna Taylor, and Ahmaud Arbery had been murdered by white police officers and armed civilians, a friend of mine in state government said that Social Services had problems placing foster children because some people were frightened of contracting the virus, while others were too nervous to venture out amid acts of civil dissent. Farid and I volunteered, submitted to tests, and received an emergency license. That's how we came to care for Heather. Her mother's a nurse who is currently being treated for Covid-19 in Saint Francis Memorial Hospital's ICU.

I carry Heather around our apartment, kissing her. She grabs at my hair and laughs. Farid films her on his phone, so when her mother recovers she can see how her little girl grew day by day. Heather's mother is Wendy Saeueng, RN, and until recently Wendy worked the ER at Saint Francis. Heather's eyes are the color of a brown bear, and she's just as strong as a bear, as I imagine her mother now has to be. The doctors tell us that Wendy's prospects are middling to fair.

While Farid warms the milk, I dance for Heather, something like how my mother used to dance for me. Heather watches me continually, like a spy. When she cries, I don't leave her to her own devices, like the baby books say you should. I rush to her and sing *coo coo coo*, but sometimes that doesn't work. Farid tucks her into a sling so her head rests against his chest. He walks around the living room, reading out loud from Cicero's letters until she falls asleep.

"I think she likes the sound of a heartbeat," he says quietly. "It reminds her of her mother."

After Heather no longer needs us, maybe we'll adopt.

When I submit this brief to you, I know you won't read it, Regional Supervisor. No one's at the office. The courts are closed. Marchers fill the streets. Also, in the years since the Woolsey Fire sent a panic through the administration, we seem to have moved on from Santa Susana. The plans for placing the laboratory on the Superfund priority list now malinger on indefinite hold. For this reason, among others, I intend this document to serve not only as a review of community impacts but also as my resignation notice.

It's strange, writing a report for no one at all, though maybe when I finish it I'll give it to Farid, or send it to the people I interviewed. Or maybe I'll compile all of these words, somehow, into a book. I think if my mother were alive, she'd make its perfect reader. I believe I know what she'd say if I told her about this project, and the people that I met, and asked for her thoughts after she turned the last page.

A long time ago, before the earth existed, before the sky, before the desert, before the moon, the angels were perfect. They flew through the stars, talking to each other in numbers and poems, because that's how the angels think, about the higher things, the beautiful things. But sometimes they were still sad. The angels worried like the rest of us, about what would happen when they died. About getting old and sick, or losing their jobs. Or not having anybody to love. Most of all, they missed their brother, Satan, because he'd made them laugh. Satan was the funniest angel of them all. He'd make them drink martinis and dance in a motel room to radio music, and clap his hands and say, *olé*. But God rejected Satan. Not because the old terrible archangel was a womanizer. And not because he stole people's money or drank all their whiskey or broke their hearts. God cast Satan into hell because

Satan said that something in Paradise had gone terribly wrong. The angels were frightened they'd have to follow their brother into the fire, but they continued to whisper among themselves that God never cared if they cried, or about how scared and angry they felt, and how much it hurt. So God went like *that*, gesturing with his mighty hand and blessing the angels, and then all they could do was sing. Joyous songs. The most pretty songs. Songs that God decreed would seem to be wholly without meaning, as they couldn't be translated into a language intelligible to the divine ear. Soon, the angels forgot the taste and sound of their own thoughts, as they could no longer put their pain into words. Nor, as time paraded forward, could they understand the tangled appeals of the people suffering and struggling on the earth below. Yet the people, as they will, prayed on. Their rejected supplications tumbled from the heavens and plummeted back down to our troubled forests and tainted oceans, and our seething cities and ruined soils. Our sweet and tender globe caught their calls for justice, and here they remain, having landed in the shape of stories that only we mortals can still hear.

NOTES

Under the Energy Employees Occupational Illness Compensation Program Act, the federal government may award medical costs and up to $250,000 to people were harmed by exposure to toxins while working at certain Department of Energy facilities. Starting in 2009, employees who worked in Area IV of the Santa Susana Field Laboratory in the 1950s were named to a special cohort under the program, which meant that they do not have to prove causation in order to be eligible. See Petition 93, https://www.cdc.gov/niosh/ocas/etec.html#pet93. In 2017, employees who worked in Area IV of the Santa Susana Field Laboratory from January 1, 1965, through December 31, 1988, were added to this category. See Petition 234, https://www.cdc.gov/niosh/ocas/etec.html#pet234.

However, in order to qualify under the program, employees must prove that they worked in Area IV for a total of 250 days and suffered from a specified cancer. See Energy Employees Occupational Illness Compensation Program Act (EEOICPA), Public Law 106–398, 114 Stat. 1654, 1654A-1231 (October 30, 2000); Claims for Compensation Under the Energy Employees Occupational Illness Compensation Program Act, https://www.federalregister.gov/documents/2001/05/25/01-13113/performance-of-functions-under-this-chapter-claims-for-compensation-under-the-energy-employees; and Area IV of the Santa Susana Field Laboratory, Centers for Disease Control and Prevention, https://www.cdc.gov/niosh/ocas/etec.html#pet234.

The conceit that the Santa Susana Field Laboratory was about to be registered on the federal Superfund National Priorities List after the

Woolsey Fire is fiction. The government has deferred so naming Santa Susana on the grounds that EPA standards would be lower than state standards. See Michael Hiltzik, "Santa Susana Toxic Cleanup Effort Is a Mess," *Los Angeles Times*, June 14, 2014, https://www.latimes.com/business/hiltzik/la-fi-hiltzik-20140613-column.html. ("In 2009, Linda Adams, then the director of the California Environmental Protection Agency, rejected an offer to list Santa Susana as a federal Superfund cleanup site because the federal standards didn't meet the state's requirements. She feared that contaminated runoff could harm surrounding farmland and residential communities.")

The book's assertion that the EPA let Atomics International and Rocketdyne monitor themselves for five decades is true. See *O'Connor v. Boeing N. Am., Inc.*, No. CV 00–0186 DT RCX, 2005 WL 6035256, at *1 (C.D. Cal. Aug. 9, 2005). ("Due to a lack of funds on the part of the Environmental Protection Agency ('EPA'), the Rocketdyne Facilities went unmonitored by the EPA for the better part of five decades and the facilities were left to monitor themselves.")

The federal government is unlikely to be found legally responsible for any harms caused by Santa Susana due to the "discretionary function" rule limiting liability under the Federal Tort Claims Act. See *O'Connor v. Boeing N. Am, Inc.*, at *10. ("It is axiomatic that the United States enjoys sovereign immunity and cannot be sued unless it unequivocally waives its immunity. *Irwin v. Dep't of Veterans Affairs*, 498 U.S. 89, 95, 111 S.Ct. 453, 112 L.Ed.2d 435 (1990). Congress expressly waived the government's sovereign immunity in the Federal Tort Claims Act ('FTCA'), but excepted from the waiver 'discretionary decisions' of the federal government. 28 U.S.C. § 2680(a); Earles v. United States, 935 F.2d 1028, 1030 (9th Cir.1991). A discretionary decision is one in which a government actor takes an action that involves consideration of social, economic or political policy."). The government also proves immune from claims stemming from Santa Susana insofar as the harmful actions were committed by private actors, that is, people who were not employees of the federal government. See *Via v. United States*, No. 3:08CV742 DPJ-FKB, 2012 WL 694761, at *2 (S.D. Miss. Mar. 1, 2012). ("Under the FTCA, the government has waived sovereign immunity and can be sued for acts committed by 'any employee of the Government while acting within the scope of his office or employment.' 28 U.S.C. § 1346(b)(1). 'This consent to be sued, though, does not extend to the acts of independent contractors.' *Broussard v. United States*, 989 F.2d 171, 174 (5th Cir.1993) (citing 28 U.S.C. § 2671) (other citations omitted).")

Lawsuits against the federal government for Santa Susana may also be barred by the two-year statute of limitations. See 28 U.S.C.A. § 2401 (West) (b). ("A tort claim against the United States shall be forever barred unless it is presented in writing to the appropriate Federal agency within two years after such claim accrues or unless action is begun within six months after the date of mailing, by certified or registered mail, of notice of final denial of the claim by the agency to which it was presented."). As a general rule in cases involving injuries like those incurred by Santa Susana victims, "under the FTCA, a claim accrues when the plaintiff knows of his injury and its cause." See *Gibson v. United States*, 781 F.2d 1334, 1344 (9th Cir.1986) (internal quotation marks and citation omitted). In addition, as a general rule, ignorance of the involvement of government employees is irrelevant to accrual of a federal tort claim. See *Dyniewicz v. United States*, 742 F.2d 484, 487 (9th Cir.1984); *Hensley v. United States*, 531 F.3d 1052, 1056 (9th Cir. 2008).

As of this writing, Santa Susana remains contaminated. There have been sporadic cleanup efforts. The most recent of these appear to have been initiated on May 21, 2020, when the Department of Energy announced that it would demolish several buildings on the site. See Monte Morin, "Cleanup to Resume at Troubled Santa Susana Field Laboratory Site," *Los Angeles Times*, May 21, 2020, https://www.latimes.com/environment/story/2020-05-21/cleanup-to-resume-at-troubled-santa-susana-field-laboratory-site. Nevertheless, this is a far remove from total remediation. See also "Boeing Required to Prove Santa Susana Cleanup Is Working," *Los Angeles Daily News*, August 12, 2022, https://www.dailynews.com/2022/08/12/boeing-required-to-prove-that-santa-susana-cleanup-is-working/. ("The lion's share of the cleanup work . . . has still not begun amid legal battles and feuds over government standards.")

In the fall of 2021, a study headed by Marco Kaltofen of the Department of Physics at Worcester Polytechnic Institute found that "highly contaminated radioactive particles" descended to residential neighborhoods from the SSFL site during the 2018 Woolsey Fire. See Olga Grigoryants, "Study: Radioactive Elements Reached Neighborhoods near Santa Susana Field Lab during Woolsey Fire," *Los Angeles Daily News*, October 21, 2021, https://www.dailynews.com/2021/10/21/study-radioactive-elements-reached-neighborhoods-near-santa-susana-field-lab-during-woolsey-fire/. Officials and residents have expressed frustration at the continued lack of cleanup and anger that action under a 2007 consent decree, which ordered NASA, Boeing, and the Department of Energy to remediate the region by 2017, had not yet begun. Grigoryants, "Study." See also "Boeing Required to Prove." ("The years of delay have sparked criticism from government officials, activists . . . and highly organized and fearful residents in the area. Activists and neighbors have blamed enduring health issues on the contamination.")

Lawsuits have been brought against Santa Susana's present owner, Boeing, though some plaintiffs ran into trouble establishing causation because of a previous destruction of records. See *O'Connor v. Boeing N. Am, Inc.*, at *29. ("Consequently, while Plaintiffs' expert has opined that Defendants breached the standard of care in their operation of the Area I Burn pit operated at SSFL, and likely emitted a variety of chemical carcinogens, due to Defendants' violations of regulations and permit requirements, and Defendants' failure to maintain records, and their destruction of records, Plaintiffs are unable to provide the dose calculations for emissions of carcinogens from SSFL Area I Burn Pit.") In 2006, Boeing reportedly paid $30 million dollars in a settlement. See "Boeing to Pay $30M to Settle Santa Susana Field Lab Lawsuit," *Business Journals*, January 12, 2006, https://www.bizjournals.com/losangeles/stories/2006/01/09/daily30.html#:~:text=The%20Boeing%20Co.%20will%20pay,diseases%2C%20according%20to%20media%20reports.

For Daniel Hirsch's scathing analysis of the Santa Susana site and the Woolsey Fire, see Daniel Hirsch, "A Failure of Governmental Candor: The Fire at the Contaminated Santa Susana Field Laboratory," *Bulletin of the Atomic Scientists*, February 21, 2019, https://thebulletin.org/2019/02/a-failure-of-governmental-candor-the-fire-at-the-contaminated-santa-susana-field-laboratory/.

For legal theory that would usher in a more meaningful human right to clean air and clean water in the United States, see, for example, Gerald Torres and Nathan Bellinger, "The Public Trust: The Law's DNA," *Wake Forest Journal of Law & Policy* 4, no. 2 (May 2014), at page 83. ("The concept of the public trust doctrine is simple: certain natural resources—such as air, water, and the sea—that are essential for all humans are held in trust by government for the benefit of all people, including future generations. Government is the trustee for these resources, the trust res, and has a fiduciary duty to protect the resources for the beneficiaries of the trust . . .")

The quotation about Xerxes whipping the waters is an adaptation from Herodotus, Vol. III, Loeb Classical Library Volume 119, translated by A. D. Godley (Cambridge, MA: Harvard University Press, 1922).

The quotation from Sappho has been translated by Julia Dubnoff, https://www.uh.edu/~cldue/texts/sappho.html#:~:text=but%20my%20 tongue%20is%20frozen,ears%20make%20a%20whirring%20noise.

The format for this novel derives from P2Solutions, "Santa Susana Field Laboratory Former Worker Interviews," November 2011, https://www.etec.energy.gov/Environmental_and_Health/Documents /WorkerHealthFiles/Former_Worker_Interview_Final_Report.pdf. This document contains the results of 132 worker interviews and was compiled at the behest of the Department of Energy so that the DOE could "learn more about historical operations at the site" ("Former Worker Interviews," page 1).

ACKNOWLEDGMENTS

The author thanks and remembers Dr. Eila Skinner, Dr. Tina Kooper-smith, Fred MacMurray, Thelma Diaz Quinn, Maggie MacMurray, Maria Adastik, Walter Adastik, Dr. Joshua Sapkin, Dr. Sia Danesh-mand, Marisa Siegel, Ginger Barber, Ladette Randolph, Brad Morrow, Speer Morgan, Evelyn Somers, Sacha Idell, Marc McKee, Andrew Tonkovich, Elizabeth McKenzie, Catherine Segurson, Ben Huberman, Nina Zweig, Adam Zimmerman, Eric Miller, Sarah Preisler, Reneé Vogel, Kathleen Kim, The Mesa Refuge, David Leonard, Susan Leonard, Héctor Tobar, Michael North, Lauren Willis, Chris Abani, Victor Gold, Rubén Martínez, Christopher Hawthorne, Elizabeth Baldwin, Ryan Botev, Chris Jarvis, the Yaddo Corporation, The Barbara Deming Memorial Grant/Money For Women, The Lighthouse Works, Willapa Bay AIR, the Huntington Library Fellowship Program, Loyola Law School, Jesse Gomez, Cathy Sudo, Colin Washington-Goward, Marina Castañeda, Soua Nia Moua, Liz Luk, Anne Gendler, Anne Tappan Strother, Olivia Aguilar, Babs Brown, and my dearest Andrew Brown.

Yxta also thanks the following publications for publishing sections of this novel:

Portions of "Introduction" were published originally in *Longreads*.

"Interview with Carlos Mejia" was published originally as "When the Prophet Gazed upon the Face of the Lord" in *Ploughshares*'s Solos series.

"Interview with Elisa Oumarou" was published originally as "The Simplest, Most Important Things" in *The Southern Review*.

"Interview with Barry Scott" was published originally as "The Big Picture" in *Chicago Quarterly Review*.

"Interview with Yaoxochitl Sudo" was published originally as "Item #4" in *Santa Monica Review*.

"Interview with Greg Wiśniewski" was published originally as "No Good Work" in *Conjunctions: Dispatches from Solitude*.

"Interview with Rudy Dimatibág" was published originally as "Happiness Is a Moth" in *Missouri Review*.

"Interview with Viola Singer" was published originally as "The Method" in *Catamaran*.